Praise for Dos Santos

~Finalist 2013~
International Latino Book Award for Historical Fiction

From Readers:

"I wanted to be there with them. I felt like I was there with them. The end was so heartbreakingly perfect. What a stunning accomplishment! And I feel I learned a lot as well."
MR, Ithaca, NY

"Detailed descriptions that allow us to live and feel the essence of our Taínos, a beautiful love story interwoven among images and dialog full of emotion, moving realism that reflects the raw stuggle that formed us as a people."
MJC, San Juan, Puerto Rico

"The conclusion is a marvel because it transforms a tragedy into a bridge of hope....What a success!"
EJS, San Juan, Puerto Rico

"The best documented narrative regarding our history as a people, descendents of a mix of races as we are. I believe it should be compulsory reading for all Boricuas who love their land."
CQ, Puerto Rico

"It's a really great story you have to tell and you tell it well. I couldn't stop reading."
PFC, Cornell University, Ithaca, NY

"Extremely well wri‑‑‑‑ the human story is fascinating and well developed, an‑ ‑‑‑‑ught provoking. The st‑ ry real and very moving."
CRO, Albany, NY

Fernando de Aragón

DOS SANTOS

A Novel

7/17

LEPICAN PUBLISHING
ITHACA, NY

¡ Ceiba Vive !

ISBN: 978-1-466-33536-3

Published by: Lepican Publishing, Ithaca, NY
Printed by Create Space

First Edition: November 2011

Design and layout by Fernando de Aragón and Norma Gutierrez

Cover design by Norma Gutierrez

PUBLISHER'S NOTE
This is a fictional work inspired by real events. While some of the facts are true to the history of the European settlement of Puerto Rico, most of the plot and the principal characters in the story are fictitious. More details can be found in the afterword.

www.dossantosnovel.weebly.com
Facebook: Dos Santos - Novel

Fernando de Aragón

Dos Santos

Dos Santos is Fernando de Aragón's first novel. He studied environmental science and planning at Rutgers University and holds a Ph.D. in Energy Management and Policy from the University of Pennsylvania. The dynamics of the Spanish/Taíno cultural encounter in lands currently occupied by Haiti, the Dominican Republic and Puerto Rico have been a passionate interest of the author for many years. Born and raised in Puerto Rico, he currently lives in Ithaca, New York with his wife Jacki, their daughter Julia and son Trevel.

Visit the author's website at:
www.dossantosnovel.weebly.com

About the Illustrator

Dos Santos was illustrated and designed by Norma S. Gutierrez, a graphic designer and faculty member at Tompkins Cortland Community College. Ms. Gutierrez created the pelican logo for the author's company, *Lepican Publishing*, to brand his independent literary ventures. She is based in Ithaca, New York.

Visit the illustrator's website at:
www.behance.net/NormaGutierrez
graphicsbynorma.com

For All First Peoples

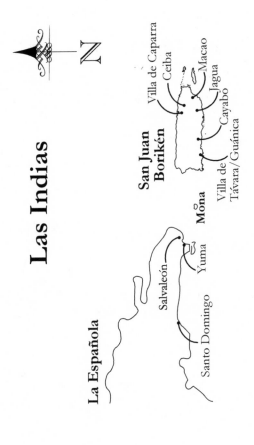

DOS SANTOS
Part I

Desde un profundo océano
Hasta la superficie del mar
Como montaña infinita
Que el sol su cumbre quiere agitar.

Paraíso escondido
Que nadie llego a tocar
Hasta que del Orinoco salieron
En busca de paz y tierra a cultivar.

Este mundo Caribeño,
Con paisajes milagrosos,
Costa pura y agua bendita,
Guarda la puerta a un mundo sagrado,
Con sus cemis y su caciques Borincanos.

Francisco Xavier de Aragón
From his poem '*Atlantis Caribeño*'

I

NIGHT FIRE

A large fire crackled in a shallow depression in the sand. The faces of the men sitting around the fire were lit in dancing light, so they seemed in constant motion even when they sat still. Half a dozen of them sat on rocks and on the sand, each with a cup in hand. Bright sparks leapt into the clear tropical night every time a faggot tired of holding its place in the flames.

"Who's running low?" asked Rodrigo, lifting the gallon jug. All cups went up in unison and Rodrigo let out a hearty laugh. "I could have guessed," he said.

The group had gathered on the beach in anticipation of their expedition that was set to start the next day. Arriving at that beach following different paths, most of the men were strangers to each other. Soldiers, sailors, laborers, a cook; none there was of the gentry. Through lifetimes of struggle, violence and dogged determination, destiny brought them together. The next day they would set out as companions on a journey, seeking to realize the promise of the New World.

The conversation flew above the fire, the excitement of anticipation in the men's voices. Sometimes in the darkness you could not tell who was speaking. But it didn't matter—that night they shared what they had in common.

"I hear there is more gold than was ever found here," said one voice.

"And the Indians are better workers," bounced another.

"And the women...I can't wait!" The men laughed and paused to drink rum.

"I'll be glad to work under Don Juan," said a burly voice in a whisper that could not be heard outside the circle. "The governors have made a mess of La Española, I think Don Juan will do better."

"As long as I make my gold I won't care who is in charge," came a response. "I don't want power. Being rich will be plenty for me."

10

"Well said," answered several voices amid laughter.

"Rodrigo," called one of the men standing up. "Thanks for the rum."

"You heading back?" asked Rodrigo.

"Yes, I can't stomach the rum the way I used to."

Rodrigo smiled, eyeing the bottle in his hand. "All right, see you tomorrow." Then turning to the group, "Well boys, we get to drink his share." No one complained.

II

YUMA

At port in the Village of Santo Domingo, a caravel named the *Santa María de la Regla* floated on high tide waiting eagerly to set sail. Overhead, steady trade winds propelled harmless clouds across the sky. The protected waters of the harbor were calm and glassy. Forty-two passengers and a crew of eight crowded the ship's deck, shouting back and forth to those few gathered at the dock. For many on board, these were their last moments in Santo Domingo and their last opportunity to talk face to face with friends they were leaving behind.

A lone man with an unmistakable bearing of authority parted the crowd as he approached the gangplank. "Captain Gil," he shouted to the man waiting to receive him on board. "We depart as soon as you are ready. I would appreciate if you do not delay."

"We are ready now, Don Juan," Gil responded, and started barking orders to his crew.

Standing with other passengers near the bow, Antonio Dos Santos watched every development attentively. His demeanor was calm but the tightness in his stomach betrayed, if only to himself, the excitement he felt at being a member of this expedition. Antonio was thirty-seven years old and taller than average. His thin but sinewy musculature hinted at hidden strength, as did his wide brow and square jaw. A pair of narrow green eyes peered at the world as if constantly searching for something. Wrinkles on his sun baked skin were proof of a lifetime of exposure to the elements, first as a sailor on Portuguese and Spanish ships, and later as a laborer in the first European settlements in the New World. On that placid July morning of 1508, Dos Santos was about to embark towards his dreams. In Santo Domingo he was leaving behind years of work and unfulfilled promises.

Calls of farewell arose from the dock as the *Santa María* left its moorings. Antonio waved at no one in particular and at everyone and everything at once. Good-bye, he thought, to the island of La Española which had served as his home for twelve years, good-bye to Santo Domingo with its stone churches and ramshackle homes, good-bye to the green mountains that had inspired his dreams, good-bye because he could get nowhere in that land.

Antonio had traveled to the New World with the second voyage of Admiral Cristobal Colón, late in 1493. He spent the next two years working in the settlement of La Isabela on the north coast of La Española. During that time he managed to learn the language of the native Taíno Indians from those who had been captured by the Spaniards and worked as slaves. This skill had helped Antonio join expeditions to explore the new country, opportunities he welcomed as respite from the hard labor of construction and the unhealthy conditions in La Isabela. From the beginning, the budding settlement had been cursed by disease and political tumult. Any opportunity to explore the countryside had been accepted without hesitation by Dos Santos.

In 1496 Antonio was ordered to join the Admiral's brother, Bartolomeo, on an expedition to the southern coast of La Española. The long, arduous trek across the island had ended with the founding of the Village of Nueva Isabela. Six years later, after being leveled by a massive hurricane, the settlement was moved to a new permanent site and rechristened as Santo Domingo under orders from a new governor. With a better harbor and easier access to known gold deposits, Santo Domingo offered the promise of riches that the previous two settlements could not fulfill.

During the cross-island trek, Dos Santos had seen the fertile countryside of Española and was convinced that the time had come for him to settle down. He had become obsessed with the idea of owning land and establishing his own homestead. Antonio participated eagerly in the construction of new settlements while he chased his dream. After a life of travel and working for the gain of others, he was ready to work for his own fortune. He meant to become a permanent settler in this new world, not just another gold digger seeking to return to Spain a rich man. After all, Spain had nothing for him; no family, no friends, no home to

13

return to.

Antonio remained in Santo Domingo working in construction and trying desperately to save enough money to obtain land. Unfortunately, land ownership was granted by the governor on the basis of title, or as reward for service, or in return for favors. Antonio did not have the standing required to receive land within the small but pretentious society of Santo Domingo. His only hope was to bribe a government official to speak on his behalf. But Antonio feared losing all his money in this risky endeavor. In the corruption of Santo Domingo, he could easily die by "accident" and no one would question it.

It was late in 1507 when rumors began circulating about a possible expedition to the neighboring island of San Juan Bautista. Word was that Juan Ponce de León had been on an exploratory trip to San Juan the previous year and was now ready to establish a permanent settlement. Antonio had met Ponce de León during the ocean crossing from Spain. In La Española, Ponce de León earned the reputation of being an astute businessman, a fierce fighter and an honorable and fair leader. Antonio was convinced that his chances to get land would improve under Don Juan's leadership. When the time came to organize the San Juan expedition, Antonio's request to join the group was promptly accepted. His experience as a sailor in years' past, his time in Santo Domingo, and his knowledge of the Taíno language were excellent qualifications. A couple of nights of drinking and friendly revelry with the expedition's draft agent were also helpful in his effort to enlist.

Once again on a ship, the deck rolling under his feet felt familiar. Antonio's life as a sailor was long past. He found it hard to believe it had been 15 years since he arrived in La Española; however, his legs retained the memory of years living aboard ships. He walked to the bow to get out of the sailors' way and to find a comfortable place to spend the first stage of this trip.

As soon as the ship cleared the dock, the captain tacked due south-southwest towards the mouth of the harbor and the reef beyond. With the wind behind her, the

Santa María slipped effortlessly out of the harbor through a passage in the reef and on to the broad swells of quiet, deep blue waters. When the white sands along the coast were lost over the horizon, the vessel once again changed directions to the east, and Captain Gil began the tedious task of navigating his ship against oncoming winds. Their first destination was the Village of Salvaleón and its port at the mouth of the Yuma River, on the eastern province of Higüey. There, in the region that the Spaniards settled under the leadership of Ponce de León, the *Santa María* was to pick up supplies for the crossing to San Juan.

"I hope the Indians in San Juan are not like the ones here," said one of the men who had joined Antonio at the bow. They sat on barrels and coils of rope, trying to find bits of shade from the sails to protect them from the hot tropical sun. "They are weak and rebellious," he continued. "When I get an *encomienda*, I want good workers to search the rivers for gold."

"Who says you are going to get an *encomienda*?" interrupted another mockingly. "Just because you are in the first ship over doesn't mean you stop being a lowlife."

"Speak for yourself, you fart. I intend to find gold in San Juan and become a rich man. Is that not why we are all here?"

All the men nodded in agreement. Each went on to tell his story of what he would do with his gold, certain that he would get rich in the new land. Antonio listened amused and said little. He understood the feelings of these young men; he had had the same dreams and illusions once. But as the oldest in that group and the one with the most years in La Española, he knew that very few untitled men got rich mining gold. Governors reserved the most promising sources of gold for themselves; other mining permits were issued to titled men or in order to gather political favor. Rarely were commoners like them granted mining rights for gold. His years of experience had taught him that, in many ways, they were little more than slaves—particularly since Indians had become rare, with those unlucky enough to be captured dying within weeks of starting work under the white men,

15

and the rest seeking refuge away from Spaniards.

But why ruin his shipmates' dreams, thought Antonio. Let them think they could get rich. Who knows? Maybe some of them would. He was certain of one thing: the only wealth he wanted was a piece of land to call his own; let the king keep his gold.

Strong winds kept the captain and crew busy tending the sails and maintaining course. Antonio noticed this and offered to assist the sailors. Captain Gil, who valued having an extra pair of experienced hands, eagerly accepted his offer. This also meant Antonio got to spend most of his time above board, which he enjoyed better that being below decks taking inventory of supplies.

Early on the evening of the third day of the voyage the captain took a measurement from the ship's compass, and then braced himself as he took a reading on the sextant.

"It is time," he mumbled to himself and ordered a change of directions to the north. The ships crew went immediately into action handling the sails.

"Now we'll have the wind more astern and we'll make better time," he said to Antonio, who happened to be steering the vessel at the time.

"Where is Yuma?" asked Antonio. "I've never been there."

"It's at the mouth of a river at the land end of that peninsula," Gil explained, pointing to port at the distant silhouette of the land they had been circling for the last day.

The *Santa María* rocked on the waves as it changed directions. Swiftly the crew adjusted the sails and these snapped to work with the more favorable wind. In contrast with the slow pace they had had to endure previously, the ship seemed to be flying over the waves. The passengers noticed the change and gathered on deck to find out what was going on.

"Captain Gil informs me that if God continues to give us this wind we will arrive in Yuma by the morning of the day after tomorrow." Ponce de León's announcement brought shouts of approval from the deck.

16

By mid-morning of the second day, as predicted, a call from the crow's nest alerted the passengers that their destination was within sight. All aboard moved to the port gunwale to look at the land. A column of smoke could be seen where water and land touched, providing a navigation aide for the captain. Within hours, the *Santa María* came to anchor close to a narrow beach with dark sand. The harbor was little more than a large cove with a narrow entrance, but it provided adequate protection from the waves and tides. The sandy beach extended approximately two hundred meters from its western edge, where a small cliff blocked the sand, to the east where the Yuma River emptied quietly into the sea. A long, rectangular building could be seen among the trees at the base of the cliff, which rose vertically from the sand behind the structure and served as a backdrop to the beach. Beyond the river, the coastline stretched to the southeast, providing a natural barrier to stiff trade winds. To the west, the outcropping of rocks that marked the end of the beach area extended as far as the eye could see.

From the ship the passengers could see a group of men at the beach waiting for the ship's arrival. Two small boats were placed in the water and began to approach the ship. The visitors climbed up a rope ladder and were helped on board.

"Gerardo, my friend, it is good to see you again," exclaimed Ponce de León as he grasped his friend's hand.

"Likewise, indeed," said Gerardo, pausing to savor the encounter with his friend. "It looks like you are finally going to Borikén," he said, using the Taíno name for the island of San Juan.

"That's right," said Ponce de León, a broad smile on his face. "How is my family?

"They are fine. They wait for you in Salvaleón."

"Then you received my message from Santo Domingo?" Don Juan asked, eager to verify what he had already guessed.

"Yes, I did, and everything is ready. In fact," said Gerardo with a grin, "you'll have enough supplies to start another war with the Moors."

Everyone gathered around laughed at the remark. The crew and the passengers were in good spirits at the end of the first leg of their trip. The availability of supplies improved the prospects of their expedition.

"It's good that everyone is here," said Ponce de León in a loud voice so all could hear. "We will take two days of rest and..." Before he could go on he was drowned by cheers. "Enjoy them," he continued. "I can't tell you when will be the next time I can give such orders." The men quieted down. "We will then load the ship with supplies and head out soon thereafter. We'll meet at the beach early in the morning, three days from today." Another quick cheer sent everyone in different directions. Accompanied by Gerardo, Ponce de León left the ship, to visit his family.

Antonio took Ponce de León's advice in earnest and spent most of the next two days relaxing around the beach. Several large trees provided shaded areas that were perfect for hanging a hammock and resting comfortably. In the mornings, before the sun was high, he would go fishing. Rodrigo, his long time friend and the ship's cook, agreed to prepare the fish Antonio caught as long as he would share them. Using small fish that he found trapped in rocky tidal pools as bait, Antonio was successful in catching enough fish to give some away to his shipmates. Each evening after serving the crew, Rodrigo used the best vegetables, which he had saved for himself and Antonio, to prepare special meals that they ate under the bright light of the tropical moon as gentle breezes danced around them. Nights were spent with music and stories, accompanied with rum bought at the Village of Salvaleón.

Few of the men welcomed the morning of the third day. Ponce de León arrived early to wait for the rest of the group to gather as agreed. He drove a sturdy wooden cart pulled by a single horse, packed with the first load of supplies. Before long, the company was together and everyone looked fit and ready for work. Ponce de León divided the men between the ship, the small boats that would ferry the supplies to the ship, and the warehouse on the beach, where the supplies were stored. For three days the men struggled with a wide

18

variety of items, all carefully selected and catalogued for the expedition. Ponce de León understood the importance of being well supplied when starting a settlement away from immediate assistance. Once in San Juan they would be on their own for extended periods of time. Agricultural and construction tools and supplies, weapons, munitions, and a variety of other non-perishable articles, including some food items, were loaded first. Perishable food items and livestock would be loaded immediately before departure.

"Once again I leave to secure more supplies and await additional passengers," Ponce de León told the gathered men. "I will be back soon, and I assure you, we will depart then."

A week passed uneventfully. The men did not expect Don Juan to be gone for so long. They were restless, eager to depart and face a future they had convinced themselves was filled with fortune. Antonio went on long walks and spent time with his shipmates. Several men arrived over the week to join the expedition. They brought news of Ponce de León, who continued coordinating the expedition from his family home.

During that time Antonio visited the Village of Salvaleón. It was a small settlement with a mix of small wooden houses and Indian style huts called *bohíos*. He noticed the well delineated signature plaza, flanked by a small wooden church. Adjacent to that was the foundation and initial stone work for a more permanent house of worship. At the edge of the village, Antonio passed by a small homestead. An older man struggled installing a roof over a small barn that also served as a chicken coop.

"Amigo, you look like you could use a hand there," said Antonio.

"I could use two if you have them," responded the old man with a look of anticipation.

"I have some time."

Between the two of them, and with Antonio's knowledge of construction, they were able to complete the work before sundown. That night Antonio slept in a comfortable hay mattress protected by his handiwork. When he departed for Yuma, he received two live chickens from the grateful homeowner.

It was the eighth day since they last saw Ponce de León. The morning sun hid behind a heavy bank of water-laden clouds so dense, it was incomprehensible that they could float in the air. By midday it began to rain lightly but it was plain to all that more serious weather was approaching. The hilly topography provided the *Santa María* with shelter from the strengthening wind.

Late in the afternoon, a group of men from the expedition gathered at the half empty warehouse where they built a fire and managed to keep dry. Some of the men cooked, others played cards and others gathered in conversation.

"Anyone interested in going to the ship?" asked Antonio out loud.

"Are you crazy? What for?" responded a young man sitting by the fire.

"Just asking. I rather not row alone."

"I'm afraid you are alone this time Dos Santos," said a large muscular man smiling. "We'll watch from here so we can tell Captain Gil what happened if you are carried out to sea."

"Thanks for your concern," said Antonio mockingly as he left. He walked to the back of the building, collected a burlap bag he had left there, and headed for the beach. With some difficulty, he pushed one of the ship's dinghies into the water, climbed aboard and started rowing. The wind forced him to pull more to one side but overall it helped propel the dinghy to its destination. After securing the boat to the side of the ship, he tossed the burlap bag to the deck. Then, drenched from head to feet, he climbed the rope ladder up the side of the ship.

"Rodrigo!" he called out as he entered the ship's hold through the forecastle.

"Who's there?" came the response.

"Dos Santos. I have a surprise for you."

"Don't tell me you were out fishing in this weather," rumbled Rodrigo. "I cannot believe you like fish that much."

His laugh echoed in the solid timber that made the walls of his small galley. He was a heavy man with a stubble beard and a greasy look that never changed. Antonio liked him for his sense of humor and admired him for his ability to make a meal out of almost anything.

Antonio placed his burlap bag on the sturdy utility table, right in front of Rodrigo. "What's this?" asked the cook.

"See for yourself."

Rodrigo lifted the end of the bag and out came two chickens, wings flapping and feathers flying.

Rodrigo's laugh could be heard by the men on the beach. "This is a treat indeed. Where did you get these birds?"

"They were payment for a day's work," explained Antonio. "I met a man in Salvaleón and helped him with the roof of his barn. The difficult part was keeping the other men from finding the chickens. They would have demanded that I share them with them."

"Instead, you will share them with me? That is very considerate of you."

"Someone has to cook them. And anyways, we have a deal."

"And a good deal it is," said Rodrigo as he grabbed a chicken head in each hand. With one quick jerk, the birds were stilled and he began feathering them one at a time while holding them out the galley porthole. The men, watching from the beach, wondered at the rain of feathers coming out of the side of the ship.

Once again Rodrigo used his magic and before long exquisite aromas filled the ship's hold, luring the only two other men on board to the galley.

"Come in," said the cook. "I knew you would find your way here sooner or later." He paused. "It's a good thing you didn't wait 'til later or all the food would be gone," he said with laughter in his voice. "Antonio, meet Gabriel and Miguel. I'm sure they bring a hearty appetite. I hope you don't mind sharing your chickens."

"Not at all," said Antonio nodding to the men.

"What are you cooking?" asked Gabriel, the older looking of the two guests.

"Señor Dos Santos here was kind enough to bring two chickens, which I am making into a rather thick stew," responded Rodrigo turning the contents of a kettle with a wooden spoon that would look gigantic in the hands of most other men.

The four men kept each other company in the warm, dry galley while the stew thickened. Outside, the once distant storm was now visiting the shores of Yuma. Rain poured in steady streams while powerful, steady winds pushed the ship taut against the anchor line, holding it surprisingly steady. After some time, Rodrigo announced that the stew was ready and they moved to the sleeping quarters. Other than the cargo hold, this was the largest compartment in the ship. It usually felt cramped because there were so many people there, but that day, with only the four of them, it seemed spacious. At the center of the room sat a heavy wooden table with thick legs and four old chairs. Rodrigo placed the stew kettle in the middle of the table. Antonio carried a large loaf of bread and a jar of water; the other two men brought wooden bowls, cups and spoons. They sat and ate and bragged about their good fortune in what, to most eyes, would look like a terrible day.

"It's an art to turn a day like today into something memorable," said Rodrigo leaning back on his chair unable to eat another bite. "I think we've done well today."

The other men smiled, and nodded in agreement with the comments of the philosophizing cook. It was satisfying to know they had found a comfortable, safe spot literally in the midst of a storm.

"Where are you two from?" Antonio asked the young men sitting with him.

"We are from Seville," answered Gabriel.

"Both of you?"

"Yes. We are brothers."

Antonio nodded with the realization that the similarities between Miguel and Gabriel were not a trick of his imagination. Both had the same toothy smile, narrow eyes and wavy hair, but Gabriel had jet black hair while Miguel's was brown.

"I was born in Seville," said Antonio quietly, as if revealing a deep secret. "In the back room of the Mesón de los Tres Toros. But I left there when I was a child. I've only returned once since then, when I passed through the city on my way to Palos to join Colón's second voyage."

"Sounds like you don't have too many fond memories of Seville," said Rodrigo.

"I worked at the Mesón's tavern from the moment I could walk. I was pushed around and harassed by patrons and by the owner of the place. I slept in a room behind the tavern that was little more than a closet. When I played, it was in a muddy alley," Antonio spit out the words with anger. "I heard enough stories at the tavern to know that there was a better world out there," he continued gesturing with his hands. "When I was nine my mother sent me away to an uncle in Lisbon. I was happy to go." He paused. "That was the last time I saw her."

There was quiet in the room. The wind could be heard outside and the tension of the ship against the anchor line could be felt through the strained wood. At that moment the wind went still.

"Do you feel that?" asked the cook sitting up on his chair.

"What?" responded Miguel, looking around as if expecting to find someone else in the room.

"The wind....it's changed," said Rodrigo. After many years aboard the *Santa María*, he could detect even its slightest change in attitude.

The other men sat up on their chairs and listened to the sounds of the wind, the sea and the ship. The ship tilted slightly to port and began to rock on the surf, which was becoming heavier with every passing moment. The bowls and cups were tossed off the table.

"I'll go on deck and take a look," said Antonio.

"We're with you," said Miguel, tapping his younger brother on the shoulder.

Rodrigo filled the empty kettle with their utensils

23

and went to secure the galley. "Let me know what you see," he yelled at his three companions as they headed up the stairs to the deck.

Night was almost upon them. The sun, an item of faith that whole day, had already set unseen. It was not raining hard when they stepped outside, but the strong wind made the drops sting when they hit the skin. Antonio walked on deck and felt disoriented. He staggered over to the port gunwale and latched on to the sail ropes. To stern he could see the dark silhouette of hills on land. The wind had shifted to the southeast, eliminating all protection offered by the landmass. The ship sat fully exposed to the wind and the increasingly turbulent seas.

Suddenly the deck jerked violently to stern. Antonio's legs flew from under him leaving him dangling from the ropes like a wet rag. He looked behind to see Gabriel and Miguel slam against the forecastle walls.

"The anchor is loose," yelled Rodrigo. He stood braced against the door frame of the forecastle, bleeding from a wound on his head.

"You're hurt," called Antonio.

Rodrigo nodded, dismissing his injury with a wave of his hand. "Where's the ship headed?"

Antonio looked towards land and recognized the familiar rocks, just west of the beach, where he had spent so many hours fishing. "We're going to hit the rocks. We better leave the ship and try to swim for the beach. But we have to go now!"

Rodrigo shook his head. "I'm not a good swimmer. I'll let the ship take me to land." The two brothers, recovered from their blows stood hanging on to the sides of the ship, which continued to be tossed by the waves.

It started to rain harder. Antonio wiped his face with one hand only to have sea spray and rain cover it again. He pulled out his knife, cut four sections of rope and stumbled across the deck to his companions. "Here, tie these on and attach them to the starboard gunwale," he said handing everyone a length of rope. "Rodrigo is right; the risk of drowning is too great. And anyways," he said with a cocky smile. "I don't want to get wet." Rodrigo looked at Antonio and then laughed in a booming voice that defied the chaos of the storm and gave confidence that they would survive this ordeal.

They had secured their safety lines and looked at the hills as they got closer. It did not take long for the ship to hit the rocks. First the vessel hit bottom and its forward progress was slowed. Then it halted suddenly, jarring the four passengers. The ship tilted slightly to port. Waves began pounding the starboard side. Sea spray rained over the gunwale and soaked the men in salt water. Antonio slid to the port side, never letting go of his rope. He saw that the vessel had run aground on rocks that were normally above water. Using the ship as a breakwater they could wade over to the rocks and then to high ground.

Antonio called the other men over and explained his idea. Once again Rodrigo protested, but this time Antonio insisted. No one knew how much longer the storm would last, and overnight the waves and rocks could pound the ship to pieces. Somehow or other they all had to get to land. Using a length of rope they lowered themselves; Gabriel and Miguel went first, then Antonio helped Rodrigo and finally Antonio crawled down the rope. The water was waist high and churning in all directions. Moving slowly and with great effort they reached the water's edge. The two younger men immediately started climbing the rock face that met them there. They were battered by waves but managed to reach the top with nothing more than a few bruises.

"Come this way," yelled Gabriel waving with his arm.

Rodrigo, followed by Antonio, started climbing where Gabriel had indicated. With encouragement from above and below the cook managed to reach the top of the rocks. Soon they were all gathered together beyond the reach of the waves. Sea spray mixed with rain continued to pelt them as they looked back at the *Santa María*. The masts remained intact and the hull, although grounded, seemed to be taking the pounding of the waves without additional damage.

"Hey, hello! Are you well?" The calls came from a group of men that approached them, leaning against the wind.

"We are fine," Rodrigo answered in his booming voice. "The ship lost its anchor. Now we know what we'll be doing tomorrow."

"I say we go for shelter," said Antonio to the cook. "There is not much that we can do here now."

Most of the men remained behind, fascinated by the sight of the grounded ship, while others, including Rodrigo and Antonio, returned to the warehouse in search of dry comfort.

"I'm just glad we ate all the stew," said Rodrigo to Antonio. Both men smiled. The storm had gotten the best of them after all, but the memory of the stew kept them warm inside.

The storm passed some time before dawn, allowing a bright, contrasting morning to unfold. The waters of the cove were glassy and calm. The sand of the beach was windblown smooth and even. In some ways things looked tidier than before the storm. The ship's disaster seemed like a bad dream until the members of the expedition looked west, towards the rocks, where dream turned to reality.

Ponce de León arrived late that morning bringing additional supplies in a heavy cart pulled by a team of oxen. He cursed out loud, flailing a fist in the air, when he saw the ship. "We leave tomorrow," he announced defiantly for all to hear. "Captain," he called out to the shipmaster. "I need an evaluation of damages to the ship." One by one Ponce de León gave orders to his officers. Soon all the men were working to get the *Santa María* afloat again.

Captain Gil's report to Ponce de León was received with enthusiasm. The ship had alighted itself on a gap between the rocks and sat on a patch of sandy bottom. Amazingly, there was no visible damage to the hull.

About a third of the provisions were ruined by the storm and cast overboard. Those supplies that survived the storm were moved to land to lighten the ship and allow it to float higher with the incoming tide. A team of oxen toiled incessantly moving supplies from the rocks to the beach where the ship's carpenter supervised construction of two wide rafts to use in reloading the ship.

The men's work paid off. Even before the tide reached its zenith the ship was already beginning to float loose from the grip of the rocks. At one point all the men were called to the water. With the help of gentle trade winds and a calm sea they pushed the ship over the rocks that trapped it and out to deeper water. Once again a cheer cut through the air. The vessel floated lightly on the smooth water as its crew scrambled aboard. The sight of the ship afloat made the men confident that Ponce de León's implausible departure schedule could indeed be achieved.

Work continued until dark, when Ponce de León himself gave the order to rest. The men were exhausted but their imminent departure kept them in high spirits. They sat around the warehouse eating roast pork, which Rodrigo had been cooking all afternoon over a pit of smoldering embers. A robust fire burned in a shallow depression in the sand, illuminating the sweat covered faces of the men, making them shine. After eating, sleep came easy for most as tired muscles demanded rest. A small group gathered around the fire to discuss their expectations for the island of San Juan, but even they soon disbanded. After the crackle of the fire died down, the only sounds were the whisper of the soft breeze and the lapping of tiny waves on the sand. The night passed in welcome calm.

"Up, men," came the call from Ponce de León. He sat on the back of a horse, his hands casually holding the bridle, smiling as he looked over the sleepy company.

The morning, so young that a few stars still showed in the lightening skies, had come too soon for the slumbering men. The same muscles that worked so hard the day before were tight and unwilling to move. Antonio blinked in disbelief at how quickly the night had passed. He felt like he could sleep for another two days.

"Today we finish loading the supplies," announced Ponce de León. "We depart with the tide this afternoon."

The few cheers that received the announcement

were drowned by the groans and moans of men trying to get their bodies to function. The breakfast of porridge and bread, clearly not Rodrigo's best effort, did little to encourage the men to face the day ahead. Eventually, however, with encouragement from Ponce de León and his officers, the company was organized once again into work parties.

The men worked efficiently, loading the supplies gathered on the beach onto the rafts at waters' edge. Once again the weather held. Gentle breezes and calm waters allowed the ship to come close enough to the beach that ropes could be used to pull the supply rafts back and forth between the loading and unloading parties. By midday all the available supplies, including small livestock, had been ferried to the ship. Antonio, who had been working on the beach, was looking forward to an afternoon nap before departure.

"You think those rafts will hold me?" Rodrigo asked Antonio as he approached from the warehouse. The big man carried a burlap bag with the cooking utensils he had rescued from the ship the previous day. His question was made in jest, but with an undercurrent of real concern.

"I suppose," said Antonio.

"I need to get to the ship."

"Hey!" called Antonio to the ship as he walked with Rodrigo to the waters' edge. "We have a passenger for you. Make sure you treat him well—I'm hungry."

Rodrigo threw his bag on the raft. He then helped Antonio push the raft out to the water and climbed aboard. Antonio joined the rest of his work party on the beach, amused by the sight of the heavy man, sitting straight and unmoving in the middle of the raft, floating towards the ship.

"How's he going to climb aboard?," asked one of the men.

"The ship may roll if he tries to climb up the sides," said another, eliciting chuckles from the group.

When the raft reached the *Santa María*, a rope was lowered. Rodrigo tied it to his bag and his supplies were promptly lifted aboard. Fearful of overturning the raft, Rodrigo crawled on hands and knees to the rope ladder dangling from the side of the ship. With difficulty the large man wrestled with his bulk to keep his balance as he stepped off the raft. He grabbed the rope ladder with his powerful hands and dangled for a second as he sought a foothold. Aboard ship, men gathered on deck looking over the gunwale at the unfolding spectacle.

"I say he doesn't make it," cried one crew member. "Who says otherwise?"

Four men responded at once and in less than half a minute every man on the ship had a stake on the ascension of Rodrigo. Catcalls and cries of encouragement followed the cook's every move. Antonio, seeing what was happening led the men at the beach in rooting for Rodrigo. Sweating profusely and feeling embarrassed, Rodrigo struggled up the rope ladder. His hands gripped the ropes tightly so he would not fall if his feet faltered. Finally he reached the wooden beams of the gunwale railing. With great effort and a loud grunt he pulled himself to his feet behind the railing. A huge cheer received him as he stepped over the railing to stand on deck.

"Pipe down you bastards," said Rodrigo in a commanding voice that silenced the men. "Which of you bet against me?" he asked seriously.

There was no response; but the look of confused fear on the faces of the men who stood together at the stern of the main deck gave them away. Rodrigo glared at them.

"I'm going to enjoy cooking dinner for you tonight," he said menacingly, then lifted his burlap bag and headed for the galley. He paused at the deck door. The smile he flashed before going below deck told the men that his apparent anger had been a prank. But it also made clear that he continued to hold a fair amount of power in the ship and that he had more than one way to deal with anyone who stood against him. There was nervous laughter on deck as the cook moved out of sight.

III

AGÜEYBANÁ

The sun was well above the horizon when Captain Gil gave orders to raise anchor and unfurl the sails. An hour earlier Antonio had his nap interrupted by orders to board the *Santa María*. He was as glad as anyone to have the expedition moving again. In spite of the mishap with the ship and the loss of precious supplies, the crew and passengers were in high spirits.

As soon as the ship left the protection of the harbor it began to sway on large, gentle swells. The steady wind raised only a few whitecaps to break the deep blue of the sea. It did not take long before all expedition members were assigned to a variety of chores, including taking inventory of supplies, cleaning the animal waste and assisting the crew; however, most of the time was spent idling, telling stories, gambling and sleeping. When he got bored, Antonio would go below decks and offer to help Rodrigo. The cook, who enjoyed his company, always managed to find work for his friend.

In the afternoon of the fourth day the *Santa María* reached Mona Island, midway between Española and San Juan. Mona protruded from the sea like a fortress, with sheer, towering white cliffs rising from the water on all sides except the southwest corner of the island. There, sand had accumulated at the base of the cliff to form a beach, which was covered with a thicket of thorny vegetation. The interior of the island was an uninviting, parched plateau.

Approaching Mona, the *Santa María* cautiously sailed around a large bird- covered rock, which dwarfed the ship. The rock island offered protection from the open seas, while creating the only good anchorage on Mona. The ship dropped anchor behind a coral reef whose dangerous teeth could be seen through the crystal clear waters. Just beyond the reef lay Mona's beach.

"Excuse me, sir," said a young officer, Ponce de León's personal assistant, interrupting a discussion between his commander and Captain Gil. "There are Indians on the beach. They look like Taínos."

"How many?" asked Ponce de León.

"Three that we can see. They sit in the shade of that sea grape tree," he indicated pointing towards the largest tree on the beach.

"Arm five men and tell Juan González that I will need his services as an interpreter. Make sure Dos Santos is among the escort, he knows the native language, too."

"Yes sir," said the officer crisply, before he left to execute his orders.

"We need clear access to this beach," Ponce de León reminded Gil. "This will be the staging point to resupply our settlement in San Juan."

Within minutes the ship's two dinghies where headed towards shore to meet the Taínos. "Keep your eyes open," Ponce de León ordered his men. "There may be other Indians hiding in the bushes. We don't want this expedition to start with an ambush." Ponce de León was not sure what to expect from the natives of San Juan. In Española, the Spaniards and Taínos had been involved in an ongoing war, and although the Europeans had superior weapons, the Taínos, with their knowledge of the land and their astuteness, had proven strong opponents. Ponce de León wanted to colonize San Juan without conflict, but as an old soldier he knew better than to face a potential enemy without caution.

The calm waters allowed the small boats to beach without difficulty. Quickly the men disembarked. "Stay close together behind us," Antonio heard the order from an officer accompanying Ponce de León. Juan González, the interpreter, was the third man at the head of the group. The Taínos emerged from their tree shelter as the Spaniards approached. They wore short loincloths and adorned their arms with bracelets made from seashells. Their bronze skin was brightly painted in a variety of patterns and shapes.

"I am Juan Ponce de León. I am here on my way to Borikén," said the Spaniard through his interpreter, using the Taíno name for the island of San Juan.

One of the Indians stepped forward. He was of average height for a Taíno, which made him shorter than most Spaniards, of medium build with well-defined muscles. "We are *caciques* of the great Agüeybaná," translated González using the common Taíno word for chief. "My name is Sibanacán."

"We know of *Cacique* Agüeybaná and seek to meet him so we may honor him."

"That would be good," said Sibanacán. His serious countenance concealed his concerns and the deliberations in his mind. "We can lead you to him," he offered after a short pause.

"We welcome your assistance. Do you have other people you want to travel with us?" asked Ponce de León in an effort to find out if there were more Indians on the island.

"No. Only the three of us will travel with you. When do you depart?"

"Before sunrise tomorrow."

"We'll be back then." Moving together, as if following a secret cue, the Taínos took a step back, then turned and walked into the scrub vegetation.

"Well done" said Ponce de León to González once Sibanacán and his men were out of sight. "It will save us a lot of time if these Taínos can lead us directly to Agüeybaná." He then turned to one of his officers. "Take the men and inspect the area," he ordered. "I want to know if we are alone on this beach. And just to be cautious, make sure the men are armed when they come ashore."

Spaniards prospecting for gold had explored Mona in previous years. They'd built a small stone building and dug a well that produced fresh water of surprisingly good quality considering the arid nature of the island. Antonio, along with the other men on the landing party, inspected the stone structure and surveyed the beach area without finding any sign of Taínos.

As soon as the beach was declared safe, Captain Gil had the ship's empty water casks brought on deck and then placed in the dinghies for transport to land. A small wooden cart was also floated to the beach to use in transporting the full casks from the well to the beach. Working efficiently together, the men had the water casks replenished and in the ship's hold within an hour. The rest of the afternoon expedition members were free to spend as they pleased.

A few men, including Antonio, took time to bathe with fresh water at the well. They took turns using wooden buckets to douse themselves. When it was his turn, Antonio first rinsed his clothes. He scrubbed and rinsed, pouring cool water over his head to wash away the salt and sweat that accumulated with every passing day at sea. After gathering his clothes, Antonio started walking back to the beach accompanied by young Miguel. They stopped short when confronted by the sight of the setting sun, half hidden by the offshore rock island. A dark band of clouds cut the sunlight into distinct rays, which shot up gigantically across the sky. The silhouette of the ship at anchor could be seen in the foreground, with a myriad of sea birds darting in the air around it. "There is some beauty in this harsh little island," he murmured to Miguel, who nodded in agreement. At the beach they sat on the sand to watch the spectacle unfold.

"Sitting here after a bath I realize that I am no longer a sailor at heart," confessed Antonio to Miguel. "Maybe I'm getting old but I'm not enjoying the crowded ship."

"It's not so bad," said Miguel. "And remember it's just a short time until we get to San Juan."

"I know. I guess I'm being a bit impatient to get there and see what awaits us." Antonio said no more but in his mind he could see a small house with planted fields. He would have to wait for the *Santa María* to arrive in San Juan, but he wondered if he would have the patience to wait for his dream to become reality once he got there.

Other men gathered beside them in silence. Later they built a fire and spent much of the night exchanging stories although, eventually, all conversations shifted to San Juan and the fortunes that waited there.

The three Indians stood on the white shell sand looking like shadows under the diffuse starlight. "They've arrived," called the lookout from the bowsprit.

"Send a dinghy to pick up our guests," ordered the captain to the waiting crew.

All had been made ready to quickly embark for San Juan after the arrival of the Taínos. Well before sunrise, the ship raised anchor and headed due south until it cleared the reefs next to Mona's beach. Once in deep water, the *Santa María* changed course to east-southeast fighting the prevailing winds, looking for San Juan. The cliffs of Mona reflected the dawn light as they sank below the blue horizon of the tropical sea.

Sibanacán and his two companions spent most of the time on the bow of the ship. All they were seeing—the ship with its sails, ropes and intricate woodwork—fascinated them, but most of all they seemed to enjoy looking out over the railing and having the wind in their faces. Juan González and Antonio, on their own and under orders from Ponce de León, made time to talk with the *caciques*. They learned that Cacique Agüeybaná continued to be the island's most powerful leader but that he was elderly and not in good health. His brother, also called Agüeybaná, a strong-willed man in his prime, stood ready to take over the leadership. According to the *caciques*, most Taínos knew about the presence of Spaniards from stories that had been told since the first landing by Admiral Colón in Borikén in 1493. Additional visits by Spanish ships, mostly to the west coast of Borikén, along with news brought from Taíno traders traveling to Española, had kept interest alive about the new visitors to their land. Neither González nor Dos Santos could determine if the Taínos from Borikén had a predetermined opinion about the Spaniards. Sibanacán maintained a neutral attitude that neither interpreter could penetrate.

"Land to port!" cried the lookout from atop the ship's main mast.

It was the morning of the third day since they left Mona Island. Like magic, every expedition member, even those working deep in the ship's hold, heard the call and came on deck to crowd excitedly around the port railing. Without the advantage of the mast's elevation the men had to wait until the ship floated to the top of a swell to catch a

34

glimpse of land. But every time they did they shouted and cheered.

"There it is," exclaimed several voices at once.

"Are those mountains or clouds?"

"They are mountains, you fool," rang the anonymous response to the anonymous question, even though no one could tell for sure what it was they were seeing. After a while the men tired of craning to see land and returned to their duties. However, throughout the day expedition members kept an eye towards the north as the land that would be their new home, their new adventure, came closer and closer.

On the after-castle Ponce de León and Captain Gil looked closely towards the coast, trying to identify an appropriate place for a landing. "Dos Santos," said Ponce de León to Antonio, who was manning the helm at the time. "Bring Sibanacán. Let's find out what he knows about the whereabouts of Agüeybaná."

"Yes, sir."

Another crewman took over the ship's wheel as Antonio went to carry out his orders. Soon he was back with the Taínos.

"Stay here and interpret for us," Ponce de León ordered Antonio, who did not fail to notice the importance of the trust being placed on him. "Do you recognize the coastline?" Ponce de León asked Sibanacán as he pointed towards land.

"I do. This is not far from where I have my *yucayeque*." Antonio used the Taíno word for village, which, like so many other Taíno words, had come into common use in Española.

"Where is Agüeybaná's *yucayeque*?"

"Farther along, beyond the place where the land makes a narrow opening and where the big fish swim."

Captain Gil and Ponce de León looked at each other and then at Antonio. "Are you sure about what you are translating?," Don Juan asked Antonio.

"I understood every word," said Antonio, somewhat upset with having to defend his abilities. "What I told you is what he said."

Ponce de León turned to Sibanacán. "Can you tell us when we reach the place?"

"That is why I am here." responded the Taíno in all seriousness. "The place where the land makes a narrow opening is past that land," he said pointing to a promontory that could be seen in the distance ahead of the ship. "After that, it is not far to our destination."

Captain Gil used the information from Sibanacán to steer around the promontory. As the highland mass slowly moved to the west "the place where the land makes a narrow opening" came into view. Sibanacán was referring to the mouth of a harbor where two massive headlands faced each other, leaving a narrow gap to the sea. Captain Gil proposed entering the harbor and exploring it, but was overruled by Ponce de León, who was eager to meet with Agüeybaná. As the ship sailed by, the captain could see the calm waters inside the bay. He made a mental note to explore this harbor at a later date, for it seemed so perfect.

The *Santa María* was now sailing close enough to the coast that its passengers could pick out details from the land. The vegetation appeared similar to what they'd left behind in Mona, small trees and thorny bushes growing on rocky soils. The rough topography produced headlands and rock formations extending out to sea, where they were battered by waves. Wherever the rocks were missing, small beaches with pure white sands reflected the sunlight so they could be seen clearly from the ship.

"Land ahead," called the lookout.

"What is it?" asked Captain Gil.

"Looks like small islands, right before that point ahead." The man signaled in the direction of what he was seeing.

"Turn to starboard," ordered the captain. "We'll seek deeper water," he said to Ponce de León. "Your Indian can tell us when to turn back towards land."

"I don't want any delays," said Ponce de León impatiently.

"It will be less delay than running aground," responded the captain sharply. "We don't have any charts of these waters, and I am not going to allow some half-naked savage to lead us through them." Captain Gil stood his ground. He respected Ponce de León's position as leader of the expedition, but when it was time to sail, he was in charge of the ship.

"Do what you must." Ponce de León pursed his lips, holding back his anger. He walked over to the gunwale and focused his eyes on land, lost in his own thoughts.

As soon as the *Santa María* reached deep water the captain tacked to the east-northeast. Within minutes Sibanacán approached Antonio. "That is where the big fish swim," he said pointing towards a crescent shaped bay the ship was passing by.

"What do you mean by that?"

"When the days are shorter large fish gather here. They dance on the waves and blow water in the air."

Antonio nodded, realizing the Taíno was talking about whales. "Where is Agüeybaná?" he asked.

"In Cayabo, where a river reaches the sea, not far from here. That is where Agüeybaná can be found."

Antonio relayed the information to Captain Gil who once again directed the ship closer to land. All eyes were either looking for reefs in their path or searching the coast for the river. A few hours later, with the help of Sibanacán, the river was spotted. A band of mangrove trees traced the shallow flow of the main channel, which was barely visible from the ship. Gil was pleasantly surprised that the river emptied into a small but well-protected bay, a detail that Sibanacán had failed to mention. Where the river met the sea there was no turbulence or other indication of a meeting of fresh and salt water, except for a series of shallows created from silt carried by the river. A collection of small coral islands created a barrier against open water swells. Captain Gil decided to drop anchor as close as possible to the beach, staying to the west of the river.

As if sprouting from the sand, four Indians appeared on the beach. They stood together, looking towards the ship with obvious curiosity. On board, one of Sibanacán's companions waved towards the men on the beach and then, without warning, gracefully leaped over the gunwale and into the sea. Members of the crew called out excitedly for the Taíno to stop but, swimming strongly, he quickly reached the beach.

"Never mind him," shouted Ponce de León. "Get the dinghies in the water." He then signaled his assistant to approach.

"Yes, sir."

"Prepare a well-armed landing party of ten men. Also, go in my cabin and bring the wooden chest that sits under the bed."

"Yes, sir."

Everyone on board was excited to reach San Juan. Antonio tried to remember fifteen years back, during his initial crossing of the Atlantic with Admiral Colón. At that time they had sailed all along the southern coast of San Juan, finally making a landing on the west coast. Antonio never got an opportunity to disembark during the two-day stay, but he remembered a beautiful land with tall mountains and lush green forests. And he remembered the stories from those who had made it to land. They talked about seeing a village with a street, a plaza and well-tended fields with a wide variety of vegetables. It always amazed Antonio that San Juan lay forgotten for all these years, considering it was so close to La Española. Except for a handful of preliminary excursions, the island remained untouched by Spanish hands.

Antonio knew that Ponce de León's expedition offered the opportunity to take control of his own future by being one of the initial settlers. Unlike in La Española, this time he was approaching this endeavor with a plan for himself and the experience to carry it out. The naiveté of the young sailor of fifteen years before was gone, not to impede the achievement of his goals.

Antonio joined the landing party escort on the main deck, and together with Ponce de León, Captain Gil, Sibanacán and his one remaining Indian companion, made ready to visit Agüeybaná. Antonio was armed with his sword and knife, and was given a round shield and spear to carry. Ponce de León and two of his officers were dressed in light

38

armor with chest and back plates, shin guards and helmets. It took two trips in the dinghies to transport everyone to shore. Once assembled, with spears raised high and banners flapping in the wind, the company was an impressive sight for the Taínos to behold.

Following the lead of Sibanacán they marched east, towards the river, until they reached a trail heading inland. Without hesitation Sibanacán entered the trail that traced the boundary between upland vegetation and the marsh grasses bordering the river. Eventually the marshes disappeared as the river, no longer affected by tidal waters, was reduced to a small stream running along the middle of a mostly dry riverbed. The foliage around the trail also changed as they moved inland. The thorny shrubs found near the beach were replaced with widely spaced trees. Tall grasses, easily reaching above a man's waist, blanketed every inch of ground. "Keep your eyes open for a possible ambush," came the general warning from the head of the column. The reminder of the obvious danger was not needed, all eyes were already alert and all hands held their weapons in steely grips.

Agüeybaná's *yucayeque* sat on a rise overlooking the riverbank. The visiting party was familiar with the arrangement of the Taíno village, not unlike to those in La Española. Several dozen of the traditional Taíno dwellings, *bohíos*, surrounded a central open area. They varied in size, but all were round in shape with walls made of the trunks of saplings laced together, and covered with conical thatched roofs. Children could be seen running among the *bohíos*. The sound of their giggles carried over to the approaching Spaniards. Smoke from open fires scented the air with the aromatic smell of burning wood.

A large group of Taíno men gathered at the trail blocking the approach. Several of them wore impressive feathered headdresses along with bracelets and necklaces, some made of gold, accentuating their bronze skin, which was covered with brightly colored paint in a variety of designs. Many of the men were naked, while others wore nothing more than short loincloths. Most had their skin covered with markings and painted symbols. An older man

39

standing in the center of the group wore a long loincloth that stretched to his ankles and had a large, delicately wrought, golden disk hanging from his neck. Antonio recognized the *guanín*, symbol of authority used by the *cacique*, and guessed that he was looking at Agüeybaná. The Europeans advanced towards the Taínos and stopped at a comfortable talking distance.

Sibanacán was the first to approach the Taínos. "Agüeybaná," he said. "I bring to you the white men. They have returned to our land and seek to meet with you."

"You are welcome Sibanacán," responded Agüeybaná. "I will speak with these visitors."

Sibanacán signaled for Ponce de León to approach, which he did in the company of Captain Gil and Juan Gonzalez, who served as interpreter. "My name is Juan Ponce de León," said the Spanish leader through his interpreter. "We come to this land to share it with you as peaceful neighbors."

"If you come in peace, then you are welcome," said the old chief.

"I bring you gifts as a sign of our friendship." Ponce de León signaled for his chest to be carried forward. The Taínos looked with curiosity as he opened the box, pulled out a pewter goblet and presented it to Agüeybaná. "It is used for drinking," he explained as the *cacique* admired the gift with a smile on his face. Ponce de León produced other items, mostly cheap trinkets to the Spaniards, which he had carefully selected to be novelties to the Taínos.

The rest of the meeting was cordial. Agüeybaná once again welcomed the visitors to his land and agreed to meet with Ponce de León the next day. The landing party left the meeting under the curious gaze of everyone in the *yucayeque*.

"That went very well!" exulted Ponce de León to his officers. "Tomorrow I'll give him some more gifts and next thing you know he'll be growing food for our settlement and telling me everything I need to know about Borikén."

The return to the beach was more relaxed for the men in the company. They bragged and joked about their

40

future plans in the island, confident that they had just made a good beginning with Agüeybaná. Arriving on the beach, they were met by most of the expedition members who had come ashore to get the feel of solid ground under their feet. That evening the mood was festive. The men built a large bonfire and gathered around it to tell stories. Before the night was out, a guitar and a flute created enough music for several of those present dance around the bonfire accompanied by the rhythm of clapping hands.

IV

EASTERN PASSAGE

Antonio was disappointed that he was not asked to go to the Taíno village the next day. Feeling more at ease after their initial encounter, Ponce de León opted to visit Agüeybaná with only a few of his officers and Juan Gonzalez who once again served as interpreter. During that second visit, Ponce de León exchanged names with Agüeybaná, a Taíno custom that assured mutual friendship between the participants. With this new status, Ponce de León was able to secure fruit and other produce from the Taínos. Meanwhile, Antonio and the rest of the crew worked to provision the ship with water and whatever other fresh food the men could gather from land.

During the night, after three full days in San Juan, the weather started to turn. Dense clouds covered a sky that in previous days had shone with the light of a million stars. The ship lay at anchor exposed to the wind from all directions except the north, where the island of San Juan provided some shelter. The low-lying peninsulas enclosing the harbor did little to block the wind. The harbor did provide some protection from the powerful open-sea waves that could be seen in the distance, crashing thunderously over reefs. The harbor waters remained covered with whitecaps, and strong waves battered the beach where a few days before they had celebrated their arrival at Borikén. The men on board awoke to the dreary feel of a wet, overcast day. Above the constant whine of the wind they could hear Captain Gil shouting orders to his crew as he ran from bow to stern, fighting the waves and wind which sought to cast the *Santa María* onto the beach.

The storm intensified as the morning progressed. All aboard were kept busy moving perishable provisions to the upper holds and securing loose items. Sometime around noon the rising tide and the unrelenting wind combined to overwhelm the two anchors holding the ship secure. With a sudden lurch, the ship began to move towards the beach, the anchors dragging ineffectively below the waves. Near chaos reigned on board. Men ran to and fro, fear palpable on their faces. Everyone felt the keel scraping sand. The ship tilted slightly to port. The waves kept a constant pounding against the starboard side. Water seeped into the ship from every crack, and now and then a large swell sent arush of water over the prostrated gunwale. Every available man was sent to help bail water and seal cracks. Even Rodrigo, whose main responsibility was the galley, showed up to work on the lower deck.

By evening the worst of the storm had passed. Captain Gil continued to give orders to bail water and protect the supplies. Eventually the exhausted men each found a place to crawl into for the night after a dinner of dry bread, water and, if lucky, a piece of the Taíno gift fruit.

Dawn arrived early and bright. The *Santa María* was once again beached clear out of the water. The storm tide and waves had receded, leaving the ship high and dry on the sand. Captain Gil picked up where he left off the night before, barking orders to get the men moving. Before any breakfast, all hands were unloading supplies on the beach to dry and to lighten the ship. It was almost midday when they stopped to eat a thick stew prepared by Rodrigo.

After lunch the main goal was to return the ship to the water. The high tide was expected in the afternoon, but it would barely reach the ship. To help the tide, Captain Gil directed the digging of a wide trench extending from the water's edge and encircling the ship. Once again all expedition members worked together using a variety of improvised digging tools. Within two hours the trench was completed and soon began to fill with water. Ropes were tied to the ship and the men began to pull. However, the trench filled with sand as much as with water. The task of moving the ship became a painstaking, inch-by-inch effort. Some men were digging out sand, others pulling, all of them cursing under the intense tropical sun.

By nightfall, the ship sat at water's edge. Captain Gil knew the ship would be afloat by noon the next day; he also knew that there was no more available strength to continue work at that moment. After another stew, this time full of fish and other seafood, sleep came quickly, no songs, no boasting, no games.

The next morning moans and groans were heard as tight and aching muscles were forced to wake. Antonio was not looking forward to the work that lay ahead. Everyone could see that overnight the ship had settled in the soft sand; there was plenty of digging to do. After relieving himself in nearby bushes, Antonio splashed water on his face and took a short walk to loosen up. To his left he could see the bay's wide opening to the sea. Not far ahead there was a shallow area with a rock formation lining the shore. Next to the rocks, mangrove trees grew into the water. The branches of the trees held half a dozen dazzlingly white egrets. The water near the mangroves was teeming with small fish splashing and jumping through the air, a dark shadow chasing them. Inland, beyond the mangroves, the vegetation was scrubby and coarse.

"This part of the island is dry and not very inviting," thought Antonio, already cataloguing his observations, thinking ahead to the day he would settle his own land in Borikén.

Sudden calls from the *Santa María* interrupted Antonio's observations. He jogged back to the company and joined in the digging. Gil had been wrong in his estimate. It wasn't until the late afternoon high tide that the crew was able to float the *Santa María*. A few of the crew leapt on board and set the sails in a way that aided the crew as they coaxed the ship to deeper water.

"Shit. Finally!" exclaimed Rodrigo once the ship's keel was freed. He was tired of sitting exposed to the hot sun, while cooking over an open fire. No one would be happier to be back on board.

By noon the following day, the supplies had been returned to the ship. Several Taínos who had been curiously watching the events of the previous days showed up before the ship's departure with baskets full of fruit and produce. Ponce de León expressed his appreciation for this gesture and in return presented the Indians with a gift of a length of cotton fabric. That done, the ship set sail again.

Captain Gil was glad to be back at sea. The wind was blowing steady and brisk. The seas were relatively calm but white caps dotted the water's surface. Gil led the ship straight out, away from land as if wanting to stretch the ships sails and get away from the place that almost trapped the expedition.

When the coastline dipped below the horizon and the mountains became a hint in the distance, Ponce de León approached Captain Gil. "Captain, I would prefer sailing closer to the coast. We can't learn much about the island if we sail in the open ocean."

"You are right, but the ship needed the open water after being caught on the beach. We were fortunate we didn't suffer more damage. Next time the weather threatens I am heading out to sea. We've been beached twice in this expedition and I don't intend to let it happen again," said Gil frustrated by the second grounding of the *Santa María* in such a short time.

"That's fine, Captain. However," continued Ponce de León with an amused smile, "I don't have your sea legs. I wouldn't mind if you let me off on land before heading out in a hurricane."

"It's a deal," said Captain Gil, then he gave the order to turn the ship about.

The waters were deep and the *Santa María* was able to sail close to the coast. Antonio enjoyed spying on this new land. In the distance the tall mountains rose to form an impressive wall paralleling the coast. He noticed the rugged coastline offering numerous excellent anchorage areas. The *Santa María* sailed into some of these to explore their potential. Antonio observed that the vegetation on land continued to be the kind you would find in dry areas. Although they had seen numerous streams emptying to the sea, it was clear that this southern side of San Juan was dry and would present some challenges to anyone trying to farm there.

After two days the *Santa María* turned to a more northeasterly direction. The coastal plains ended. Instead,

45

mountainous terrain stretched to waters' edge, meeting the sea with naked cliffs topped with abundant vegetation. The scrubby vegetation of the south coast was no longer evident. In its place there was dense jungle, verdant and mysterious. Off to starboard, in the distance, the passengers could see the outline of a large island. The waters they were sailing now were shallower and the ocean changed from a deep blue to a light aqua-green.

The islands east of San Juan were settled by the fierce Carib Indians. Ponce de León ordered additional day and night lookouts as a precaution. To date, every encounter of Spaniards with the Caribs had been violent. Starting with Admiral Colón who, on his second voyage to the New World, disembarked on an island they named Santa Cruz. There, they had been ambushed by a large band of Caribs. These fearsome natives fought as if possessed by the devil. Only their superior weapons allowed the Spaniards to overcome the ambush. From Taínos in La Española they learned that the Caribs periodically raided neighboring islands, taking prisoners to their own villages. It was rumored that Caribs practiced cannibalism with their male prisoners and kept the women as slaves. Now that they were to be neighbors, Ponce de León expected there would be more frequent encounters with Caribs.

On several occasions the lookouts spotted canoes in the distance. Ponce de León ordered the ship to sail close to shore in hopes of intercepting one of these groups of natives, but the canoes never came close. On one clear day the *Santa María* sailed along the coast until late in the afternoon, when Captain Gil dropped anchor in a protected bay with a small river emptying into it. The horseshoe-shaped bay had tall, jungle-draped cliffs embracing the waters. At the beach a ribbon of fine golden sand met transparent waters. The ship rested on glassy calm waters. The waters were so clear that, even in the dimming light of early evening, one could see the anchor chain clear down to the anchor. Some of the men were sent up river to replenish fresh water supplies while others fished.

Busy with chores, no one noticed the three Taínos

who emerged from the trees near the mouth of the river. The group gathering water were so startled by the Indians that they nearly overturned their dingy. Quickly they rowed to the ship and soon Ponce de León was on his way to shore with a small party, including Antonio. As they approached the beach, Antonio observed that the Taínos were dressed in formal attire according to their customs. The Taínos were all men wearing feather headdress. One had a loincloth while the other two were naked. All had their bodies painted in colorful patterns such that it was difficult to notice their nakedness. They carried weapons, bow and arrows and *macanas*, a heavy sword-like wooden club. Most interesting to the European visitors were the golden ear and nose rings worn by the Indians.

Ponce de León approached the Taínos respectfully, Antonio at his side to serve as interpreter. They learned that there were numerous villages in this part of San Juan; the local *cacique* was called Humaca; and gold was found by carefully looking in mountain streams. The Indians learned that the white visitors were servants of a powerful king and that they intended to settle in Borikén. The meeting was short. Apparently satisfied with what they learned, the Taínos suddenly and swiftly reentered the jungle and vanished.

In the small community of the ship it was not long before everyone knew of the Indian's gold, and grand stories of available riches formed quickly. The encounter served to re-energize the members of the expedition, whose muscles still remembered pulling the ship to sea just a few days before. Chores were completed faster and the Captain's orders were followed with crisp efficiency.

Sailing the east side of San Juan proved somewhat challenging. Close to shore there were numerous sand banks. The unknown waters were relatively shallow, requiring constant sounding and a vigilant lookout in order to keep to the reef-free areas between the large island of San Juan and several small islands to the east. The wind direction forced the ship to tack repeatedly to find a favorable angle for the sails. In spite of the sailing challenges, there was not a man on board who did not appreciate the beauty of the crystal clear waters ringing virgin islands with white, sandy beaches. To the west, San Juan was crowned by tall mountains that tumbled towards the sea, ending in imposing headlands, all covered by a carpet of thick vegetation. Overhead, a wide variety of birds danced playfully above the ship, curious about this small floating island.

Nighttime was imminent as the *Santa María* approached a narrow passage to the open sea north of San Juan. Captain Gil, preferring to have full light as he made the crossing, decided to drop anchor in the protected waters of the small, unnamed island that marked the end of the eastern passage. Most sailors and passengers enjoyed the opportunity to bathe in the clear waters that held the ship as if in molten glass. Antonio removed his shoes and joined his shipmates jumping off the bulkhead. The water felt refreshing after a hot day of unrelenting sun. He could feel his every pore contract in response to the cool water. Re-energized, Antonio swam to the beach. He was surprised to find that the white sand fringing the island was rough to the touch. Looking closely he noticed it was not really sand, but crushed shells and coral. Nevertheless, it was fine enough that he could walk on it without a problem.

The ship's deck lights were already lit when Antonio climbed the rope ladder along its side. He was the last man out of the water. After wringing his shirt he went below decks to change into dry pants and then headed to the galley. The swim and walk had awakened his appetite and he was counting on his friend Rodrigo to smuggle some food to him.

"Don Rodrigo, what do you have for a hungry sailor?" asked Antonio in his friendliest voice.

"Go away!" barked Rodrigo. "There is nothing like a swim to open a man's appetite and I've had everyone stopping by for a handout." Looking away and continuing with his chores Rodrigo kept talking. "You'll eat when everyone else eats. And don't expect anything other than what we've been eating – fish stew and old bread."

Antonio knew better than to say another word.

The next morning everyone was awakened by the

alarmed calls from the lookout on deck. "Something is moving on the beach. They are coming out of the water!" The young man, still a teenager, could not hide the fear in his voice. Captain Gil, and even Ponce de León, came on deck to find out what was going on, fearing a possible Carib raid. All could see the movement on the beach. There was a shared suspense as the men looked through the early dawn shadows trying to figure out what they were seeing.

"They are turtles, you fools!" boomed Rodrigo's voice. "They are laying eggs".

That statement of the obvious released the tension that was felt by all, and mostly by the lookout who, with no knowledge of these animals, had been overtaken by deep-seated superstitions. Now he faced weeks of teasing and ridicule from his shipmates.

Once the turtles were identified, Captain Gil sent a contingent of men to butcher half a dozen animals and bring the meat and eggs to the ship. The opportunity to replenish their stores of meat and to have fresh eggs could not be missed.

The sun-bleached coral sand turned red under the slit throats of the upturned turtles. Their fins flapped in the air slowly as if waving good-bye after a long visit. Eventually the blood reached the water sending plumes of red as calling cards to all sorts of predators. Before the butchers were back on board, the waters around the *Santa María* were infested with sharks.

Late morning Captain Gil ordered to unfurl the sails and raise anchor. With extreme care, the ship sailed around the coral reefs that circled most of the small island that served as their anchorage and proceeded to round the imposing headlands at the northeast end of San Juan. Beyond that point, the *Santa María* assumed a westerly heading with favorable winds from stern. Now sailing in the deep blue waters of the Atlantic, the captain could relax his guard and allow the ship to move confidently among the whitecaps.

With the sun low on the horizon, and after consulting with Ponce de León, Captain Gil pulled the ship closer to shore to look for safe anchoring. Ponce de León's notes from

49

his previous exploratory trip indicated that their destination, a large enclosed bay, was not far away and they did not want to miss it by sailing at night. Eventually, the *Santa María* found protected waters between a small rock island covered with sea birds and a sandy headland that transitioned into a shallow reef where it met the water.

That night, all aboard the *Santa María* were in good spirits; their bellies where full of fresh meat, the ship was safely moored and they were near their destination in San Juan. A cool, soft breeze blew steadily from the northeast, making it very comfortable on deck. Antonio settled himself on a coiled rope near the bow of the ship. The soft lapping of waves on the beach could be heard in the background and overhead, scattered clouds could not hide the intensely starlit sky. With Antonio were the brothers Gabriel and Miguel and a couple of other men who had wandered over looking for players in a game of dice. Gabriel's eyes lit up when he saw the dice.

"He likes playing, I see," said Antonio to Miguel, who had moved closer to get away from the game.

"Ever since he was a little kid. And I'll tell you something— he is good. I've learned not to play anytime he is around."

"I'm not a big player," said Antonio, amused by the game in front of him. "I find I lose most times, and I work too hard for what I have to give it away like that. In any case, thanks for the warning about Gabriel."

Using the deck as a table, Gabriel and his two adversaries where concentrating deeply on their game. Their calls and shouts attracted a small crowd. At every roll the voices went up and soon side bets were taking place. Antonio stood up to get a better look at the action. Gabriel's sour expression indicated that things were not going well for him. Following a few intense plays Gabriel reached a decision point; a final roll would decide if he made modest gains or lost all he bet. After a scramble to make final wagers, the small group of men went suddenly very quiet. Gabriel looked at his brother who offered an encouraging smile. He kissed the dice and rolled with an expert flick of the wrist.

50

Two seconds later Gabriel threw his arms over his head and called out in a shout of victory. A close game! Not a very lucrative one, but a win nonetheless. The other two players walked away cursing their bad luck, while the men who bet for him congratulated Gabriel for his excellent play and inspiring good luck.

The next morning there was a high level of excitement building among the crew. The offshore line of coral, which forced the ship away from the coast along the northeast coast of the island, now lay closer to the beach. This allowed the *Santa María* to sail relatively close to land. Mangroves, sea grapes and other coastal vegetation could be seen clearly, interspersed with sandy beaches. This gentle ocean front pattern was broken abruptly at a rocky cove, which seemed to lead to a lagoon. Thereafter the land along the waterfront rose steadily to form a formidable rock cliff with waves breaking threateningly over coral and rocks at its base. Even though the dark blue water was obviously very deep, Captain Gil ordered the ship to move farther out to sea. "I'm not pulling the ship out of any more rocks," he swore to himself.

"There it is," exclaimed Ponce de León pointing ahead. "See where the cliff goes down to the water? That's it, the entrance to the bay. On the other side there is no cliff. See?"

"I see," responded Captain Gil. "Stay on course and prepare for a turn to port," he called to the helmsman. The second officer reacted to the command by shouting out orders to the sailors, getting ready to engage in the intricate dance of sails and ropes and straining wood that allowed the ship to move with deceiving ease over the waters.

Within a half hour the ship was rounding the headland identified by Ponce de León and entering the bay that was their destination. All aboard were on deck to witness the arrival. The ship moved cautiously at half-sail. Men at the bow concentrated on the water ahead looking for signs of rocks or sand banks. As they sailed further into the bay, the Captain's expression transformed into one of awe. "This is an amazing harbor," he said to Ponce de León. "We

51

could anchor the whole Spanish fleet and still have plenty of room to maneuver."

"I knew you would appreciate this place Captain," Ponce de León said with a smile. "We need to explore the area and try to find an adequate location to set up camp."

The *Santa María* carefully set out to sail around the bay, which extended east from its mouth in a huge oval shape. The strong voice of a sailor repeatedly sounding the waters and calling out its depth was like a slow drumbeat in the background. The cliffs facing the open ocean served to block most of the wind, providing for smooth waters in the harbor, while allowing enough of a breeze for the ship to sail. On several occasions, the Captain ordered to drop anchor and small rowboats approached land, looking for a high, dry place that they could use as a home base.

To the north, the land with the cliffs was too exposed and rocky, and had no obvious source of fresh water. At the deepest, easternmost point of the harbor the rowboat followed what looked like a small river, but found its way blocked by dense mangrove forest. To the south, the Spaniards found nothing but mangroves and extensive marshes. The men who visited these areas were chased away by swarms of mosquitoes. The western edge of the bay included a narrow sand spit that could be seen from the ship. The waters on that side of the bay proved too shallow for the *Santa María*.

Towards the end of the day, the Captain moved the ship to a quiet spot on the north side of the harbor, not far from the opening to the ocean. Most men went ashore and could be seen climbing on rocks and swimming in the calm waters. Ponce de León and Captain Gil stood together near the ship's wheel.

"I had every expectation that we would find an adequate place to camp along a harbor of this size," said Ponce de León. "I must admit I'm disappointed. I'm eager to get off this ship and get on to the business of establishing a colony."

At this last Captain Gil could be seen to stand a bit straighter and look at Ponce de León.

"Nothing against your ship, Captain," said Ponce de León noticing the Captain's reaction. "Please take no offense. You must understand, I am a man of land and I have a mission to settle this island. If I misspeak, then you are hearing the voice of my impatience."

"I understand how you feel," said Gil, relaxing his posture. "How do you wish to proceed?"

"There are some other anchorages further west, not far from here. However, none are as grand as this harbor."

"I should think not," interrupted Gil. "This place is truly extraordinary."

Ponce de León smiled at the Captain's interruption. It was obvious that the man had a sailor's appreciation of this protected body of water and its potential for a new colony.

The next day, the ship sailed when only the slightest glow could be seen on the eastern horizon. Moving slowly through the mouth of the harbor, the *Santa María* quickly gained speed when entering the deep ocean water and facing the full force of the trade winds. By late afternoon, the *Santa María* was pulling into a small harbor where a river emptied to the sea. The next morning, the ship was unloaded and everyone except the crew was moved to land.

That night, their first on the island of San Juan, there was great excitement. A large fire was built, and the men gathered after eating. They talked about the new settlement and what they would be doing over the coming days. As the night progressed they noticed the curious sounds that surrounded them. In particular the low-sharp rhythm of a two-note song that sprang all around them. The song seemed to originate from a thousand places at once. The sound was gentle and although some of the men let their superstitions bring fear to their hearts, eventually the sound faded to the background along with the more familiar crickets and other insects. In the next few weeks, the men would find the source of the night music in a tiny tree frog they named "*coquí*," after its song.

Late that night, the often-repeated stories of dreams of fortune and gold were retold, bringing comfort to the

53

men and reminding them of why they were there. Antonio listened, knowing that his own story and his dreams were different. He dreamed of having a place to call his own. He had no dreams of great haciendas and riches, just the freedom of being his own master. Never, since being sent away by his mother, had he ever been truly independent. He had always been at the mercy of someone else: an uncle who did not want him, shipmasters, captains, governors, admirals, all directing his life.

Antonio's mind wandered to his first experience on a ship. Within months of arriving in Lisbon, his uncle, an ambitious but unsuccessful merchant, had placed Antonio with a local ship master in exchange for a few silver pieces. Rodolfo Pedroza, his first ship master when he was still a boy of ten, was overbearing and abusive and cared nothing for any of his crew, including young Antonio. For three years Antonio suffered under his command, until one day, during a trip along West Africa. They sailed a short distance up a river to replenish their fresh water supplies. Antonio disembarked along with others wanting time off from their musty ship. He wandered off on his own, following a stream, and found a small grotto with water falling like silk into a stone-lined pool surrounded by tropical flowers and foliage. The fourteen year-old boy had never seen a more beautiful place and he delayed returning to the river. When he finally got back he found that Master Pedroza had abandoned him. The ship was gone.

Fear gripped Antonio as he realized his predicament. More than anything he was afraid of spending a night in the jungle, so he made his way downriver hoping to reach the sea. He reached an area of extensive sand dunes in time to see the last rays of what must have been a spectacular sunset. Ahead of him he could hear the waves breaking. Wanting to leave the jungle as far behind as he could, he walked on the sand towards the breaking surf. On the dune closest to the water he found a large bush and crawled under its foliage, made a shallow depression in the still warm sand and fell asleep with the waves' rhythmic song in the background.

Antonio awakened to see the last stars fade in the

westen horizon. He was surprised by how well he had slept and attributed it to the great sense of relief he felt from being free of Rodolfo Pedroza. He sat for a long time in the same shelter where he slept, looking over the crashing surf and thinking of many things. It was still early in the morning when Antonio saw a group of men laying fishing traps by the mouth of the river. He approached nervously.

He was hungry and thirsty. With hand signals, he was able to explain his situation. The fishermen had seen the ship the day before and had little problem understanding where this pale skinned boy could have come from. Antonio observed the fishermen at work for a long while. One of the older fishermen, Fulaya, was the first to approach Antonio. He offered fresh water, bread and fruit to the boy who accepted with trembling hands. Afterwards Antonio stayed with Fulaya and spent the rest of the day helping with the traps and nets. Late in the afternoon, as the men were packing their gear and catch, Fulaya approached Antonio and invited the boy to come with him. Antonio's relief was obvious and Fulaya smiled kindly. The old man was a respected elder in the fishing village of Dikya, where the Koumba River met other rivers on their way to the ocean. He lived with his wife and three daughters and was happy to welcome another male into the household, regardless of his strange origins. Fulaya was able to bring Antonio into Dikya with little difficulty. The young man was not a threat and had already proven an able worker; further, Fulaya had agreed to house him so the boy was not a burden to anyone else.

Dikya was Antonio's home for three years. Every day he grew stronger and every day he was more help to Fulaya and his family. In Dikya he learned how to integrate himself into a completely different society and developed a deep respect for these so called "primitive" people. In Dikya he also learned to love for the first time as he fell for Ayainda, Fulaya's youngest daughter.

"Ayainda, you will help Anto," said Fulaya to his daughter using the boy's newly given name.

"Yes father." Ayainda smiled in response, having no idea what to make of this new chore.

55

At first it was not easy. Ayainda and Anto had to invent a new language to help them communicate until, little by little, Anto learned the language of the villagers. Ayainda was a good humored girl of 12 and she found Anto's efforts to fit in quite funny. Everyday activities the villagers took for granted, like the proper way to eat fish stew or how to pour water from a clay jar, became amusing adventures with Anto. The first time he decided to join the other young men at a dance became a humorous story that was repeated for generations. Poor Anto was so clumsy he knocked down several other dancers before he was pulled away by Ayainda. Fortunately, Anto was a quick learner, and although he never stopped needing Ayainda's help dealing with the challenges of moving into a new culture, he did become much more self reliant.

One day, a European ship sailed up the Koumba River and Antonio was faced with the biggest decision of his life. From the day he was abandoned he had hoped to be rescued. But at that moment, with the opportunity to leave floating on the Koumba, he wondered what that meant. Would returning to a ship's crew under someone like Pedroza be better than staying in Dikya, where he was part of a family and respected? And what about Ayainda? But, did he want to spend his whole life fishing at the shores of the Koumba? He had already seen much in his young life and he knew there was a large world beyond Dikya, one that had a strong hold on his imagination.

Antonio swam to the ship and met with the shipmaster Francisco Dos Santos. Dos Santos was a thin man of medium height whose appearance was dominated by a thick mane of long black hair. Once over his surprise at meeting a white boy in the middle of an African wilderness, this bright, honest man immediately grasped Antonio's dilemma and, taking a liking to the young man, convinced him to join his crew. To facilitate this, he offered to wait a day to let Antonio get his affairs in order.

Antonio struggled with his decision. However, Fulaya made the transition easier.

"Anto", he called, waving his hand to call the boy

next to him. Anto walked slowly to the man that was like a stepfather to him. "I can see that you are troubled. Talk to me."

"I have the opportunity to leave, but I'm not sure I should go".

"Do you have any doubts about staying here?"

"Some", said Anto quietly. "I always thought I would leave, but", he paused, "I like it here, with you and Ayainda and the others."

"I know. But you are young. You have a long life ahead of you". Fulaya put one of his calloused hands on Anto's knee and looked into the boys' eyes. "I never thought you would live here your whole life. Your world is a different one, out there on that boat." Fulaya waited, looking for a reaction in Anto's face. "You can go back to your people. But remember, you will always have a home here". Fulaya's big black eyes were filled with tears that would not drop.

It was not easy saying good-bye to the people who had helped him and had offered him so much. Most difficult for Anto was saying good-bye to Ayainda. He would miss her more than anyone, especially after that last night when she quietly crawled into his bed knowing they would never be together again.

Within two days, the Spaniards had built a rough *bohio* they would use for shelter. Ponce de León then ordered the ship to return to Mona Island to pick up supplies scheduled for delivery to that location. Ponce de León had made arrangements with his people in Yuma to use Mona Island as a supply station for the expedition to San Juan.

The night before the ship was to depart, Antonio met with Rodrigo at the cook's kitchen. "Mi amigo, it seems to me that we'll be parting ways tomorrow," said Antonio slapping Rodrigo's beefy shoulder in a friendly gesture.

"Yeah, but we'll be back before you know it."

Antonio sat on a stool and rested his elbows on the counter used by Rodrigo to prepare his foods. "What do you think of this place?" he asked.

"In all honesty," answered Rodrigo, "I think you'll be out of here in a few weeks. There's good access to water and

57

some flat land that seems arable, but the anchorage is shit! And a new colony needs access to ships and commerce."

"I think you may be right but I hope you are not. I have plans for this island and am ready to get going." Antonio's eyes betrayed his excitement about finally starting a settlement in San Juan. "I already scouted the area and you are right, the land here is good. Soils are loose and not too rocky and the forest is not too dense. I could have a small farm producing within a year."

Rodrigo looked at Antonio as if he hated what he was about to say. "I think you are getting a bit ahead of yourself. You know how things work; first we build the governor's house, then the priest's house, then, maybe, a building for the men. They always find other priorities than what is good for us sailors and workers. You saw it in Santo Domingo, they use us until we die." After a pause he continued as if he just remembered something he meant to say. "And you better start shitting gold if you think you will get any land for yourself. Land is for the rich lords to get richer."

Antonio grew serious and looked at his own hands, calloused and rough from years of working for other people's gain. He knew Rodrigo was right. "I know what you are saying, but I have a plan. I don't intend to spend much time working for others on this island."

Rodrigo smiled at his friend and reached down to pull out a pint bottle from a cabinet. He filled two small cups with the contents. "Here's to your future in San Juan. I hope you are your own master the next time I see you."

"*Salud*," cheered Antonio, and he grimaced as the acrid rum burned his throat.

Rodrigo's predictions on the fate of the expedition were correct but not precise. The *Santa María* departed as scheduled. Meanwhile, Ponce de León organized the men to accomplish the tasks required of a new settlement. Some men hunted, fished and gathered fresh foods; others explored the area and planned for future vegetable and grain plantings; another group spent time building rudimentary shelters and facilities for the settlement; and yet others were sent upstream to pan for gold along the river and its tributaries.

The latter task, although least important for the immediate survival of the settlement, was critical for the morale of the men. The tiniest speck of gold was enough to validate the sacrifices and hard work of establishing a new settlement. It didn't take long for the prospectors to return with evidence that the colony in San Juan was a worthwhile endeavor.

As the summer advanced into fall, the trade winds became stiffer and the ocean waters rougher. When the *Santa María* returned, the value of a good anchorage became evident. The narrow pass through the reefs and the small harbor, barely adequate with calm seas, presented the ship master with a great challenge in the new season. The difficulties in securing the ship and unloading provisions led Ponce de León to consider finding a more suitable site for the settlement. It took the expedition leader a month longer than the ship's cook to realize that a new settlement needs secure anchorage.

During an encounter with curious Indians, Antonio had learned that the river by the new settlement was called the Ano River. He also learned that further east there was a larger river, the Toa, within a days' walk. With this information Ponce de León led a group of men, including Antonio, in search of the Toa River and better conditions for a permanent settlement, including a better harbor. For two weeks the men explored the area but could not find what they sought. The Toa River was substantially larger than the Ano, but still too small to be considered navigable by even the smallest caravel. In addition, it emptied into the ocean among treacherous unprotected shallows. A harbor west of the Toa showed some promise but the reefs protecting it from the open ocean were too hazardous to risk sailing through.

Ponce de León and his men returned to the Ano River settlement with plans to make improvements to help ships bringing supplies. Once again Ponce de León sent the *Santa María* for provisions to Mona Island. In the meantime, he ordered the construction of a dock and a road to connect the settlement to the waterfront. What nature didn't offer on its own the Spaniards were seeking to provide through their work.

The *Santa María* arrived back at the settlement to find a simple dock ready for use and numerous other improvements. That same evening it began to rain softly. However, from the coastal outpost one could see dense clouds accumulating over the mountain tops along the center of San Juan. It was easy to guess that the mountains were getting a lot more rain than they were at the coast. The rain continued steadily for two days. The roof of the *bohio* that served as the main shelter started to fail and eventually it was no easier staying dry inside than outside the shelter. The Ano River swelled overnight and began to overflow its banks. Before dawn, the settlement was ankle deep in water and everyone had been woken by the watchmen.

Ponce de León held a quick meeting with the shipmaster and then turned to give out orders. "We can't leave in the ship because of the low tide and the darkness. Load everything you can carry and gather at the eastern trail."

"Where are we going?" called an unidentifiable voice out of the darkness.

"Back to the large harbor we explored weeks ago," answered Ponce de León. He was not used to having to explain his orders. However, on this occasion he felt it was prudent. "Now hurry," he snapped, "this flood is coming on fast."

Captain Gil and his men left without delay, finding they had to wade through chest deep water before swimming the last stretch to the ship. Meanwhile the other men rescued supplies and equipment from the flood. Two carts were loaded with all they could carry. Still the group of men and their leader had to hand carry some of the supplies in their hasty escape from the floodwaters.

Wet and short-tempered, they walked eastward through a sunless dawn. They barely stopped to rest until they reached the Toa River late in the morning, just as the rain ceased. The swollen river blocked their route and Ponce de León decided to take the opportunity to rest the men and reorganize the expedition so they could travel better.

Antonio and the brothers Miguel and Gabriel unloaded the carts and then reloaded them carefully. They were able to accommodate all the equipment so the men could walk unburdened. Scouts were sent up and downstream in search of a ford to cross the river. Both teams reported that the river current was too strong to consider a crossing that day. Ponce de León was familiar with mountain-fed rivers and knew that within a day or two the waters would recede. So they set camp, and waited for the island to drain itself.

After a night of tired sleep the men welcomed the new dawn with its promise of warmth and the opportunity to dry out—but, not before crossing the river. With a horse pulling and men pushing, the carts were coerced across a rocky ford with a swift current that sought to cut the men at the knees. Once across, the group advanced at a rapid pace. The ground was level and the vegetation could be cleared without much difficulty. By late afternoon they arrived at a small ridge and from the top they could see the harbor that was their destination, still a few miles away. Ponce de León, relieved to see the familiar panorama, ordered his men to set camp alongside a gently flowing creek with clear water. Although he considered pushing to reach the settlement site, he thought it better to give the men time to gather themselves. The men drank, washed and ate and all but the night watch were asleep not long after dark.

By midday the next day the group had hacked a trail through the mangrove trees lining the harbor shoreline. Within a week they had built another *bohio* for shelter just inland from the mangroves, a dock at the harbor and cleared a road connecting both. Within four weeks, well into November, Ponce de León decided to move the settlement once again. Humidity, mosquitoes and poor access to fresh water had made the bay-side settlement impractical and uncomfortable. After searching the area they found a better location on a hillside, open to breezes and with nearby potable water. The main inconvenience of the new location was that it was half a league from the harbor and not far away enough from the mangrove swamp to keep the mosquitoes away. Ponce de León named the new settlement Villa de Caparra and immediately ordered the construction of his house and a jail, to be made out of stone, a church and the extension of the road leading to the harbor. It was November 1508, and from this outpost Ponce de León expected that Spain would rule San Juan Bautista for many years to come.

DOS SANTOS
Part II

Así dicen las historias que me contaba mi abuelo,
De un mundo en paz y tranquilo,
De un pueblo lleno de un amor profundo,
De un sol y una luna que mi isla cuidaban.

¿Donde está la india taína?
¿Donde está su hombre con valor?
Mucha gente no los encuentran
Por que no los buscan dentro de su corazón.

Francisco Xavier de Aragón
From his poem '*Los Seres De Tu Pasado*'

V

THE CELL

There were only a handful of structures in Villa de Caparra. One of the strongest was the stone jail. It was also one of first built and by far the smallest. The prison was purposefully located where it was exposed to the relentless tropical sun from mid morning to sunset. It consisted of a single square cell, two meters to a side. The clay floor in the cell was mostly dry except for a corner where the prisoners relieved themselves. The stench of the waste was alleviated by a weak flow of fresh air entering the cell through two windows, which amounted to no more than small slits in the stone walls.

The cell was occupied by two men. The younger man, Rodolfo, was a corporal with the regular army, no more than 25 years of age, tall, of medium build with dark hair and brown eyes. Two days earlier he got drunk and, during a heated argument, punched a sergeant who made the mistake of making Rodolfo's mother a topic of discussion. He was awaiting court martial, scheduled for the next day. He expected, and hoped, to get some lashings, and not to be demoted in rank. The latter would mean a loss of face with the other men and a reduction in pay he could not afford. The lashings he figured as instant punishment and after a week of sleeping on his stomach everything would be the same as before. Regardless of the sentence, he swore never to drink again, at least not in the company of superiors.

Rodolfo's cellmate was Antonio Dos Santos. Antonio lay on the ground, a festering bullet wound on the left side of his back. Caked dirt and blood covered his matted brown hair and his tattered clothes. Only his narrow green eyes offered a contrast to his beaten condition. They radiated an inner peace that clashed with the diseased appearance of his body and the poor outlook for his future—for Antonio was the first prisoner scheduled for execution in the newly settled island of San Juan Bautista.

It was close to noon and both prisoners were quiet.

65

Rodolfo stood by the window facing the wind. Antonio, too weak to stand, preferred to lie down near the door. This was poorly hung and the wide gaps along the frame allowed for outside air to sneak into the cell and dilute the pervasive stagnation.

"I've been here two days and you haven't said much," blurted out Rodolfo suddenly. "I hate to see anybody in your condition, but if what they say about you is true, you probably deserve it."

"What are they saying about me?" asked Antonio in a whisper.

"According to the sergeant, before I knocked him down of course, you betrayed the crown and the governor. But worse, you betrayed the Holy Church and God himself. He said that you renounced God and accepted the god of the Indians. If this is true, I'm probably sinning just talking to you."

"Relax," said Antonio calmly, barely looking up. "Your soul will not suffer because you talk to me. I'm not going to seduce you from the church." He paused to painfully move to a more comfortable position. "If you want," he said, hesitating, "I will tell you what happened to me." Lying there in the heat, next to his waste, Antonio realized that no one knew why he did what he did. He never got a chance to explain himself at his cursory trial, not that it would have mattered. Now his cellmate offered the only opportunity for someone to know his truth. However, he feared that Rodolfo would dismiss him.

"Sure," responded Rodolfo to Antonio's relief. "Tell me your story. It will help time go by. It drives me crazy to be locked up."

Antonio smiled. Slowly he sat up leaning against the doorframe. In this position his wound was somewhat more painful but he could breathe better. He then proceeded to tell Rodolfo how he had come to this predicament.

VI

THE DREAM

Like most other men, Antonio worked hard in the construction of Villa de Caparra. Among other work, he built the roof of the jail that was later to hold him captive. Whenever an expedition was planned to explore the surrounding region, he was invited along as an interpreter. He always found exploring new lands an exhilarating experience. The expeditions not only served as a reprieve from the exhausting labor at the village— they also gave him a chance to explore the country where he was certain he would finally settle. In these journeys he became familiar with the geography of the area and established contacts with some of its native inhabitants.

After two years in Caparra, Antonio began to notice similarities with the situation he had left behind in La Española. Once again, political squabbles where slowing down progress in establishing the colony. Ponce de León had been appointed interim governor by the king the previous year and, almost immediately, the appointment was challenged by Diego Colón, the son of the late Admiral Cristobal Colón, who laid claim to all the lands discovered by his father. Diego Colón, on his own initiative, named Juan Cerón as governor and Miguel Díaz as sheriff of the island of San Juan. The moment the two men arrived in Caparra to claim their positions, Ponce de León arrested them. The next ship out of the harbor carried Colón's men back to Spain in chains. After a year of dispute the king made a proclamation granting full governorship to Ponce de León. Nevertheless, there were rumors that Diego Colón would continue to pursue his claims to the rule of the island. Ponce de León, in order to fight the impending challenge to his position, was pushing for the accelerated construction of Caparra, and was anxious to begin other settlements around the island.

Antonio didn't want to spend any more time in construction of new settlements, but the political situation was damning him to just that. He was convinced that the only way he could improve his condition was to become a landowner and he had a plan to achieve this.

"Governor, sir," announced the secretary formally. "Antonio Dos Santos to see you. He claims you know him."

"Let him in and tell the accountant I need to see him today about these records," responded Ponce de León without lifting his eyes from his work. After receiving the title of interim governor a few weeks earlier, he was making an extra effort to ensure all paperwork was filled out correctly; the emissaries of the crown were renowned for their meticulousness. All products of the colony were to be recorded and all taxes would definitively be paid. If he was to retain the titles and grants he required to develop this colony, he needed to impress the crown with his ability to manage it properly. Keeping good records and clear accounting would surely expedite any petitions to the king.

Antonio entered the small office in the governor's house. Facing him was a sturdy wooden desk where the governor sat busily writing in a ledger. Behind the governor was a window overlooking the village. Antonio moved up to the desk and waited nervously. He knew he was taking a chance with what he proposed to do and didn't know how the governor would react.

Ponce de León finished writing and carefully put his pen away so no ink would drip on his papers. He looked up at Antonio, stood up and came around the desk to greet him. "It's good to see you, Antonio," said the governor. He was a hand taller than Dos Santos, with broad shoulders, and a pointed black beard speckled with white hairs. The governor carried himself with the confidence of a veteran soldier. He liked talking to men like Antonio. Through them he got an idea of the mood of the colonists. In addition, they reminded him of the days when he was more a man of action and less an administrator.

"Thank you, sir. Please excuse me for bothering you. I have a request," Antonio hesitated a second and caught his breath before continuing. "It's more like an offer I would like to make to you."

"This sounds interesting. What have you to offer me?" said the governor with a smile.

Antonio spoke quickly. "I would like to explore the island for you."

"What do you mean? We are all here to explore and settle this land," he said noticing the nervousness in Antonio. "I have known you since our trip with Admiral Colón. I know you are a bright man. Just relax and tell me what you have in mind. Here, sit down," said the governor pointing to a chair next to his desk. He then returned to his own chair. "Go on," he said to Antonio.

"Well, sir, I've noticed that most of the effort in the colony has been dedicated to building Caparra and searching for gold. The only exploration that has taken place has been along the northern coastline. If you allow me, sir, I would like to be your scout. I communicate well with the Taínos. Two of them have offered to guide me into the mountains. I could go and explore and report back to you. This way you would have the advantage when laying claim to the best lands."

Ponce de León looked closely at Antonio for a few seconds that seemed like an eternity. "Would you be working for me or for the crown?" asked the governor unexpectedly.

This question terrified Antonio. It put him in the position of choosing between the governor and the crown. "I would be working for you, but always for the glory of the crown" he said carefully.

"Well answered, Antonio," exclaimed the governor slapping a hand on his desk. "And what would be in it for you?"

"Well, sir, all I want is a little land. A few hectares where I can raise some crops, keep some animals and maybe even have a family." Gauging the reaction of the governor, he continued. "You'll excuse me sir, but after the years in Santo Domingo and the work we've done here, I am tired of building. I helped build three settlements in La Española and I've worked hard here, but the next building I put up I want to be my own. At my age, I wouldn't mind settling down some."

The governor sat back and looked out the window at the budding village. Antonio waited quietly for the governor's reply. He had said his part. Now it was up to Ponce de León to accept or to call him a fool.

Antonio did not realize how much Ponce de León sympathized with his desire to work the land. Ponce de León was rare among the *conquistadores*, one who recognized the need to establish self-sustaining permanent settlements in the new colonies. As governor, he knew that having farmers, millers, smiths and other tradesmen was as important as finding gold. He himself had made his fortune, not from gold, but from selling food provisions to ships traveling to Spain from Santo Domingo.

"I like your idea," said the governor, turning away from the window. "I want you to leave as soon as possible. Leave quietly. I'll tell your foreman that you have been assigned to work for me."

"Thank you, sir. I can leave in three days."

"Come back tomorrow at the same time. I want to give you instructions on what to look for. You may go now," said the governor, returning to his desk. "And remember, this is a private matter."

"Yes sir, I understand. Thank you. Good afternoon, Governor." Antonio turned and walked out of the office. He kept a straight face until he was outside. As soon as the hot afternoon sun hit his face he greeted it with a smile. His mind was full of a thousand thoughts and plans. For his efforts in exploring the island, which he enjoyed doing anyway, he would become a land-owner. The money he had saved would be sufficient to get seed and maybe even buy a couple of animals. He knew that he would work twice as hard when he labored for his own gain. For the first time in his life he felt that his future had some purpose, and he liked the feeling.

Elated by his success and with a wonderful feeling of relief from completing his visit to the governor, he moved south across the village. Those who saw him had to look twice to recognize him. Antonio was not known as a lighthearted person, but that afternoon he floated across Caparra with an unexplainable smile on his face. Beyond the wall that served as a defensive perimeter, he met the trail that headed inland. After a short walk, he turned into another trail leading to a small clearing used as an encampment by the Taínos when they visited Caparra to trade. Antonio was certain that the encampment and the trading visits were also used by the Taínos to keep an eye on the Spaniards.

In the time since the foundation of Caparra, relations with the Taínos had remained mostly amicable. Several *caciques* had visited Ponce de León in the village. Antonio had served as interpreter on these occasions and he knew the Taínos were mostly curious about the white people, but also cautious. He was certain they knew about the harsh treatment received by their kinsmen in La Española.

As he approached the small clearing, Antonio saw two Taíno men. From a distance he called out a greeting. Antonio knew the Taíno to be peaceful people but in La Española he also learned they were capable of fighting. It was prudent to not surprise them when approaching their camp. The Taínos responded and Antonio was glad to see they were the same two men he had talked to a few days back. He had made arrangements with them to serve as guides in his excursion into the island.

"Greetings, friends," said Antonio as the men, dressed in simple loincloths and adorned with shell jewelry, came closer. He had met them several times before. They seemed to be always together, at least when they visited Caparra. In his conversations with them he got the sense that they were truly curious about the newcomers to their world. On a previous visit, when Antonio asked them to guide him into the interior of the island, they responded enthusiastically.

"Greetings," responded Taibaná and Moné in unison. The Taínos were generally shorter than the Spaniards, with straight black hair and deeply bronzed skin. Taibaná was above average height for a Taíno and of slender build. His companion, Moné, was relatively short with broad shoulders and a stout, muscular constitution. Both had their hair cut evenly around their heads, not unlike the style Antonio had seen used before by Taínos in La Española.

"I have spoken with my *cacique*. I will go with you to visit your people," said Antonio without delay. He knew the Taínos to be succinct in their communications, which helped Antonio, since his vocabulary was limited and it was easier to be concise.

"Good," said Taibaná. "We are ready."

"I need three days. Then we can leave," explained Antonio.

Taibaná looked at Moné who nodded in consent and then signaled his agreement to Antonio.

"I am grateful," said Antonio. "We'll meet here."

Once again Taibaná and Moné nodded in agreement, then waved and turned back to their camp.

Antonio looked at them as they walked away. Ever since his days in Africa he had admired native people. He envied what, in his eyes, appeared to be uncomplicated lives. Their concerns were fundamental: ensuring shelter, food and safety. From Antonio's perspective they seemed to achieve these goals with minimal effort. They were a strong contrast to Europeans. Often, Antonio wondered if their more elaborate clothes, buildings, tools and armaments truly offered a better life.

He spent the next two days preparing for the journey. He did not own many possessions and it didn't take long to sell them. Antonio was a veteran of several land expeditions and he knew how important it was to travel light. He packed a bag, keeping in mind that he would have to carry it himself over mountainous terrain.

As planned, Antonio met with the governor one more time. Ponce de León described his desire for flat land with a dependable water supply, near a good harbor or with easy access to Caparra. He had plans to raise crops and cattle which he could ship to Spain. He wanted high quality property which he could use to provide for future generations of his family. Finally, they decided that Dos Santos would return after six months.

His last night in the village, Antonio went out after

midnight and quietly buried all the money he had saved over the years. He found a spot away from the village, where it would remain undisturbed. He planned to return to these savings when he had his land. After camouflaging his treasure site, he promptly returned to the small shack he shared with some other men. Anticipation and anxiety kept him from sleeping even though he knew he needed to rest for the long day ahead.

Before dawn, while his housemates enjoyed their deep morning sleep, Antonio gathered his old sword, his dagger, and his carefully prepared travel bag before silently stepping outside the house. He headed for the south end of the village, casually acknowledging the morning greetings of those who were up at that time. His acquaintances had been informed he was now working for the governor and would be going on a long trip. Everything was set for his upcoming venture. Antonio knew that the moment he stepped beyond Caparra's defensive wall, he would be ending a stage in his life and starting a new one that would hopefully carry him the rest of his days.

He was in a pensive mood as he strolled towards the clearing where his new companions were located. By the time he reached the campsite of Taibaná and Moné, the clouds on the horizon were beginning to turn white, losing the golden colors of dawn. The trees around him stood motionless but resounded with the song of birds and *coquí*, whose two-note song seemed to flourish everywhere in the island.

"Greetings," said Antonio to the Taíno men. As he looked around, he noticed that they were packed and ready to leave. Their diligence surprised him; it left no room for the possibility of delay.

"Greetings, Antonio," responded Taibaná. Moné nodded in greeting to the Spaniard. As usually happened in their conversations, Taibaná was the principal spokesman. Moné was always attentive, but remained quiet most of the time.

"If we leave now we can reach the *yucayeque* well before sunset," Taibaná informed Antonio, who was eager to enter this new stage in his life and didn't want to delay

73

its start.

"Good," said Antonio. "I am ready."

A slight smile transformed Taibaná's face. It was obvious he was eager to move on. Antonio braced himself. He realized they would have to keep a grueling pace to reach the Taíno village that afternoon. Antonio liked the spirited young Taibaná. He was friendly, intelligent and interested in learning about the Spaniards. Although Antonio barely knew him, he thought that Taibaná embodied many of the qualities he would like to see in his own son, if he ever had one. He looked forward to his potential friendship with this young Taíno.

Moné said something to Taibaná, too fast for Antonio to understand, then collected his pouch and his weapons and started walking south. Taibaná, already carrying his stone club and his bow and arrows, turned to Antonio and waved for him to follow. In this fashion, they followed a narrow trail into the heart of Borikén.

VII

CEIBA

The two native men walked at a quick steady pace through the woods. On occasion they stopped to allow Antonio to catch up. Although he was strong, Antonio was not athletically fit and had difficulty maintaining the pace set by his companions, who were younger and physically in their prime. Around midday, with the sun directly overhead, they stopped by the side of a small stream to rest and eat. Moné swung his bag in front of him as he squatted. From it he pulled out a collection of fruits and some unleavened bread, *casabi*, made from cassava roots. Without hesitation he passed the food around for his two companions to share. Antonio was familiar with the *casabi* from his dealings with the Taínos in La Española. Although he found it somewhat bland, it was hearty and good travel food. He was happy to accept what he was offered. He had brought some bread and hard cheese from Caparra but thought he would save it for another occasion.

After the quick meal, Antonio walked over to the stream to refill the leather wine skin he stole from one of his housemates to use as a canteen. With obvious curiosity, Taibaná followed him to the stream. Under the watchful eyes of Taibaná, Antonio opened the canteen and filled it. Then he replaced the nozzle and pulled out the small stopper that allowed a narrow stream of liquid to emerge from the container. Squeezing the leather sack, Antonio let out a jet of water that reached clear across the stream. Taibaná stood back with eyes wide open. Antonio smiled broadly and offered the sack to Taibaná. The Indian took the canteen and squeezed. The water spray hit Antonio right between the eyes. Taibaná dropped the bag and stepped back. He feared what the Spaniard's reaction may be. Moné, watching from a distance, took a few steps forward.

Antonio instinctively turned away from the water and brought his hands up to his eyes. He cleared the water from his face and turned back to look at Taibaná. Intentionally, he gave the young man a serious look for just a second and then broke down in laughter. Taibaná looked at his friend Moné, back at Antonio and then started laughing himself. The release of tension between them was palpable.

Most of the afternoon they walked south and east at a steady pace, crossing over several ridges of small hills. Antonio was getting ready to ask his companions to stop for a rest when suddenly the forest vanished. They had arrived on a wide, semi-circular clearing bounded by a river on the far side from where they stood. Right before them were lush gardens. Two wide paths, resembling streets lined with small trees, dissected the area crosswise. Between the cultivated parcels and the river was a Taíno *yucayeque*.

The settlement was shadowed by a pair of gigantic trees that grew side by side, towering beside the easternmost *bohíos*. The branches from the trees extended over half the *yucayeque*. Each tree had a convoluted root system reaching high above the ground, buttressing the massive tree trunks that emerged from them.

Below the trees, the *yucayeque* consisted of approximately twenty *bohíos*, set in an oval around a central plaza called the *batey*. The *batey* was clearly delineated by stones, some low to the ground, some standing tall, which where placed to form circular and triangular patterns around the central rectangular space. All the structures were built of wooden poles and thick grasses. The roofs, in the shape of long inverted cones, were framed with poles and covered with well-tended grass or palm leave thatch. At the west end of the *batey* was found the *cacique*'s house, the *caney*, which was larger than the *bohíos* and rectangular in shape.

"This is my home," revealed Taibaná with a mix of pride and joy. Now Antonio understood the eagerness of the young man to get going that morning.

"It is beautiful," said the Spaniard. Once again, his memories of Africa returned. This Taíno settlement reminded him of the village that long ago had been his home for several years. Antonio appreciated the orderliness of the *yucayeque*, a strong contrast to the chaotic form of the settlements were he had lived since he came from Spain.

76

La Isabela and Nueva Isabela, in Española, had both been abandoned before becoming well established; and Caparra was but a year old. Only Santo Domingo, after several years, had begun to take a form and stability that could please a visitor.

"Does the place have a name?" Antonio asked Taibaná.

"Ceiba," he responded. "Like the trees that guard the *yucayeque*." Eagerly, the young Taíno started to move to the right along a trail circling the cultivated lands, which the Taínos called *conucos*.

They approached the settlement from the west side and went directly to the *caney*. Once the travelers were spotted, word spread quickly to all the residents in the *yucayeque*. Within minutes every *bohío* was empty and the three men were surrounded by the villagers who were talking excitedly and curiously examining the bearded white man. Tired and with the nervous excitement of being the center of attention, Antonio saw the faces looking at him melt into a composite of these people with their bronzed skin, high cheek bones, dark, narrow eyes, and thick, straight black hair cut evenly around the head, some with a hank of hair dropping straight down their backs. In addition, he couldn't help but notice that most were naked, their bodies adorned with bright colored symbols and markings.

Antonio was beginning to feel somewhat overwhelmed when suddenly everyone went quiet. Three serious looking men approached. The one in front wore jewelry which identified him as the *cacique*. Antonio recognized him but said nothing.

"Welcome, Taibaná. Welcome, Moné," said the leader in a strong voice which matched the impression made by his wide shoulders and square torso.

"We are glad to be home, *Cacique* Gurao. We bring a visitor. He is one of the white men who wants to live with us. He speaks well and knows how to laugh. His name is Antonio," said Taibaná explaining the presence of the white man.

Gurao looked closely at Antonio. His intelligent eyes

seemed to absorb every detail of this strange man who had entered his *yucayeque*. Slowly, but confidently, he circled his new visitor while continuing his inspection. Antonio stayed calm and allowed the *cacique* to look him over.

"I have seen you before at the white man *yucayeque*," stated Gurao as he finished his inspection.

"I am honored you remember me," said Antonio surprised to be recognized. Early in the settlement of Caparra two *caciques* had approached the village. One of them was Gurao. On that occasion Antonio had served as interpreter for Ponce de León. That initial contact had been a friendly one and relations with the Taínos continued to be relatively peaceful.

Gurao nodded slightly. Antonio could tell the *cacique*'s mind was busy considering his decision on whether or not to welcome this stranger into his village. Suddenly he announced his decision in a loud voice so everyone could hear, "Antonio, you arrive with friends. You are welcome here in peace."

"I am grateful *Cacique* Gurao," responded Antonio respectfully.

Without delay, the *cacique* turned and entered his *caney* followed by his two escorts. This ended the ceremony and instantly the three travelers were surrounded by the inquisitive crowd. Taibaná was mobbed by a group of women which Antonio latter learned were his sisters and his wife. Moné was formally greeted by several men and a shy looking young woman. Meanwhile, Antonio was the center of attention for the many who had heard about the new people in their land but had never seen one.

After a few minutes Taibaná took Antonio by the arm and led him to his *bohio* on the opposite end of the *yucayeque*, closer to the huge ceiba trees. Moné followed closely. When they started to move the crowd dispersed, everyone settling back to their daily chores. Only the small children continued to follow, giggling friskily as they crossed the *batey*.

Taibaná lived in a *bohio* covered by the expansive branches of the ceibas. These provided shade until late in the afternoon when golden sun rays managed to sneak through under the covering branches. Adjacent to Taibaná's home was a second *bohío* occupied by his parents and two sisters. A well-worn path connected both homes. The lush foliage enveloping the *bohíos* also served to bring them closer together.

The area around the entrance to the *bohío* was carefully arranged, with planted flowers and a colorful hedge. Inside, the *bohío* was surprisingly open and spacious. Two hammocks hung from supporting poles, some house wares were neatly stacked on the floor or shelves while other hung from the roof. Up high, near the apex of the conical roof, Antonio noticed a mesh bag hanging, full of what appeared to be bones.

Antonio was intrigued to get this close look of the Taínos. In Española the relations between the Taínos and the Spaniards had been bellicose from the beginning. He had the opportunity to visit several *yucayeques* in the early days of the settlement. However, these were formal visits, when he served as interpreter and white men were viewed with suspicion, if not outright animosity. The only time he got to establish more personal relationships with Taínos was when they worked and lived with the Spaniards, usually as slaves.

"You will stay here with me and Mayaco," said Taibaná to Antonio, gesturing to his wife. Mayaco was a beautiful, petite young woman. She had the hair and skin tone typical of her people, but it was the way her face lit up when she smiled that accentuated her attractiveness. She clung to Taibaná's left arm like she would never let go. "We will hang an extra hammock later," he concluded smiling as he looked into his wife's adoring eyes.

Responding to an unspoken sign, Moné tapped Antonio on the shoulder and signaled to be followed. As they stepped out of the *bohío* a woven tarp covered the door from the inside. Antonio smiled quietly to himself.

A radiant silver sunset silhouetted hills that hid the far horizon. As darkness approached, fires were lit in front of the *bohíos*. Moné led Antonio next door to Taibaná's parents' home. There, they were greeted and offered food—a thick vegetable stew, casabi and fruit. It had been a long day and

79

now that the excitement of arriving in the village was passing, Antonio remembered how hungry he was. Following Moné's lead, he ate what was offered. Taibaná's parents and his two sisters eyed the Spaniard curiously, but did not attempt to establish a conversation. This did not bother Antonio, who wanted to concentrate on his food.

After eating, they expressed their appreciation and walked to the river where they washed and relieved themselves. As they returned to the *bohios* they saw Mayaco and Taibaná standing by the fire outside his parent's home. Without ceremony Moné took his leave from Taibaná and his family and headed for another *bohio*.

"He will sleep in his woman's bohio," explained Taibaná answering Antonio's questioning look.

"Are you tired?" asked Mayaco, sensitive to her guest's needs.

Antonio paused for a couple of seconds before answering with a definitive, "Yes."

Mayaco led him to the *bohio* that would be his home in Ceiba. She showed him his hammock and made sure he had all he needed for the night. Laying down on the hammock, his body's demand for sleep overwhelmed him swiftly. He fell asleep thinking of how surprised he was by the kindness and gentleness of Mayaco. He had been living among ornery men for too long; he hadn't realized how much he missed the company of women and their ability to bring gentleness to a man's life.

One by one the fires around the *yucayeque* were extinguished and all human sounds grew quiet. It was time for nature to serenade her children. Frogs from the river, together with the land-bound coquí and crickets combined to create a night song of mystifying complexity. The music surrounded the whole village in a lullaby that carried its gentle people into the depths of sleep.

The next morning Antonio opened his eyes and suffered the trepidation common to those who awake in a strange place. He looked around and noticed he was alone in the *bohio*. He took a few minutes to recall the events of the previous day and his mission to explore and learn about this land. With some care, he got out of his hammock and walked outside. People were all about, engaged in different chores. They could be seen fishing by the river, tending the *conucos* and fixing their *bohíos*. A small group of people gathered around the *cacique's caney*.

Not seeing any of his companions, Antonio returned to the *bohío* and had a quick breakfast of the bread and cheese he carried from Caparra. As he stepped outside once again, he met Taibaná.

"You sleep long. Do all white men sleep like this?" asked the Taíno jokingly, but not without curiosity.

"No. I was tired from the long walk. I usually get up early," explained Antonio.

"Today you stay with me," said Taibaná abruptly changing the subject. "Later you meet Gurao."

That day, already shortened by sleeping late, went by in a whirl. Antonio got to see much of the village and met many of its inhabitants. He found he was having some difficulty getting used to the Taínos and his surroundings. His previous short visits to *yucayeques* had provided inadequate preparation for the differences in lifestyles he was witnessing at Ceiba. Most difficult for him was the Taíno custom of not wearing any clothes. He noticed that most adults wore some type of jewelry made of shells, stones or wood. Most of them also painted their bodies in bright colors. However, except for married women or for protection when performing certain tasks, Taínos commonly moved around naked. This made an impression on Antonio, who was used to the conservative Spanish dress code. Although he knew beforehand that the Taínos did not cover themselves, he had never experienced the situation of being the only person wearing clothes. He couldn't help feeling self-conscious.

He found it particularly difficult getting used to seeing women naked. The New World settlements did not have many women. Often, months went by when the only women he saw existed in his minds' eye. Now, all of a sudden Antonio found himself in the midst of a community with beautiful women who enjoyed wearing nothing but paint markings for cover. Antonio's attitude, nevertheless, was a positive one. He had never shared the opinion of many of his fellow sailors that the Indians were like animals. His experience in Africa had taught him to appreciate native cultures and he knew the Taínos had much to offer. After a few hours of visiting and talking to different people, the casualness of the Taínos communicated itself to Antonio and he began to feel more at ease among them.

Antonio noticed that people kept busy but that there was no rush in their activities. Whatever they were doing, they seemed confident and tasks were done with ease. The Taíno social structure included *nitaínos,* who served as assistants to the *cacique* and held a position of importance, and the *naboría,* who were the working class of the Taínos. The *naboría* worked under the direction of the *nitaínos.*

The laughter of children was a constant sound in the background. Throughout the afternoon, men, usually in groups of two or three, arrived in the village with the prize of their hunting and fishing forays. The fowl and fish were handed to women who were cooking over separate fires.

Late in the afternoon, a stern looking young man brought word that *Cacique* Gurao wished to meet with the visitor. Without delay, Taibaná led Antonio to the *cacique.* Gurao's *caney* had a gently sloping roof extension on the south side, facing the river and the hills beyond. A group of men were sitting in the shade of this roof, surrounding a small fire and smoking from a pipe similar to others Antonio had seen in Española. The two men walked up to the sitting group and waited to be acknowledged. After another round of the pipe, Gurao gestured the newcomers, inviting them to sit down.

"Greetings, Antonio," pronounced the *cacique* formally. He sat on a *dujo,* an elaborately carved low chair, with his back to the house and facing the river. On his chest hung a *guanín,* the strangely carved gold disk symbolic of his authority as *cacique.*

"Greetings, Gurao," responded the Spaniard cautiously after sitting facing the *cacique.* He was not sure what to expect from this meeting with Gurao, but he knew that it was important to show respect to the *cacique.* His fate was in this man's hands. With support from the *cacique*, he could move on to other villages and continue with his mission; without it, he could die in this *yucayeque* and no one in Caparra would know or care.

Gurao proceeded to introduce his three companions: two elders and Yuquiel, the shaman or *behique* for the *yucayeque*. The two elders sat together to the right of Gurao looking like twins. They had deep wrinkles in their faces and wisps of white highlighting their otherwise black hair. Yuquiel sat close to the *cacique* opposite the elders. He was a small man with alert eyes and long hair to the middle of his back. He was adorned with several amulets hanging from his neck and bracelets on his ankles and wrists.

"Your people have been in Borikén for over a cycle of seasons. You are the first I see alone. Why did you leave your people?" asked Gurao wasting no time in getting to the point.

Antonio got the same feeling he had while interviewing with Ponce de León. He knew his answers would dictate the actions of the *cacique*. "I am new in Borikén. You live here. I travel to learn about you and about Borikén so we can be good neighbors."

"Will your people stay in Borikén?"

"Yes. They build Caparra as their home." Antonio wanted to be honest but he saw no benefit in giving too many details. As it was, he had no idea how Gurao was accepting his answers. The *cacique* sat stoically, not a hint of his thoughts showing on his face or tone of voice.

Gurao was quiet for a few moments before asking his next question. Among other things he was considering what to do with his visitor. Should he allow him to stay? Did he pose a danger to his people? Gurao had met the *cacique* of the white people and remembered him as a big man with pointy hair on his chin. He also remembered Antonio as the interpreter and the deference he showed to his *cacique*. From his observations, Gurao was certain that Antonio was not a person of much stature with his people. Influencing him would not impact the actions of the white men in Caparra. Nevertheless, he offered the opportunity to learn more

83

about the newcomers. In addition, he thought, as a single man he was no threat to his *yucayeque*, which was Gurao's primary concern as a *cacique*.

"Tell me about your people?" he said finally.

Antonio waited an instant to gather his thoughts before responding. "Our *cacique* is Juan Ponce de León. He is a great warrior. We live in *yucayeques* like Caparra with houses of wood and stone. We eat vegetables, fish and meat. We have *conucos* like yours to grow our food. We also have animals that we grow at home for food.

"We have *yucayeques* in Aytí," continued Antonio using the Taíno word for Española, "but our homeland, called Spain, is far away over the sea. We travel in canoes, much bigger than yours, which carry many people and things."

Gurao already knew most of what the Spaniard said. He had seen the large canoes that carried the white men, and the stone buildings in Caparra. The presence of white men in neighboring Aytí, had been reported at the gatherings of *caciques*. Gurao was interested to know that the white men grew their own food. On his brief visit to Caparra he had seen some small *conucos*, which did not look productive. He also did not understand how you could grow animals at home. There were no large mammals in Borikén, thus, the concept of animal husbandry was absent in the Taíno culture of the island.

"What animals do you grow?" asked Gurao.

"We have many animals; some for food and some for work. I do not know their names in your language," responded Antonio.

Gurao nodded in understanding.

Acting on an idea, Antonio leaned over to the fire and grabbed the end of a piece of wood. Using its fire-hardened tip he began a crude drawing of a horse in the clayey soil. The Taínos around him observed with interest. After a couple of minutes he stopped, pointed to the figure and explained that it was a horse. Gurao stood up to look over Antonio's shoulder. "I know that animal. He was standing behind your *cacique* when I went to Caparra. I thought it was a monster," he exclaimed.

"We use horses for work. They are very strong. They carry us and move heavy things," explained Antonio.

One by one Antonio drew rough outlines of common farm animals for his hosts to see and explained how they were used. Gurao could only recognize dogs, the only other animal he had seen in his short visit to Caparra. He suspected that the other animals were the same ones that white men were observed releasing on a beach on the western coast of the island several years before. *Cacique* Urayoan had reported seeing these strange animals in the vicinity of some western *yucayeques*.

Antonio was feeling more comfortable now. It was apparent that the *cacique* and his aides were just curious about their new neighbors and their ways. Their questions were basic and reasonable considering they were completely unacquainted with Europeans.

After returning to his seat, Gurao was approached by the shaman and they had a brief whispered exchange. The *cacique* turned to Antonio, "Tell me about your gods and their powers". Obviously, he was seeking to placate the curiosity of Yuquiel.

Antonio's feeling of confidence was suddenly deflated. Religion was another subject he preferred to evade. Issues of religion and politics had a way of leading to trouble. Antonio had seen more people suffer for their opinions and beliefs than for any other cause. Once again he decided that the truth, if limited, would be the most prudent strategy to answer questions on religion. "We have one god and he has all the power," said Antonio.

"How can this be?" interrupted Yuquiel. "One god that is responsible for the good things and the bad. This is not possible."

Gurao gave Yuquiel a brusque look and then signaled Antonio to continue. "We have *behiques* called priests. They teach about God. Our God is good, we are like his children." Antonio kept his dialogue simple because he was missing much of the vocabulary needed to explain religious terms and because he had no idea how to begin to explain the tenets of Catholicism to the Taínos.

Yuquiel was about to say something when the *cacique* stopped him. "This is enough," he said with finality. "Some other day we will speak again". Turning to Antonio he said, "You are welcome to stay in Ceiba." Without blinking, his eyes shifted to the young Taíno sitting with Antonio. "Taibaná," he said clearly, "he is your guest." He finished his statement with a dismissing gesture. Taibaná immediately stood up and Antonio followed. Gurao directed his attention to other matters and without another word, the two men stepped outside the *cacique's* presence.

Antonio felt relieved that the questioning was over. As far as he could tell all went well; he did not insult anyone and he was accepted as a guest in the village. He was not sure what was expected of him as a guest, but he counted on Taibaná to let him know.

VIII

AIMÁ

Two weeks passed and Antonio could not remember the last time he had been this relaxed and happy. Maybe, he thought, not since his time in Dikya, with Ayainda, in Africa. His seventeen years in the New World had been full of work and disappointment. He had spent the prime of his life chasing a dream, with nothing to show for it. Now these simple people were showing him that there are destinies other than the harsh one he set for himself in trying to achieve his dream. It was ironic that the simple life of the Taínos seemed to provide all that he could ever want without the complications of the Spanish system of land ownership. Antonio could see much that was worthwhile in the way the Taínos led their lives.

As a guest in the *yucayeque* Antonio was made comfortable. He slept in Taibaná's *bohío* and shared in the life of his host's extended family. The Taínos were a gregarious people, so it was not difficult for Taibaná's family to absorb another person into their household. Having the white man as their guest brought a level of distinction to the family and elevated their stature in the *yucayeque*.

As Antonio had hoped, he and Taibaná had become good friends. They shared much time in a variety of tasks around the *yucayeque*. Together they fished at the river, helped gather wood and palm fronds for a new *bohío*, and worked on the thatch roof of their own dwelling. Antonio liked the joyful way in which the young Taíno led his life. It was obvious to him that Taibaná was exactly where he wanted to be—where he needed to be.

Deep down, Antonio was jealous. He'd never had a chance to find that level of comfort with himself. Always there had been somewhere else he'd rather be, something else he'd rather do. As a child he lived in extreme poverty, his mother never had time for him, and his neighborhood was rough and simply ugly. Good childhood memories were preciously rare: his mother's hand on his forehead while laying half-asleep in bed; a goodly patron telling him stories of his adventures at sea; finding a coin under a table. Later, life as a sailor was a constant struggle for survival as he shared meager resources with men who were older, bigger and nastier than himself. It did not help that shipmaster Alfonso Pedroza held a special place in his dark heart for the younger members of his crew. His situation became less precarious under Francisco Dos Santos, who didn't need threats and violence to command his ship. Nevertheless, life as a sailor remained competitive and rough, each man having to prove himself through strength and skill and no small measure of conniving.

Being with the Taínos, he was beginning to feel that maybe he had found his place at last. His contract with Ponce de León did not leave his mind. His long lived dream of owning land held on stubbornly in his mind. However, for the first time, Antonio questioned its wisdom. He wondered if there were other roads he could follow. Long before, in Dykia, he faced a similar choice in life. Then he was very young and a world of opportunity and the support of a good man, Francisco Dos Santos, guided his decision to move on. Now, with a lifetime behind him, he felt comfortable considering a change of his plans if the opportunity presented itself. He wondered if the Taínos were showing him the way.

That morning Antonio woke up before sunrise. Taibaná and Mayaco were still asleep. He noticed that the usual night song of the forest seemed hushed. Quietly he lay in his hammock giving sleep every opportunity to win over his wakefulness, but it did not happen. He decided to go by the river to wash and await the dawn. Carefully he slid off his hammock and out of the *bohío*. The village was quiet. Overhead, above the branches of the protecting trees, the moonless sky was clear of clouds and covered with a blanket of stars.

He walked towards the river, silently moving past the neighboring *bohíos*. As he approached the water the silhouette of a woman emerged from the starlight. As he got closer he called out softly so as not to startle her.

"Who's there?" asked the woman in a voice Antonio thought he recognized.

"Antonio, the white man," he responded.

"Didn't my brother give you a comfortable hammock?" she said with a quiet laugh.

"Aimá, is that you?"

"Can't you tell," she responded playfully.

"What are you doing out at this time?"

"I was waiting for you," she said, without hesitation and in all seriousness.

Antonio felt a rush of sensations move up his back and then shoot down to the bottom of his feet. Something in the way she said that last comment exposed him to feelings he had not experienced in a long time. He knew about Aimá's romantic misfortunes and had allowed himself to fantasize about her. However, until now, he had never sensed that she might be interested in him.

Aimá was Taibaná's older sister. She was a handsome woman, with robust features. Tall compared to other Taíno women, she had full breasts that perfectly complemented her generous hips and gently rounded belly. Aimá had never married. Twice, years before, she had suitors; both times the men died while courting her. One died in a skirmish with the Carib, the other, while sharing a hammock with her. Since then, no man had sought her favor. She fought the sadness of her loneliness with the strength of her renowned sense of humor. At times her powerful laugh could be heard across the *yucayeque*, drowning out the rambunctious noise of children at play. She shared her bountiful spirit with all in the village, especially the young. The love she couldn't share with children of her own she gave in abundance to the ones in the village.

As Antonio reached her she turned to face the water and sat on a rock that had been used for that purpose many times before. He sat next to her. The starlight was strong enough that they could see each other clearly surrounded by shadows. The river gurgled gently at their feet as its waters moved eagerly to the sea.

"How did you know I would be here?" he asked.

"I did not know, but here you are," she said.

She saw the perplexed expression on his face and

89

looked away to the river. After a moment she continued, "Some nights I come here to look at the river. It is better than being alone in my hammock. Tonight I knew the river would bring me a gift."

"I could not sleep either. I came here to await the dawn. Maybe the river has also given me a gift."

"Do you accept your gift?" Aimá asked, sitting up straight and turning to face Antonio, hiding nothing about herself.

Antonio felt a rush of excitement that almost paralyzed him. After a few seconds that seemed like a long time, he shifted closer to Aimá. Moving slowly, aware of every moment, he kissed her. A soft, unhurried kiss, meant to quench the thirst of two people who had not had a drink for years.

Eventually she pulled away. Taking his hand she led him upstream to a collection of large boulders that had been polished smooth by the river. There, under a blanket of stars, they made love. In their passion, their different cultures merged. There, the eternal hope of humanity was brought to a climactic reality by the gentle rocking of two bodies meeting for the first time.

It didn't take Aimá's mother more than an instant to realize that Antonio and her daughter were lovers. By the end of the day the news had spread around the *yucayeque*. Everywhere he went Antonio was met with smiles and in some cases with friendly teasing. All this activity reflected the affection people had for Aimá. They hoped the white man would provide her the companionship she so obviously craved and which none of her own people dared to give.

Antonio's relationship with Aimá did not change his routine very much; already he had been seeing her on a daily basis as he assisted Taibaná in his chores. Whenever they wanted privacy they would find it in either of their *bohios*. At night she would come to his hammock, putting an end to their lonely nights. The newfound joy of his relationship with Aimá made Antonio's desire to stay with the Taínos stronger than ever. His contract with Ponce de León felt unimportant. His dream of owning property was beginning to fade before the much more attractive option of living in Ceiba with Aimá at his side.

IX

THE HUNT

One bright morning, cooled by a strong northeast wind, found Antonio talking with Aimá in front of her *bohío*. Across the *batey*, beyond the *bohíos*, the crops were full grown and the plants were raked by the breeze. Comfortably kneeling, Aimá was expertly grinding yuca for preparation of *casabi*, the bread of the Taínos, which served as a staple in their diet. Antonio enjoyed the refreshing breeze as it touched his bare chest. He had adopted the Taíno dress for himself except his Spanish modesty required that he use a loin cloth, even when there was no practical need for it. The rest of his body was usually covered with paints in the same patterns used by Taibaná. In addition to being decorative he found the body paints helped to protect his skin from the sun and from biting insects.

Taibaná, who had been called to the *caney* by *Cacique* Gurao, approached the couple, his whole body radiating excitement. "Friend, tomorrow we go hunting for *carey!*," he exclaimed referring to the sea turtles which were a delicacy in Ceiba.

"Where do you find the *carey*?" asked Antonio.

"There is a beach one day away where many come to lay eggs every night. We will leave tomorrow before the sun goes up and be there for the night," he explained. Without pause he continued, "When we return we will have meat for everyone in the *yucayeque* and we will celebrate the hunt and this harvest with an *areito*."

These last words brought a smile to Aimá's face. The *areitos*, dance and song celebrations that could last for days, were her favorite feasts. She was glad the harvest *areito* had finally arrived; she had much to celebrate. She also knew that Taibaná was being pretentious to imply that the *areito* would honor his hunt. This *areito* was held every year to celebrate the harvest and everyone knew the *cacique* would soon announce a date for the celebration. Already she had noticed the young women gathering to make *chicha*, the principal drink of the *areito. Chicha* was prepared from the juice of chewed corn and needed to be ready days ahead of the *areito* in order for it to ferment and become powerful. However, it could not sit too long or it would become impossible to drink. Gurao loved *chicha* and he would not risk losing it. Aimá was certain the *areito* would take place regardless of the results of Taibaná's expedition.

"I will go with you to make sure your tale of the hunt is not exaggerated," she said goading her brother.

"The men for the hunt have already been selected," he replied.

"Don't worry Taibaná, no one will miss me here. In any case I can carry more meat than any of the boys you are taking with you."

Taibaná glared at her. His response was frustrated because he knew she was right. Taibaná would be accompanied by a group of youngsters. Hunting *carey* required no particular skill and it was not dangerous. Nevertheless it always proved an exciting outing for the boys of the *yucayeque*. For some it would be their first significant contribution of food to the community. Taibaná also needed people to help him carry the bags full of meat and the *carey* shells back to the *yucayeque*. Aimá, still seated, looked up at Taibaná with a childish smile that always softened her brother's heart.

"You always do what you want, don't you? You need a husband to tell you what to do," Taibaná said, and automatically his eyes moved to Antonio.

"She is not my wife, friend. But she is your sister," Antonio said to Taibaná with a smile. Antonio had been quietly enjoying the exchange among siblings and knew better than to get involved.

"Very well, you come along with us. I'll make sure you carry the biggest bag," said Taibaná to his sister.

"Thank you little brother, I'll make sure not to walk so fast you can't keep up," she said as her impish smile turned into contagious laughter that the two men could not resist joining. Aimá knew how to manipulate Taibaná to do her bidding, yet he didn't mind. He enjoyed her company more than that of many of the men and he knew he could count on her to work harder than anyone else. They spent the rest of that day organizing their outing.

Next morning, Antonio was prodded awake by Taibaná well before sunrise. Outside the *bohio*, bathed in the half-light of a small fire, a group of six boys aged 9 through 12 were busy getting ready. Antonio splashed his face with water from a clay jar and pulled out the travel bag he prepared the night before. He was advised to travel light so all he carried were some fruit and *casabi*. For this trip he put on his pants, boots, and his old sword. Going out for an overnight trip, he felt more confident in his Spanish clothing.

A short time later Aimá arrived and soon the small band was off. They followed the walking path through the *conucos*. Their departure from Ceiba was witnessed by the mature yucca, corn, peanut and pepper plants growing behind the small trees that lined the path. Farther back, hidden in the darkness, were additional plants which provided the *yucayeque* with a variety of food and fiber.

They entered the forest along the same trail that brought Antonio to Ceiba. The group lined up in a single file with Taibaná in the lead followed by the six boys, Antonio and Aimá at the rear. The dense forest blocked most of the diffuse starlight, making it hard to see the ground. The company moved quietly, as even for the nimble Taínos the forest darkness demanded their full concentration as they walked. Antonio found he had to push himself to keep up with his companions, who were all much younger than he was and familiar with the trail.

The earliest morning light found them changing trails. The new path veered slightly to the east. Antonio was not certain what their destination would be. He had explored the area around Caparra and had seen a number of beaches and lagoons east of the village. He wondered if this was where they were headed. Sometime around mid-morning they stopped by a stream to rest and eat. By then the boys were talking and teasing each other. Each one of them anticipated capturing the largest *carey*. One of them predicted his *carey* would be so big the *behique* would tell the story of how one

94

animal fed the whole *yucayeque* for days. The three adults sat on boulders by the stream. They enjoyed listening to the bantering of the boys.

Taibaná recalled going on a hunt similar to this. "We arrived at the beach late at night and found many *carey* laying eggs" he told his companions. "We worked most of the night, taking all the meat we could carry. We barely rested before heading back to the *yucayeque*. We were so tired we were not even excited about getting back home. It was the first time I had worked so hard. Not even after playing games all day had I felt so tired. However, I also remember the pride I felt when the *cacique* thanked us for bringing food for the *yucayeque*." These were valuable lessons, thought Taibaná, and wondered how the boys under his care would hold up under the hard work ahead.

They continued to move over hills and across narrow valleys. The vegetation changed from dense rain forest to a more open, dryer forest. In the latter part of the afternoon they reached the top of a ridge at a spot where a massive tree had fallen, clearing an area of canopy and opening a vista for the group. Before them, the land went down to the coastal plain below. Not far beyond the bottom of the ridge started a large lagoon which reached almost to the ocean. Antonio recognized it from a previous visit. The trail they were following skirted the west side of the lagoon. East of the trail the ground was low and the swamps made it impossible to cross on foot. To the west, in the distance, Antonio noticed the large harbor used by the residents of Caparra. It was too far to ascertain if any ships where at anchor.

"I have been to the lagoon before," commented Antonio "it is a half a day walk from Caparra."

"Do you think we will see any Spaniards?" asked Taibaná.

"Probably not," explained Antonio. "We'll be walking close to the lagoon. The Spaniards prefer the dry land to the west."

Taibaná nodded in understanding.

"Will we get to the beach before sunset?" asked

95

Antonio.

"It depends on how fast we walk," answered Taibaná.

Without warning, as if interpreting the question as a challenge, Taibaná started down the trail at a quick pace. The boys scrambled to follow with Aimá and Antonio encouraging them. Before long, they were down the hill and working hard to catch up to Taibaná.

At first they moved quickly. The ground was covered with widely spaced trees and short grass underfoot. A topography of gentle rolling hills descended towards the lagoon. As they got closer to the waters edge they came upon a sharp transition in the vegetation. The company was faced with a dense thicket of mangroves that was growing along a stream that fed the lagoon. These trees, with their spider-like roots arching from their trunks to the ground, seemed to pose an impenetrable barrier.

"Follow me like before," said Taibaná. "We will move through the trees and swim to the other side."

Without hesitation Taibaná moved right into the mangroves. The boys followed single file. With great agility they moved from root to root mimicking their leader. Antonio was slower. His larger size was an added handicap to his age when moving through the tight spaces created by the tangled roots. His sword kept getting caught on branches. Aimá patiently paced herself to keep Antonio company.

By the time they reached the narrow stream, most of the company had finished swimming across. On the north side of the stream was another thick tangle of mangroves lining the waters edge. Slowly, the two stragglers lowered themselves into the brownish water while trying to hold their travel bags dry. The bottom of the stream was covered with leaves and other dead organic matter, which mixed with fine clay to create a thick, sticky mud. Antonio made the mistake of standing on the bottom and instantly sank down to his knees. He had to pull himself out using one of the mangrove branches for leverage. He could hear the boys laughing from the other side.

"Come Antonio," called Aimá from the middle of

96

the stream. "You can't walk. Swim!"

Cursing under his breath, he let himself drop in the water and splashed the short distance to the other side. He handed his bag to one of the boys and pulled himself back up on top of the mangrove roots. Once again, the company set off walking on top of the tree roots. This time, regardless of the discomfort of the wet clothes, Antonio made sure to stay up with boys who moved playfully from one tree to another.

Beyond the mangroves, they quickly sought high ground and Taibaná ordered everyone to eat then, before it got dark. Antonio sat with Aimá and they shared their food. He felt miserable in his wet pants. He realized he'd gotten used to wearing the Taíno loin cloth and now he felt confined in his European attire.

"The ocean is behind that low rise," said Taibaná pointing to the north. "We'll go straight to the water and then walk along the coast to the beach with the *carey*."

It didn't take long before they reached the last hill before the ocean. From there they could see the waves breaking on a sandy coastline. The vegetation along the beach was mostly bushes with some scattered stands of taller trees. A narrow line of sand dunes, covered in grasses and vines, stretched right along the water's edge. At different points mangroves were growing to the water line, challenging the ocean to give up more land. The boys cheered at the sight of the ocean. The youngsters still possessed an abundance of energy and enthusiasm that Antonio found enviable.

Almost at a run, they moved to the ocean. Except for an encounter with a cluster of prickly bushes, this last push to the salt water was uneventful. Reaching the water was one more of a series of small accomplishments that resulted in celebrations from the young Taínos. The boys dropped their bags on the sand and laughing ran headlong into the calm sea. The three adults followed their example. The cool waters cleaned their bodies and recharged their tired muscles. Antonio removed his boots and emptied them of the mud he had collected when crossing the mangrove creek.

With some effort, Taibaná got everyone out of the water and ready for the last leg of their journey. Looking to the west in the fading daylight Antonio could see a headland in the distance that marked one end of the curved beach they where walking on. Ahead of them, nearby to the east, was the headland defining the other end of the semi-circular beach.

The beach was narrow, but unobstructed. Walking by the water's edge, they made better time than at any other moment of their day-long excursion. They reached the east headland in a few minutes. Ahead they could see two wide, arched beaches similar to the one they were leaving. Taibaná pointed to the second headland in the distance; that was their destination.

It was dark by the time the group reached the first sandy headland. The low promontory that was their destination could be seen through the growing moonlight, silhouetted against the stars that blended with the ocean at the horizon. There was a steady, soft breeze that kept mosquitoes at bay and made that evening the most pleasant part of their trip.

With the moon clear above the horizon, the company reached the end of the beach. An inlet, flowing with dark water originating in a dense mangrove swamp, blocked their way. The inlet itself was lined with mangroves, posing another barrier for the company. This time Taibaná led them along shallow water most of the way around the trees on the south side of the inlet. After a short swim across the main channel of the inlet, they once again reached shallow water and quickly walked around the trees on the north side.

Once out of the water, the group faced a rocky promontory twice the height of Antonio. They scrambled up the rough coral stone. Below them, facing inland, they could sense the mangrove swamp extending far into the night. Defying the moonlight, this brackish forest seemed to trap all light. They couldn't see the trees but they could feel their presence. The swamp was the source of eerie clicking and sucking sounds, nothing like the melodious night music of the rain forest. Instinctively the young members of the

98

company moved closer to the adults.

"We are almost there," said Taibaná trying to encourage the boys. "Don't worry; we don't have to cross those trees."

They followed the high ground along the promontory, which followed the coastline. The rocky soil and salty air allowed only the hardiest of plants to survive there. They continued northward along the top of the ridge, the sandy beach below them to the left, the mangrove swamp to the right. Gradually the path turned eastward, to the right, and angled down to meet the beach sand. Wind tossed waves broke against the beach. Ahead of them, looking east as far as they could see, there were tall narrow sand dunes. The mangrove trees could be seen as shadows hugging the inland side of the dunes. A variety of grasses, vines and shrubs covered the sand, helping the dunes grow by trapping and anchoring the sand.

"The *carey* will arrive at any moment," said Taibaná to the group. "We will spread out along the beach. Call out when you see one. I'll decide which to kill."

After resting for a few minutes, Taibaná left with the boys to assign them positions. Each young hunter sat alone monitoring as much beachfront as he could see in the moonlight. Aimá and Antonio remained behind at the place were they first reached the beach. As Antonio collected driftwood, Aimá skillfully kindled a fire in a depression she dug in the sand. Before long, flames illuminated the sand with a golden glow. Antonio sat next to Aimá, who lay on her back facing the stars. She was quickly lulled to sleep by the rhythmic sound of the waves.

Antonio looked to the ocean and his mind drifted to his other life as a sailor. The sea had been his companion for many years before reaching the Indies. He missed that life but knew he could never go back to it, nor did he really want to. Time had a way of softening his memories of his years at sea. It was easy to remember his time with Francisco Dos Santos and forget his terrible time with Shipmaster Pedroza. But even with Don Francisco, as he used to call him, things were bound to change.

He recalled that night when he was summoned to Don Francisco's cabin. "Antonio", he said, "I will be leaving the ship next month when we sail to Cadiz. It is time I leave this thankless life at sea and return to my home and family. I'll be happier spending the last years of my life there." Fear crept into Antonio's belly, fear of being abandoned as he had been in Africa, fear of losing this man who was the closest thing to a father he had ever known. "I care for you like a son," said Don Francisco looking directly at Antonio with a serious, yet tender expression. "If you stay in this ship you will grow into an old sailor and nothing more. The owners don't care for the crew and I can't guarantee the new shipmaster won't be a bastard." Don Francisco could read the anxiety in Antonio's face. "I've heard," he continued before Antonio could say a word, "that a Genovese shipmaster has sailed west and discovered a new route to the Indies. His name is Colón. He's planning a second trip and looking for men to crew an armada of ships." Antonio continued to stare expressionless, knowing his life was about to change abruptly and feeling there was little he could do about it. "I think you should consider joining Colón on this voyage. There will be many opportunities for a bright young man like you."

So much had happened since then; saying good-bye to Don Francisco knowing he would never see him again; feeling lonely, scared and excited about his new venture to the Indies; the struggles at the new settlement of La Isabela; trekking across La Española; building Santo Domingo and Caparra; and now this new experience living with the Taíno. He looked besides him and saw Aimá sleeping. For years now, he had wanted, and sought, permanence and companionship in his life; he wanted a home of his own. His short time with Aimá had reinforced this desire and made it seem like more than a dream. Quietly he leaned over, kissed her gently and joined her. The hike to the beach had been physically demanding. He allowed his body's need for rest to overwhelm him.

"Taibanáaaaaa!" rang the excited call from the youngest of the boys.

Taibaná stood up from where he sat on the opposite side of the fire from Antonio and Aimá. "Stay here resting if you like," he said to the sleepy Spaniard as he looked up to see what was going on. "The *carey* take time to lay their eggs. We don't touch them until then." With a slight nod Antonio turned back to reclaim his warm place on the back of Aimá's neck. Taibaná moved away from the fire to meet the excited boy.

In the next few minutes two other boys called out, the *carey* had arrived. Before long a score of the large reptiles were lumbering across the beach to the sand dunes. There they immediately began building nests as the boys watched, fascinated. In the water the *carey* were graceful as birds in flight. They spent all their lives in the liquid medium, seeking land only to complete their reproduction. On land, their movements were one dimensional; programmed by instinct to complete their one task and then return to the water. The fragile link with land in the life cycle of these ancient beings made it possible for the Taíno to harvest them with ease for their shell and meat.

Taibaná instructed the children following the traditions handed down through generations. With great respect, they selected two of the larger animals. Following Taibaná's instructions the boys did not disturb the animals as they lay their eggs. Antonio and Aimá approached as the first *carey* finished its task and started heading back to the surf. As it approached the water all the boys eagerly crowded on one side of the animal and, in a coordinated effort, lifted the *carey* and dropped it on its back. Some of the boys shouted excitedly. The old animal lay helpless, its fins flapping ineffectively in the air, its head dangling low, exposing the neck. Without hesitation Taibaná approached the creature and with a swift swing of his stone battle axe made a deep cut on the *carey*'s neck, killing it instantly. Suddenly all was quiet; only the surf remained unimpressed.

"She will feed our *yucayeque*," said Taibaná to the boys, some of whom had taken several steps back, shocked by the severity of the death just witnessed. "We will all remember her in the *areito*. And you," he said pointing to the

101

boys standing together, "will always remember her in your memories of this hunting trip."

All were quiet for a long moment. Then the oldest boy solemnly approached the dead *carey* and touched it in silent tribute. The others followed instinctively, as if asking the *carey* for forgiveness and thanking her for the gifts they were about to take from her.

"We must go to the other *carey*," said Taibaná in a gentle voice.

Knowing what lay ahead the boys were more serious in their handling of the second animal. Once again the boys crowded to one side and lifted; but they were not strong enough to overturn the large *carey*. They jumped back as they let go of the animal, which landed right side up and continued moving towards the ocean. The adults joined the young Taínos and with a strong effort managed to overturn the *carey* on the second try.

This time the death of the *carey* was less shocking to the boys, if only because they knew what to expect. After the boys repeated their spontaneous ritual with the dead beast, Taibaná divided the company into two groups to butcher the animals and prepare the meat and shells for the return to Ceiba.

Aimá led Antonio and two of the youngsters to the first kill. The Spaniard offered Aimá a small dagger he carried in his boot and showed her how it could be used. She marveled at the knife's ability to cut cleanly through the tough sinews of the *carey*. Working together with stone scrapers and the Spanish dagger they finished their work well ahead of Taibaná, who was handling the larger animal and didn't have the advantage of a steel knife. They then moved the *carey* shell to knee deep water to finish cleaning and rinsing its interior. One of the boys was sent to collect thick sea grape leaves to line the wicker baskets used to carry the meat.

Once finished with their task, Aimá's team moved over to help Taibaná and his group. While most of the company hunched over the giant shell scraping and cutting, Aimá and one of the boys began preparing the baskets for the meat. Although the work was arduous and messy the whole company was excited about completing it and returning to the *yucayeque*. The boys imagined the proud faces of their parents as they returned home with enough meat to feed everyone in Ceiba. In their excitement they were not thinking of the long hike back with little sleep. Their stamina had not yet been tested.

Aimá was beginning to wonder if the boy sent to collect leaves had fallen asleep. Why wasn't he back? "I'm going to go looking for that boy," she said to her assistant.

She started walking down the beach with her eyes fixed on the sand dunes. Suddenly, out of the darkness ahead of her she saw her young charge running desperately towards her. He didn't slow as he approached Aimá.

"Run," he called out in a panicky voice as he grabbed her hand and pulled. "Run, there's Caribs on the beach."

At the mention of Caribs a cold feeling rushed down Aimá's spine. All Taínos knew about the ruthless Carib warriors. They were the great enemy of her people.

Leading the young boy with her stronger strides, Aimá ran towards the others who were just finishing their work with the second *carey*.

"Taibaná," she said trying hard to stay in control, "there are Caribs on the beach."

"It's true, it's true, I saw them" said the boy still holding Aimá's hand. The fear in his eyes was unmistakable. He clung to Aimá while he kept rocking from one foot to the other.

Taibaná approached the boy and squatted down to eye level. "Tell me what you saw," he said in a calming voice.

"There are these many," said the boy holding up four fingers. "They were getting out of a canoe."

"Did they see you?"

"No," he said with certainty. "I was under a tree when I heard them. They were saying things I didn't understand.

"Did you see anything else?" asked Taibaná patiently.

"They looked scary and had weapons with them."

Taibaná stood up patting the boy on the head.

"What are they doing here?" asked Antonio thinking out loud. He knew the danger they were facing; Antonio had been a member of the landing party that fought its way out of the Carib ambush in Santa Cruz years before.

"This is most likely a raiding party," responded Taibaná. They must have seen the fire." He paused, obviously contemplating his next step. Taibaná knew the fate of the group depended on him. "I will not give up our meat," he stated with a firmness that left no doubt—fists clenched at his chest. "There are too many tracks and we can't try to outrun them. We must face the Caribs and defeat them!" His mind was racing, trying to figure out a way to successfully confront the enemies. It was his training as a hunter that led him to a plan. He would attract the Caribs to a trap like he would any other prey.

"You two and Antonio stay with me," said Taibaná pointing to the two oldest boys. "Aimá you lead the rest of them to the ridge overlooking the beach and hide quietly. Go now, leave everything." His tone of voice allowed no room for question.

"Be careful," said Aimá to the two men. Then she turned and ran towards the ridge leading the four boys.

Without a second glance at his sister, Taibaná directed his full attention to the two boys with him. "You will lure the Caribs to a trap," he said with what looked like a smile. "Which one of you runs the fastest?"

"I do," said the shorter of the two boys.

Addressing the taller boy Taibaná said, "You will wait by the large *carey* shell".

Turning quickly to the faster boy, Taibaná gave instructions. "Start walking down the beach until they see you. Keep your eyes open; try to see them first. As soon as they see you, run back to the large *carey* shell." Taibaná was exuberant seeing his plan working in his mind. His heart was racing. "Then, together you will run under the ridge along the sand. Stay close to the cliff face. There, Antonio and I will attack by surprise. Make sure the Carib are following you!" he stressed. "Do you understand?" Both boys nodded.

104

Placing a hand on the first runner's shoulder and looking in the boy's eyes Taibaná instructed, "Go now. Pay attention and run like you were flying."

The boy was nervous but things were happening quickly and he had no time to show doubt. This harmless *carey* hunt had turned into his personal challenge and he was determined not to fail. Confidently, he turned and started walking down the beach at a quick pace. Taibaná's heart was full of pride as he saw the young Taíno move away from him. The runner had taken his orders with no complaints, no hesitation. He knew that for a young Taíno to walk towards a band of well-armed Caribs called for exemplary courage and wondered if as a boy he would have been that brave. Taibaná did not want that courage wasted. He was beginning to feel the pressure of the risks he was taking with these young lives.

Taibaná now turned his attention to the taller boy. "You will wait for him by the shell and encourage him to run faster. As soon as you are together continue running down the beach. Run right under the cliff," he reiterated.

The boy looked at Taibaná with fear in his eyes. "You will be all right," said the older Taíno. "Remember we will be there to help you." He patted the boy on the shoulders and smiled reassuringly. "Now go!" he said, and the boy went.

"We better go hide," said Antonio to Taibaná , who would not take his eyes off the boy slowly disappearing into the darkness.

"Let's go," said Taibaná. Now that his hastily thought out plan was in action he feared for the young lives that were trusting in him. What if they failed? What of Aimá and the younger boys? With a purposeful hand gesture he waved away the hesitation. This was not a time for doubt.

They barely reached the top of the ridge when they heard the commotion from the beach. Their runner had already been spotted. The Caribs' war cry was heart stopping.

"I hope you know how to do battle, Spaniard," said Taibaná, not looking away from the beach. "I count on you for the sake of the others."

"I am not a trained warrior but I will seek to fight like a Taíno," responded Antonio.

Taibaná peeled his eyes away from the beach for an instant and gave Antonio a wicked smile. "We will jump on them as they run by," he instructed waving his stone ax over the cliff. "You must fight to kill or they will kill you."

"I'm ready," said Antonio, already holding his sword in his left hand, his knife in the right. In his mind, he voiced a silent prayer.

Antonio's mind focused sharply on the moment as the figure of a young runner emerged out of the darkness. With fear pushing him, he was maintaining his lead over the Caribs. Next to the *carey* shell the other boy waved frantically at his friend.

The Caribs were ready for battle. Their bodies were painted red with bright white lines which seemed to shine with a light of their own. Their faces had patterns which made them look grotesque. They carried stone axes and bows strapped across their chests.

Antonio and Taibaná lay flat with weapons ready. They saw the runner reach the *carey* shell to be joined by his friend. The Carib warriors were now closer to the two boys. Taibaná touched Antonio's wrist, signaling to move into a crouch position. The Spaniard's stomach was a knot of nerves and tension.

As planned, the boys ran below the ridge hiding the Spaniard and the Taíno warrior with the Caribs close at their heels.

"Go!" said Taibaná as they both jumped.

Antonio knew surprise was on their side. He noticed the Caribs looking straight ahead as he fell. As he floated down towards the two leading warriors he aimed his feet to the head of one and hoped to cut into the second with his sword. The impact of the fall stunned him momentarily. His mind however, was racing—Get up! Get up! In seconds that seemed like minutes he was up on his feet trying to gain his bearings.

To the left, on the sand, was the bloody corpse of one Carib warrior, a sword cut visible from shoulder to mid torso. In front of him, on his knees, was another warrior recovering from the initial impact. Antonio moved on unsteady legs to finish him off. Suddenly the injured man stood up, ax in hand. He ran towards Antonio and swung his weapon on a wide arc. The Spaniard ducked away and then lunged with his sword at the exposed right flank of his enemy. The rusty sword pierced the skin and ripped between two ribs into the lungs. Antonio twisted the blade. The Carib warrior collapsed as the Spaniard pulled out his weapon.

Awakened by the fever of battle, he looked to help Taibaná. Over by the water line he saw the tall boy lift a stone ax high and crash it into the skull of a Carib who lay on the sand. Beyond, near the cliff face, Taibaná was combating one of the enemy warriors. Instinctively Antonio ran towards Taibaná, a shout of victory in his throat.

The Carib and the Taíno were well matched, each holding the other at bay. Antonio's approach tilted the fight in favor of Taibaná. The Carib, seeing himself alone, dropped his weapons and ran down the beach in a panic. Taibaná gave chase, tackled the warrior from behind and broke his neck with a sharp blow of his stone ax.

As Taibaná got to his feet Antonio exhaled, releasing the elation of battle. He then sat on the beach, overtaken by the night's events. Soon the whole company joined him. All the boys seemed overwhelmed and were quiet as they stood around. What was to have been a simple adventure to get some *carey* meat had turned into a fight for their lives. For all the boys it was their first experience with violent death, and the impact was a sobering one. Only Aimá expressed any joy at the fact that they had survived without injury. She hugged all the members of the company in an expression of obvious relief. Then she moved to comfort the boy who had killed one of the invading warriors. He sat crying in huge quiet sobs next to his friend the runner. Aimá sat close to the boy whispering in his ear. Before long he stopped crying and moved closer to the others, a look of pride in his eyes. "Truly, Aimá could weave magic in the hearts of these boys," thought Antonio.

Once again, Taibaná took control of the situation.

107

"Aimá, you and the boys get all the meat ready for the return home," he ordered. "Antonio, you help me."

The two men collected all the weapons from their enemies and tossed the bodies into the water away from where the rest of the group was working. Then they inspected the Carib dugout in hopes they could use it for their return trip. The craft, carved from a huge tree trunk, proved to have ample room for everyone and all they were carrying.

Working together, they loaded the dugout without delay. Most of the boys crowded in the center of the boat, while Aimá and Antonio sat at the bow and Taibaná steered. They paddled out to gain some distance from the breakers and then turned west. Before long they were crossing the inlet to the mangrove forest and entering calm waters protected by a reef. Off to starboard Antonio could hear the waves breaking over the coral. The waters inside the bay were so calm that the small waves soaking the beach could not be heard on the port side.

Pushed by a soft but steady wind, they made good time following the coastline shadows cast by the expiring moon. Most of the boys fell asleep leaning against each other in a heap. Aimá hummed a song while Antonio and Taibaná paddled steadily, keeping time. They eventually caught up with the shadows at the westernmost sandy headland that stretched out to the sea in front of them. Just beyond was the site where they would turn inland to follow the same trail that brought them to the ocean. They beached the dugout and unloaded it without difficulty. There were no complaints when Taibaná ordered everyone to sleep the little time left until daybreak. Under the restless trade winds the exhausted travelers found easy slumber.

X

THE AREITO

Dawn arrived all too soon. The hunting group struggled as they hiked home loaded with *carey* meat, taking turns carrying the two huge shells. The boys were exhausted physically and emotionally. Their innocence was wounded. They returned home having witnessed death at the hunt and death in battle; unexpected experiences that strengthened some and scarred others.

Soon after sundown, the exhaustion they felt lifted somewhat as they walked proudly into the *yucayeque*. Friends and family emerged from *bohíos* to greet them and noticed the stone axes and bows carried by the boys. Taibaná led his charges directly to the *caney* where *Cacique* Gurao would accept their gifts for the *yucayeque*. Everyone was present, curious to learn where the weapons came from.

"We bring meat for the *areito* and weapons we captured in battle with Caribs," said Taibaná to the *cacique*. That single sentence sent a burst of energy through the crowd.

Gurao lifted one arm in a request for silence. "Welcome back," he said looking at the different members of the hunting party. "I can see in your eyes that you are tired. The day after tomorrow we hold the *areito*. We will gratefully eat the meat you bring and we will hear your story. For now, go home and rest."

Immediately a group of women moved to the *carey* meat and shells and whisked them away. The hunting party dispersed, the boys accompanied by their parents and other family members. The travelers, in the familiar comfort of their *bohíos*, were asleep before the coquí started their night song.

The next morning found Antonio better rested although his body continued to remind him of his adventures of the previous two days. His right foot was bruised where he first landed on the Carib warrior, his legs were aching from the hours of hiking and even his shoulders hurt from paddling the dugout. He limped outside the *bohio* and sat on a rock that had been placed for this purpose next to the fire pit. He observed that the *yucayeque* was a hub of activity. Everyone was preparing for the *areito*. The anticipation was palpable even to the Spaniard who was not sure what to expect. Antonio had never been to an *areito*, but he knew it was some kind of dance celebration. The slave Taínos in Española had spoken about *areitos* that lasted all night, with the participants falling asleep as they danced. The Catholic priests condemned *areitos* as pagan rituals that should be prohibited by the Spaniards. They stressed that only the holy mass carried the true word of God to people—a lesson Taínos were meant to learn on pain of death.

Antonio had never been a religious man. As a young boy he was not taught about the church, except for generalities and superstitions he picked up on the streets. Later, in Africa, he observed that different people prayed to different gods in different ways. The people of his village in Africa were some of the most decent people he had ever met and they had no idea of Jesus or Mary or the pope or any other Catholic icon. At the same time, he had seen many priests stand by while Taíno slaves and even fellow Spaniards were abused, supposedly in the name of God. Ultimately, he thought, the basic beliefs and behaviors that define the good and bad in a person were similar everywhere. He lived his life hoping that when the time of judgment arrived, God would recognize a decent man by more than just counting how many times he went to church. After living with the Taínos, he believed this more than ever. The word Taíno meant "good" in their language. Antonio thought this was appropriate since, in the most fundamental of ways, the Taínos were indeed a "good" people. Surely, he thought, God must see this.

Antonio sat a long time looking into the charred remains of a log, his mind lost in thought.

"Your body is here but your mind is elsewhere," said Aimá who had approached Antonio and stood next to him without being noticed.

The Spaniard looked up startled. "Oh! Sorry, I was thinking," he said as his mind returned to accompany his body.

"I can see that," she said as she sat next to him.

With barely a look at Aimá, he started to talk. "I like this *yucayeque*. I really can see no reason to leave. My future with the white man is full of hard work and hardship. Here I feel at home. Do you think your people would accept me if I asked to stay?" He looked into Aimá's eyes anticipating her answer.

"I have accepted you," she said softly. "You have already proven yourself a friend of the Taíno by fighting with us against the Caribs. If you are willing to live as one of us, I don't see why you would not be welcome." Antonio smiled earnestly, leaned over and gently caressed her cheeks with the back of his hand. She looked him in the eyes and responded with a soft smile.

They spent the day together resting and observing the final preparations for the next days' festivities. At the west end of the settlement, there was a square stone and wood structure called a *barbacoa* that became a center of activity in preparation for the *areito*. A group of women were involved in friendly chatter as they prepared the *carey* meat by spicing it and wrapping it in leaves. Others brought firewood and stacked it nearby. Aimá explained to Antonio how the *barbacoa* would be used as a platform to cook the meats and other foods over a wood fire.

Over by the *batey* a group of boys, under the watchful eye of an elder, were busy clearing debris, straightening stones and making sure the ground was smooth and even. Large clay jars containing *chicha* were distributed around the *batey* where everyone would have access to the drink. At odd intervals, the sounds of rhythmic chanting were heard from Yuquiel's *bohío*. The *behique* was busy preparing for the religious rituals that would be part of the *areito*.

By early evening, Antonio was again exhausted. He was amazed that Aimá looked fresh and rested, as if the trek to the beach had never happened. After a small meal the members of Taibaná's family sat outside their *bohíos* socializing in anxious anticipation of the next day. Antonio, immune to the excitement generated by the *areito*, found it

111

hard to keep his eyes open and was asleep before the stars were all out.

The *areito* began around mid-day the next day. Three drums, two made from *carey* shells and the third from a hollowed tree stump, sat on a bed of reed mats at the north side of the *batey*. The drummers, two men with similar red feathered headdresses, beat a slow rhythm using stout wooden sticks. The population of the *yucayeque*, now swelled by visitors from neighboring communities, began congregating around the *batey*. The gathering of people presented a rich spectacle of color and texture. People wore body paints in an abundance of colors and motifs representative of their rank and family ties. Most adults wore necklaces, bracelets, armbands and earrings made of colorful shells, feathers and stones. Some wore gold jewelry, which sparkled in the tropical sun. Colored fabrics had been used to make brightly patterned short skirts for the women and loincloths for the men.

It was the *cacique* and his wife however, who wore the most impressive garments. Gurao's golden *guanín* hung from his chest like a piece of the sun. As he moved, the highly polished metal disk reflected the sunlight as if on fire. His ears were pierced with multiple gold and shell earrings, and from between his nostrils hung a simple gold ring circled with beads. His upper arms had enough armbands to make them look armored. Second to the *guanín*, it was the arrangement of feathers on his head that made the *cacique* stand-out from the dazzling crowd. A multitude of pure white feathers were exquisitely arranged on his head so they cascaded down his back. Gurao's wife wore a similar headdress as she stood next to him. Her colorful skirt was similar to those worn by other women except it had front and rear panels that extended down to her ankles.

Gurao, standing in front of his *caney*, raised his arms and the drums stopped beating. "I welcome our visitors who join us for the *areito*. We celebrate our harvest with openness. Today you are one of us."

A simple look from the *cacique* signaled the drummers to start again. This time they played a faster beat. Above the sound of the drums a piercing cry was heard. The attention of the crowd moved to the walkway in the *conucos*. There, Yuquiel was involved in a dance ritual praising the season's abundant crops. Moving to the beat of the drums, Yuquiel's dance echoed the worship of generations of Taínos, a people who lived off the land and knew how to honor her spirit. In a few moments, Yuquiel ended the dance by dashing into the fields and running among the plants towards his *bohío*.

No sooner had the *behique* left the walkway than a group of about forty young men and women dressed in simple loincloths emerged from the forest running towards the *yucayeque*. The crowd around the *batey* started calling out in great excitement. Antonio had been standing quietly close to Aimá witnessing the events, not knowing what to expect next. "Who are they?" he asked.

"They are the *bato* players. This year we are having a game before the dances."

The crowd opened to allow the athletes to parade into the *batey*. The group separated into two and each team claimed an area of the *batey*, which was now transformed into a *bato* court. The colorful assembly gathered around the *batey* forming a living boundary that enclosed the players on all sides. Suddenly the sound from the fast-beating drums ceased. Once again Gurao took control of the gathering with a quick wave of an arm. From behind him someone produced a ball made from plant fibers and rubber. After recognizing the team leaders, he handed the ball to the nearest player.

Quickly, the ball was passed to the front line of players who stood facing their opponents. The spectators began hooting and hollering raising the level of excitement for themselves and the players. Without warning the ball was airborne. The game was simple but physically demanding. The objective was to keep the ball airborne without the use of hands, and pass it to the other team. The heavy ball was somewhat uneven and prone to bounce erratically. The young athletes threw themselves at the ball with abandon in their efforts to keep it aloft. Soon Antonio was caught up in the contagious enthusiasm of the crowd, which cheered every dramatic attempt to save a point. After reaching a predetermined score one of the teams was declared victorious. Members of the winning team received accolades from the crowd and *Cacique* Gurao.

By the time the *bato* game was finished the people were thoroughly immersed in the festive spirit of the *areito*. A group of musicians with a variety of instruments gathered by the drums and began to play. Instantly, there were dancers in the *batey* while others watched, their feet also moving in rhythm. A variety of percussion instruments, including maracas and drums, were complemented by wind instruments made from seashells, reeds, wood and clay. At times the musicians would move into the *batey* and dance while continuing to play their instrument. The rhythmic music was accompanied by singing from the dancers. Some of the songs in the *areitos* remembered important events and people from the Taíno past. These were composed by the *behique* and their words, part of the *yucayeque* heritage, remained unchanged. Other songs, recalling recent events, were full of improvisation and were often more festive.

Antonio stood with Aimá observing the dancers who lined up side by side in rows. One dancer in the front row served as a leader whose moves were repeated instantly by the other dancers. The dancing was accompanied with singing which followed the same pattern; first the leader sang a verse then the group repeated it. Antonio had some difficulty understanding the words of the song but eventually he realized the dancers were singing about the *bato* game, the skill of the players and the camaraderie of the teams. After the first dance, the music continued uninterrupted with different musicians taking turns with the instruments. Dancers moved in and out of the *batey* following a protocol that Antonio could not identify.

"I will dance this song," said Aimá, her body leaning towards the *batey*. "Join me."

"No!" responded Antonio quickly, exposing his nervousness. Already he felt self-conscious. Regardless of his time spent in Ceiba and Aimá's efforts to dress him as a Taíno, many of the visitors were overtly curious about him and the scrutiny made him feel uncomfortable. Dancing would only expose him more. "You go ahead. I will be watching you." He added, fearing she would insist that he dance. However, it was with relief that he saw Aimá smile and jump into the dance, a fast-moving feast of percussion, her sensuous body gracefully mimicking the steps of the dance leader.

The afternoon passed with constant music and dance. The skillful preparation for the *areito* ensured that no one had to work that day. Food and drink were ready and all were welcome to partake at their leisure. The *carey* meat was the principal dish. This was supplemented by fish, river shrimp, a variety of tubers, corn, peanuts, baskets full of fruit, and the ever-present *casabi*.

Late in the afternoon, Aimá and Antonio got some food and joined Taibaná and Mayaco who were sitting with Moné and his fiancée, Guaína. Moné, who served as messenger between *yucayeques*, was seen regularly in Ceiba visiting Guaína. However, Antonio had not seen him in weeks.

"Greetings Moné, its good to see you again," said the Spaniard while also acknowledging Guaína.

Moné reciprocated the greeting with a quick nod and a raised hand. Guaína smiled.

Not much has changed with him, thought Antonio.

"I have news...," Taibaná started to say but was interrupted by Aimá.

"What is it now?" she said, teasing her brother. "The last time you brought news we ended up in a battle with Caribs and not sleeping for two days."

"Don't forget, we won that battle. And tonight you eat the rewards of your efforts." Taibaná smiled, confident his retort would quiet his sister. "The news is," he continued without giving Aimá an opportunity to respond, "that *Cacique* Guaraca from Guayaney is calling a meeting of his *caciques* for the next full moon." Taibaná then looked at Antonio unsure of whether to continue.

"What else?" exclaimed Aimá. "You are not Moné. If you have something to say, say it."

Moné looked at Aimá with a raised eyebrow.

"There have been problems with the white men," said Taibaná somewhat hesitantly. "We go visit Guaraca to learn more, but apparently there has been fighting."

Antonio felt a knot of apprehension in his stomach. "Who brought this news?" he asked.

"I did," said Moné.

"Do you know anything else? Have Taínos fought with the Spaniards?" asked Antonio with obvious anxiety.

"You know what I know," responded Moné calmly.

"You will come with us to the meeting," said Taibaná, trying to comfort Antonio. "There we will learn what we need to know. You can expect a call from Gurao."

Antonio was visibly disturbed. After living in Ceiba, he was more aware than ever of the vulnerability of this peaceful people. Although he hoped that Ponce de León would bring a different kind of leadership to San Juan, he had seen the abusive treatment of the Taínos in La Española ever since the Europeans arrived, especially under the ruthless Governor Ovando, and he knew that Ponce de León had been a part of those efforts. There, any rebellion against Spanish rule was an excuse for the white men to strike at the natives. This heavy-handed approach resulted in the Spanish wiping out whole villages, killing the inhabitants or making them slaves. There was not much left of the Taínos in La Española. They lived in poor settlements under control of their white masters. The lucky ones retreated to the mountains, far from the Spaniards.

Antonio's mind was racing. Thoughts came to his mind unbidden and dreadfully clear. How could he have been so naive? White men would never coexist with the Taíno. They would attempt to dominate the natives of San Juan as they did in La Española. An image of the future crystallized in his mind and at that moment he realized he needed to choose once and for all: life with the Taínos or life with the Spaniards. He was surprised at his feelings and at the ease with which he made his decision—from now on he would share his fate with the Taínos. This decision was a revelation. Being honest with himself made him feel like he no longer had to keep a secret that he knew to be a lie. Although he felt the joy of one who finds his path after being lost, the fear in his heart remained.

"Aimá, you must teach me how to dance in the *areito*," said Antonio.

"I will," Aimá responded. But she also noticed that Antonio continued to be disturbed by Taibaná's news. She placed a comforting hand on his shoulder. "We have a few days before this journey," she said softly to him. "Today we have an *areito*, don't let your unhappy thoughts get in the way of the celebration. Besides, you have nothing to worry about; I will go with you to the meeting of *caciques*."

"Now he is really in trouble," cried Taibaná unable to resist this opportunity to taunt his sister.

His outburst served to release the tension created by Antonio's reaction to the news as they all laughed out loud. Even Moné smiled, enjoying his friend's obvious pleasure at harassing his sister.

"You keep quiet, you frog!" she raised her smiling voice over the laughter. "It was your big mouth that brought the bad news."

"The only bad news is that you've decided to come with us," said Taibaná.

She then shoved him and he fell backwards from his squatting position, laughing uninterrupted.

Antonio observed all of this with a smile on his face, but his emotions were conflicted. He could not shake his concern about the possible meaning of the news he'd received.

The small group of friends was still sitting together when word came that Yuquiel wanted to see Taibaná and Antonio. The two friends took leave of their companions and walked across the *yucayeque* in response to the unexpected summons. They stopped outside the covered entrance to the *behique*'s *bohio* wondering what he wanted from them.

"Greetings Yuquiel," called Taibaná after a gently rapping on the canes framing the doorway. "It's Taibaná and Antonio. You called for us?"

"Come in and sit," came the slurred response from

117

inside the dark *bohio*.

The two friends pulled aside the thick fabric covering the doorway and entered into a different world. Here lived the spirits of the *yucayeque*. The air inside the *bohio* was thick with the smoke and strong scent of plants burned in secret rituals. The *behique* was accompanied by three elders who sat quietly behind him against the far wall of the *bohio*. They looked up at Yuquiel's new guests with fixed grins pasted to their faces. The three old men made Antonio nervous with their stares. The Spaniard was not very familiar with the religious rituals of his hosts. In particular, he had been suspicious of Yuquiel.

As his eyes got accustomed to the darkness he noticed more details. Yuquiel sat on a *dujo* facing the doorway. Small rocks delineated a circle on the ground in front of him. In the middle of the circle a small fire illuminated an intricately carved *cemí* the size of a small anvil. Antonio recognized the effigy. It seemed that every *bohio* had one of these figurines, representative of the gods of the Taíno. However, this *cemí* was larger and more elaborate than others he had seen. The three-sided object sat on a wide base carved with fantastic looking heads at each end. The center rose from the base to a rounded peak with a slight indentation on top. The carvings on the *cemí* were highlighted in bright colors, the indentation on the peak was laminated in gold.

Yuquiel signaled for his guests to sit to his right. Antonio followed Taibaná's lead, making sure to stay outside the stone circle. Yuquiel then closed his eyes and remained still for a long moment. It was quiet inside the *bohio* even though the *areito* continued outside.

"Tonight," called out the *behique* suddenly, startling his visitors, "you will tell the story of your encounter with the Caribs. We are here to prepare your bodies and your minds so that your story will not falter." Without interruption, Yuquiel started to chant as he prepared a mixture of powders called *cohoba*, in a small clay dish.

Taibaná looked at Antonio reassuringly and placed a hand on one of his friend's knees. Antonio did not know if he was offering comfort or seeking some for himself.

118

Yuquiel then moved into the stone circle and performed a simple dance as he continued to chant. After going around the *cemí* once, he squatted, picked it up and moved it directly in front of his guests. He then reached for the clay dish and placed a small amount of the *cohoba* on the gold plated top of the *cemí*.

"We will first share in the power of the *cemí*, and then we will plan our story," explained Yuquiel as he reached next to his *dujo* for a Y-shaped piece of ceramic with three hollow reeds attached to each extremity.

Yuquiel placed the double end reeds in his nostrils and held it there with one hand. He used the other hand to guide the single end to the top of the *cemí*. With a quick, forceful breath he inhaled the mixture of powders into his nose. He then passed the reed to Taibaná obviously expecting the young man to emulate his actions.

Antonio got more anxious. Clearly he was going to be asked to follow Taibaná in this ritual. He knew of the Taíno *cohoba* ceremony. He had been told it allowed demons to take over your body. Antonio's mind was full of questions he had no opportunity to ask; however, he decided to set them aside. He trusted Taibaná to keep him from getting harmed. If his friend was willing to obey the *behique*, he would also. "Don't I want to join these people?" He thought to himself. "Then I must follow their ways."

Taibaná showed no hesitation. As soon as Yuquiel laid the *cohoba* on the *cemí*, he leaned over, snorted it and passed the reed to Antonio. Yuquiel looked closely at the Spaniard, as if reconsidering his decision to include him in the ritual. Antonio returned the stare and after a short moment the *behique* sat back and signaled to the *cemí*, the *cohoba* ready to be inhaled. Slowly, making sure he mimicked his friend exactly, Antonio adjusted the reed, leaned over and snorted the fine powder. Immediately, he felt the desire to sneeze; with some effort he controlled the urge.

Aimá was talking with Mayaco near the *batey* when a young boy ran by announcing the *behique* was getting ready to tell a story. The two women looked to the *batey*, their eyes exposing the anxiety they had been hiding from each other

119

since their companions left to see the *behique* sometime near sundown.

"Do you think Antonio and Taibaná will be with Yuquiel during his story?" asked Mayaco.

"I hope so. I don't like not knowing what is going on."

The two women approached the edge of the *batey* where they could get a good view of Yuquiel's *bohio*. In a short time most of those present at the *areito* were gathered in quiet expectation. All remaining light from the silver sunset was now gone. Numerous fires bathed the yucayeque in a golden light, dimming the brilliance of the stars. Shadows danced to the rhythm of the flames.

Out of Yuquiel's *bohio* ran a young man. Aimá recognized him as one of the musicians. He ran around the *batey* to one of the *carey* drums and began playing a steady fast beat. Once again the woven door of the *bohio* opened and the crowd looked around to see Yuquiel step out followed by three elders and finally Taibaná and Antonio. Yuquiel and the elders had their skin painted black with white streaks resembling the Carib's.

Yuquiel walked forward to stand within the *batey*. He raised one arm and the drums stopped. "Tonight you will hear and see the story of Taibaná and Antonio and their battle with the Caribs," he announced to the crowd in a serious voice. Then, without pause, he and the three elders moved to the opposite end of the *batey*, sat cross-legged, bent their heads down and remained still as statues. As soon as the four men were in place, Taibaná and Antonio walked into the *batey*. They came to a stop with Taibaná standing a few steps ahead of his friend.

Aimá was confused. Usually Yuquiel told the story and used different people to represent characters. This time however, Yuquiel was sitting aside and Taibaná was taking the place of the storyteller. This, she thought, was a great honor for her brother. She also noticed that Taibaná and Antonio were staring right through the crowd, as if they were standing alone in the *batey*. Had Yuquiel cast a spell on them?

120

Her thoughts were interrupted by the sound of her brother's voice. Suddenly, his eyes became animated and his posture more relaxed. He contrasted sharply with Antonio who remained behind him, stone-like. Taibaná began telling the story of the *carey* hunt. With much detail he described the early rise and the day's long trek to the coast. He told of the arrival of the *carey* and how the gentle giants gave knowledge to the young ones and meat for the *yucayeque*.

Aimá observed her brother closely. She had never seen him like this—he was totally absorbed by his own story. In fact, she thought, he was reliving it. His gestures and words were showing all the excitement and tension of the night they met the Caribs.

Next, Taibaná began to relate their encounter with their feared enemies. Out of the crowd weapons appeared. Taibaná was given his stone ax, Antonio his knife and sword, and Yuquiel and the elders were given the Carib weapons. At the point on the story where the Caribs were running down the beach, Taibaná went quiet and the drummers started pounding a fast beat. He moved to join Antonio and, with weapons in hand, squatted at the edge of the *batey*.

Yuquiel and his men collected their weapons. Carried by the drums, they ran around the *batey* shouting the Carib war cry, weapons in the air, frightening the crowd. With eyes bulging out and teeth bared, they expressed the rabid fierceness of the Carib warriors.

Aimá began to fear this reenactment. She looked to her brother and her lover and saw the same faces and emotions as in the night of the real battle. That night they fought true Caribs and four men died. She only hoped the spell cast by Yuquiel would not permit any bloodshed.

A wild scream came from the squatting men as they attacked their simulated enemies. The reenacted battle was not much like the original—it was more spectacular. In greatly exaggerated moves the men fought each other back and forth. Ultimately, the Caribs fell to their adversaries one at a time. At the death of the last Carib, the drums stopped. The crowd was entranced. After a couple of seconds, Taibaná and Antonio returned to their original positions in the *batey*.

121

There Taibaná quickly completed the story in a couple of sentences.

This released the crowd, which joined in a victory shout in approval of the story. Aimá and Mayaco ran to their mates looking as anxious as if there had been a real battle. Yuquiel and the elders quietly gathered themselves and went into the *behique*'s *bohio*. In the background, music began to play and dancers took to the *batey*; the festive *areito* resumed.

Still under the spell of Yuquiel's magic, Taibaná and Antonio joined every dance of the *areito* until dawn. When their bodies finally surrendered to fatigue, they slept for a full day.

XI

JAGUA

In the days following the *areito*, Antonio became more deeply integrated into the society of Ceiba. The *areito* had felt like a ritual of passage into the community of the *yucayeque*. With his commitment unencumbered by other loyalties, he found a new level of intimacy with the residents of Ceiba. He made an effort to learn people's names, relationships and personal stories. His level of comfort with the Taíno was enhanced by being openly accepted into their community.

"Aimá, I want you to know that I want to stay in Ceiba with you and your people," Antonio confessed one night. "Do you think I will be accepted? Can I be a Taíno?"

"I think you already are," she said. "You just need to learn to think of us as your people."

"I think I can do that," he said as he gently pulled her close.

One hot, sunny day, Aimá led Antonio upriver to a secluded waterhole adorned with a spring fed waterfall quietly splashing water to one side. The place reminded Antonio of that magical spot in Africa which lured him away from his ship a lifetime before. Together they washed in the river and enjoyed each other's company in the solitude of the jungle. During a quiet moment Aimá went to the riverbank, opened a bag she carried from the *yucayeque* and pulled out a number of clay disks and several carefully tied leather pouches. She handed the clay disks to Antonio who noticed they were carved in different patterns. She then went to an area on the downstream side of the waterhole and started digging and placing soil on a wooden plate.

"Come close," she called.

Antonio obeyed. Aimá scooped some soil from the wooden plate and started rubbing it on Antonio. The soil was very fine red clay. Aimá covered Antonio's torso, arms and legs and he turned bronze.

Aimá laid out the leather bags inside small holes she'd dug in the riverbank to hold them in place. Skillfully

123

she applied paint she carried in the bags onto the clay molds and proceeded to use the clay molds to stamp their bodies. She purposefully imprinted similar patterns in both their bodies as a symbol of their relationship. She continued until their bodies were covered. That evening they returned to Ceiba dressed in ancient symbols that spoke of their unity and brought Antonio closer than ever to the community.

Until the upcoming meeting of the *caciques*, Antonio had decided to follow Aimá's advice and try to not be troubled by the news of conflict with the Spaniards. However, in the back of his mind remained the fearful thought of Spain at war with the Taínos. He knew both worlds and understood that in a violent confrontation the Europeans would prevail. It took nine years for the Spaniards to dominate Taíno culture in La Española. Early on in the settlement, Admiral Colón made enemies with some *caciques* and allies of others. There were skirmishes and battles, and eventually both sides settled into an uneasy peace. Those years of mostly peaceful co-existence were forgotten when a new governor, Nicolas Ovando, arrived at the Village of Santo Domingo in 1502. Under the leadership of Governor Ovando the Taínos were harassed, enslaved, and treated viciously. The natives fought valiantly and honorably and had many victories against the newcomers to their land. The Spaniards fought with the advantage of deadlier weapons, horses and battle dogs, but it was lies, deceit and disease that proved their most potent weapons against the Taíno.

Governor Ovando led a crusade against the Taínos making no pretense at righteousness. It culminated in a legendary betrayal when he paid an extended visit to the revered Taíno queen Anacaona at her *yucayeque* of Jaragua, in the west end of La Española. One of the stated intents of the visit was to express gratitude to the Taínos who had warned the Spaniards of an impending hurricane, advice Ovando had dismissed in arrogance and at a great cost in lives. After the storm, the Taínos had rescued the distraught surviving residents of Santo Domingo with supplies of food. These friendly actions provided Ovando with a pretext to approach the Taínos openly. After days of living and feasting together with the people of Jaragua, Ovando called for a meeting with all available *caciques*. Most of the island's Taíno leadership gathered in the friendly confines of Anacaona's *caney*, ready for the important meeting.

Only Anacaona survived that meeting.

Ovando ordered his men to burn the *caney* and kill anyone trying to run out, except for the Queen, whom he wanted alive. At the same time he attacked the unsuspecting residents of Jaragua, resulting in a massacre beyond the comprehension of any Taíno. Anacaona was held captive and after a pre-arranged trial, was condemned to hang. But Anacaona kept Ovando from final victory by exposing his treacherous actions during the trial, and ultimately, by committing suicide before she was to hang. Undeterred, Ovando brought her dead body to the gallows trying to complete his intent of setting an example. Ovando's final plan, to have Anacaona drawn and quartered with parts of her body taken in a tour of Indian villages, was thwarted when her body was taken down from the gallows in the middle of the night by some of her many admirers, never to be found again. But the damage was done; the bright light of the Taínos of Aytí was reduced to a flicker. The lessons learned there would reverberate in future conquests led by those present, including Hernando Cortez and Francisco Pizarro.

Antonio did not participate in the events at Jaragua. He was one of those who remained at the Village of Santo Domingo, rebuilding from the hurricane. He learned of Anacaona's fate and the shameful events at Jaragua from Fray Bartolome de las Casas and other witnesses who disagreed with Governor Ovando's ruthless tactics. Like many long time settlers, Antonio grew to respect the Taíno and appreciate their knowledge of the land, their peaceful nature and their intrinsic honesty, which made them so vulnerable to deceit and lies they could not comprehend. From a more practical perspective, many understood that Taínos were needed as labor for their farms and mines. How did the governor intend to do the work needed with the few available Spanish laborers? Ovando knew the answer would come from Africa.

Antonio didn't have long to wait before Gurao ordered things ready for the visit to Jagua, a small *yucayeque* in Guayaney, that would host the gathering of *caciques*. On a cool morning, before dawn, the small band of travelers gathered by the *caney*. Taibaná and Antonio were set to accompany Gurao and Yuquiel as representatives from Ceiba. Aimá, who found a way to convince Gurao to let her go with the group, was adding some final items to her travel pack. Moné, had remained in Ceiba since the *areito,* and now planned to join other members of his home *yucayeque* at Jagua.

Mayaco and Guaína were present to see their partners off while others gathered quietly to wish the travelers well. With the stars still visible, the group left the *yucayeque* headed southwest. Moné, the most experienced traveler, led the way. Tenuous rays of morning light could be seen illuminating the tops of the ancient ceibas as they crested the first line of hills beyond the river. A soft morning breeze was dispersing the smoke from exhausted fires which had accumulated under the trees' expansive boughs. As they walked, Antonio looked back and admired the beauty of the *yucayeque*. It was truly a lovely place, fully in harmony with the world around it. He gave Aimá, walking behind him, a quick smile and returned his attention to the trail. At that moment he thought himself a fortunate man.

For most of the morning, the trail led them over hilly terrain. Rain from the previous day had made the ground slippery and Antonio had to concentrate to keep his footing on the wet leaves and clayey soil. Nevertheless, the group made good time. With Moné in the lead there was little idle chatter and no deviation from the route to their destination. Several times they came upon streams that were swollen and they had to leave the trail to find rocks or fallen trees that would give them a safe route across. In the afternoon, after a small meal, the group reached a broad valley. There, walking on mostly flat ground, the group moved swiftly south. They reentered mountainous terrain just before

126

sunset and Antonio started to wish dearly for their arrival at their final destination. Late in the evening, they crested a ridge overlooking a small valley. On the opposite side of the valley, the *yucayeque* of Jagua was made visible by its many burning campfires.

Cacique Guaraca greeted the travelers upon their arrival. Recognizing the weariness of his new guests, he immediately assigned host families to Moné, Antonio and Aimá. *Cacique* Gurao was invited to the *caney* with other *caciques*, and Yuquiel joined the assembled *behiques*.

Antonio was so tired that he did not notice the stares he received as he and Aimá walked across the *yucayeque* with their host. After a light meal and an exchange of pleasantries the couple from Ceiba climbed in a hammock and were soon asleep, wrapped in a mutual embrace.

Once the travelers were accommodated, Guaraca called on Gurao. "Follow me," he said discretely to the visiting *cacique*.

Cacique Guaraca led his guest to a nearby stream. He made certain they were alone and turned to face Gurao. "Gurao, I've known you since we were young men. You usually have a good reason for your actions. Please explain why you bring a white man to this gathering," Guaraca looked serious but hopeful. He wanted a good response from his long time friend. As host to the meeting of *caciques* he wanted everything to go smoothly. The presence of the white man was unexpected and almost certainly would create dissension among the *caciques*.

"It is my right as a *cacique* to bring assistants and company when I travel."

"Times are changing," said Guaraca showing some of his frustration. "The white man fights the Taínos on the other side of Borikén. Tomorrow we meet to determine how to respond. Your white man may be in danger if he serves no purpose other than company."

Gurao thought for a moment before responding. Then he spoke evenly and firmly, "This white man has proven himself a true friend of Ceiba. He has fought with us against the Caribs. He has participated in the *areito* and

Yuquiel chose him to tell a story. I know that his allegiance is with the Taíno. We should be able to use his knowledge of white men when contemplating our decision." He stopped, allowing Guaraca to think about what he had said. "He can be of help to us."

"Very well. We must tell the *caciques* tonight. I don't want them to be surprised when we start the meeting and they see a white man sitting across from them."

That night, while Antonio slept across the *batey*, the *caciques* had a lengthy discussion about his presence in Jagua. It took all the persuasion of Gurao's good reputation and the considerable influence of Guaraca as host *cacique* to convince the Taíno leaders of the advantages of having a white man's point of view at their meeting.

Antonio woke up rested but somewhat stiff. Aimá, he noticed enviously, looked as if she had taken a stroll around the *batey* instead of having walked all the previous day. Aimá was already at ease in the *bohío* and helping their hostess prepare a morning meal. Not long after they ate and washed, the *caciques* and their aides were called to gather at a shady glade adjacent to the *caney*.

There was no hint of rain that day but humidity lingered from a recent downpour. As Antonio walked to the meeting place, he noticed he was being scrutinized. He remembered his first days at Ceiba when his white skin was a novelty. However, this time he felt there was more than just curiosity in the stares; there was fear, and from some, there was hatred.

The meeting area was a clearing surrounded by large trees that provided shade. Most of the *caciques* brought *dujos* on which to sit. Others sat on the ground or on makeshift seats made out of logs and stones. All the principal *caciques* from the eastern half of Borikén were present. Together with their aides there were close to fifty people attending the meeting. There was a sense of purpose in the gathering which was evidenced by the lack of ceremony.

"We are gathered to discuss the news brought by *Cacique* Mabodomaca," said Guaraca, calling the meeting to order without preamble.

Mabodomaca stood up to speak. One of the principal *caciques* from the north-central part of Borikén, Mabodomaca was a man of average build with wide set eyes and a large nose dividing his face in two.

"These are difficult times," he started. "Many of us wondered about the white men when they started to visit our land. Now we know their purpose." Mabodomaca paused. His troubled eyes looked to the ground. He shook his head as if fighting troubled memories. Already he regretted the sad story he was about to tell.

The *cacique* took a deep breath and continued. "For a time a white man called Sotomayor had been trying to build a *yucayeque* near Guánica. The great *Cacique* Agüeybaná, and later his brother Agüeybaná the Brave, welcomed him and helped him. Agüeybaná the Brave even allowed his sister Guanina to live with the white man. But Sotomayor was an ungrateful man. He became unpleasant and arrogant. He expected our people to work for him and abandon their *yucayeques*. When they did not obey him, he hit them, injuring many. He demanded we work for him and forget our lives. This behavior was not natural and could not be tolerated. Agüeybaná and his *caciques* had no alternative but to challenge Sotomayor. He was killed, along with his escort in a place called Jauca, high in the mountains, inland from Cayabo."

Antonio felt a familiar knot tighten in his stomach as he heard Mabodomaca tell his story. The news was worse than he had expected. He knew of Don Cristobal de Sotomayor from Caparra. He was a young man, the son of a count and sent to San Juan by the king of Spain himself. He had been a great aid to Ponce de León and served as sheriff in Caparra for a time. Not long before Antonio departed Caparra, Sotomayor had received permission to establish a colony on the western part of Borikén, which he called Villa de Távara. Surely Ponce de León would not tolerate such an attack on a Spaniard, especially one of high rank. Often in La Española the life of one Spaniard was paid for with scores of Taínos killed or enslaved. Antonio knew the same would happen in Borikén.

Mabodomaca continued his story without pause.

"The chief *cacique* of the white men, the man named Ponce, then came and fought Agüeybaná and his warriors at Coayuco. This was a terrible battle. The white men fought with fire and their shiny knives. Many Taínos died."

At this announcement, those gathered broke into commotion. Several of the *caciques* stood up and paced outside the clearing. Others lamented with long sustained cries of grief.

Antonio looked to Aimá who had her face buried in her hands, hiding her grief. He gently put a hand on her shoulder. "Tell me," he asked softly. "What is happening?"

Her face showed her pain. "The great *cacique* Agüeybaná died not long before you came to Ceiba. Now his brother, who was a promising leader, has been defeated in battle and many others have died. It does not bode well that your people have done this."

Antonio bristled at her last comment. "They are not my people!" He exclaimed in a forceful whisper. "You know I have made my decision. I am Taíno."

They were interrupted by Guaraca who was beating a drum to call everyone back to order. "Mabodomaca is not finished," he said and signaled for the speaker to continue.

"I myself led our warriors against the white men in the lands of *cacique* Aimaco. There too, good warriors died. Another battle took place at Yahuecas." He paused, looking closely at the members of his audience. "Ponce, the white *cacique*, now demands that we accept him as our *cacique* and that we do as he says. He wants us to work his *conucos*, find gold for him and pray to his gods." Once again, voices rang out from the gathering, but this time Mabodomaca kept control of the meeting. "We must respond to the white *cacique*. That is why we are gathered here. Do we go with him or do we remain free?" After signaling Guaraca that he was finished, Mabodomaca sat on his *dujo*.

"It is time to speak and decide. We must respond to the demands of the white *cacique*," said Guaraca.

"What of Agüeybaná? Where is he?" sked one *cacique*.

"Right now he is meeting with other *caciques*,"

130

Mabodomaca responded from his seat. "Regardless of what we decide here, he will not follow Ponce."

"What will happen to our *conucos* if we work for the white man?" came another question.

"You have not had much experience with the white man in this part of Borikén," said Mabodomaca. "They do not care about your *conucos*. Their *cacique* came to my *yucayeque* and took my *conucos* from me saying that he was my new *cacique*. He then gave them to another man who took all the *yuca* by force." Mabodomaca's anger was visible in his face. "We have been facing abuse from the white men almost since they arrived. They do not respect us, or the way we live. They expect us to leave our *yucayeques* and go live with them. They say they will give us homes and food but we must follow their orders."

"What if we don't?" asked *Cacique* Humaca from Macao, Moné's *yucayeque*.

Mabodomaca began to respond, then stopped. His head turned and he looked directly at Antonio. "Maybe we should ask a white man," he said evenly. "Gurao, tell your man to answer Humaca's question."

Gurao shot an angry look at Mabodomaca. He did not appreciate being told what to do in front of his peers. However, he realized that Antonio's contribution in this discussion would be invaluable. "Antonio has good standing in my *yucayeque*. He has fought to defend our people. He is one of us!" Gurao paused and looked around the gathering ready to face any challenges. Antonio felt a deep gratitude for Gurao taking such a supportive position.

"He speaks if he wants to," ended Gurao.

Antonio, sailor and laborer, was not used to speaking in front of groups, much less a group of confident leaders at the height of their power. He was nervous, but he knew he had to speak. He had to warn his new people about the enemy they were facing. Slowly he stood up to face his audience. All eyes were on him. Few in this group had dealt directly with these latest visitors to Borikén; they were curious to hear what he would say.

"I am afraid Mabodomaca is correct," started

131

Antonio. "The white man is concerned with obtaining gold, which they value highly. They also want to teach their belief in one god. They think your ceremonies and gods are evil. A few powerful white men have *conucos*. They trade the crops with others that have no *conucos* to become wealthy and more powerful. They need people to work looking for gold and tending the *conucos,* but there are few white men to do this work. They will use the Taíno for this. I have seen it in Aytí."

Antonio's words stirred up the *caciques* who shouted defiantly. Angry faces looked at the Spaniard.

"Stop!" yelled Guaraca explosively with a sharp beat on his drum. "Let him finish."

After the group quieted, Antonio continued. "The white man is a strong enemy. They have powerful weapons and can kill many in battle. This too I saw in Aytí." That said, he sat once again next to Aimá.

Cacique Humaca then stood. "My *yucayeque* has been fighting Caribs for generations. There is no fiercer warrior. I say we do not give ourselves to the white man. If he elects to fight, we will fight."

Proud cries of support erupted from all in the group. It was obvious to Antonio that the Taíno would defy Ponce de León. It was also obvious to Antonio that they had no alternative. It was either slavery or war. In either case, he knew in his heart that the Taíno would suffer greatly—this too he had seen in Aytí.

The meeting continued until late in the evening. Each *cacique* spoke in defense of their *yucayeque* and their people. They invoked their gods and told of omens that supported their positions. None agreed to the subservient life under the control of white men. The response to the white *cacique* was unanimous: the Taínos would challenge his demands; they stood with Agüeybaná.

That night, buoyed by the spirit of their meeting, *Cacique* Guaraca sponsored an *areíto*. The mood of the celebration was defiant and boastful. The *behiques* took turns telling stories of Taíno victories against the Caribs. Yuquiel used his turn to tell the story of the encounter during
132

the *carey* hunt. After he was finished, Antonio observed a marked difference in the way the people interacted with him. Suddenly, there was less suspicion and more acceptance. Nevertheless, he remained on the periphery of the *areito*.

He was distracted by thoughts of the day's news. He knew better than anyone the challenges facing the Taíno. Now that they had been defied, the Spanish would be ruthless. The Taíno's way of life, their culture, everything they had known, was being confronted by a mortal threat. The *caciques* had no option but to resist.

"Come, share a dance with me," said Aimá in an effort to lift her lover's spirits. "This is an *areito*. You are not meant to sit here."

Antonio looked at Aimá, happy that she was there but also somewhat annoyed that she was badgering him. "I'm thinking. Leave me alone."

"What are you thinking? If you tell me, then your thoughts will leave your head and you can dance with me," she said squatting next to him with a smile on her face.

Antonio could not refuse her honesty and her beautiful smile. He reached out and caressed her face. "I am thinking about your people."

"Our people," she corrected him.

"Our people," he nodded. "They face a deadly enemy, yet they dance. I'm so afraid for the Taíno, I can barely move."

"The *areito* celebrates our decision to stand up and face an enemy," she explained in a soft voice. "If you are correct that the enemy is so deadly, then there is greater reason to celebrate. My heart is full because my people are not surrendering."

"I have thought of that. The Taíno are brave in defending their lives and their *yucayeques*. Believe me," he said looking down, "life as a slave of the white men would be painful. I can see that there is greater honor in fighting."

"Then come with me," she said standing up and reaching out with her hand. "Help me celebrate that bravery and honor. Be Taíno."

Antonio looked up at his lover. She stood straight

133

and strong and proud, wearing nothing but a simple loin cloth, her body covered in colorful designs, gold arm bands, shell necklace, and an embroidered headband holding down her thick black hair. He felt his love for her drench his body like a great wave. In his mind he questioned if he was worthy of this woman. Somehow she embodied everything he loved about these people. How could he resist her? He put his hand in hers and she helped him to his feet. They drank *chicha* and danced, sustained by the shared energy flowing through the *batey*. The *areito* continued until the sun rose over the land ruled by *Cacique* Guaraca.

XII

MACAO

After a day of rest, the visitors to Jagua prepared to return to their home *yucayeques*. Aimá however, wanted to use this opportunity to visit a childhood friend in Macao. She made arrangements for Antonio and herself to accompany Moné, *Cacique* Humaca and the two other members of their group back to Macao. So it was that, following a hearty morning meal, Antonio and Aimá took leave of Taibaná, Gurao and Yuquiel, and went to join the group from Macao. The band gathered at the eastern end of the *yucayeque* and left on their two-day trek with Moné in the silent lead.

After several hours of crossing numerous ridges the trail to Macao leveled off and became easier to traverse. The group followed the floodplain of a small river until early evening. They crossed a variety of environments, mostly savannas with patches of dense vegetation wherever a tributary stream joined the river. Early in the evening they reached a point where the ridge of hills that marked the northern edge of the valley angled to meet the river. There, the river turned sharply to the south. *Cacique* Humaca explained to Antonio that they had to cross the ridge to reach a second river that would lead them to Macao. The *cacique* decided to make camp and tackle the ridge and the rest of their trip the next day.

Immediately, Aimá set out to build a fire. Moné disappeared into the dense vegetation along the hillside returning a few moments later with a bag full of fruits. The other members of the group produced dried fish, *casabi*, and dried *yuca* which was then placed in a small bowl made from the gourd-like fruit of the *higuero* tree and mixed with water and herbs to make a mealy cream. The sky was not totally dark when the group sat around the fire to share their meal. After eating, they shared stories and a couple of songs.

Cacique Humaca was a curious man and less impressed by the Spaniards than *Cacique* Gurao. Much of the day he had been questioning Antonio about the newcomers to Borikén.

135

Systematically he inquired about all the characteristics of the Spanish settlements, including their population, type of weapons and number of settlements. Here, thought Antonio, was a general expecting a battle, seeking weaknesses in his enemy. It was obvious to Antonio that Humaca still had some questions in his mind. He was not surprised when the *cacique* moved to sit next to him.

"Tell me, why did you come to Borikén?" inquired Humaca.

Antonio took a few minutes to consider his response. "I came here to find a better life."

"Did you find it?" interrupted Humaca.

"I did," said the Spaniard, "with the Taíno." He shared a nod of understanding with Humaca and then continued. "But that is not what I, and many like me had planned. I wanted to obtain a piece of land where I could plant my *conucos* and be my own *cacique*. That is what the white men call a *hacienda*."

Humaca looked perplexed as he mouthed the word "ha-ci-en-da". "You would work the *conucos* alone and have no *yucayeque*?"

"Normally a man would have his wife and children and some workers. They would not be totally alone."

"If I had to live alone with my wives and children I would go crazy. It is good to have a *yucayeque* with people."

"Now that I live with the Taíno, I agree. But white men live a different way. They seek to make wealth for themselves and their families, not the *yucayeque*."

Humaca, an experienced *cacique*, could not understand how people could meet even their most basic needs if they were all working separately. "How do things get accomplished if you don't work together?"

Antonio could see Humaca struggling with concepts that were totally foreign to the Taíno way of life. Once again he paused to organize his thoughts. "Our principal *cacique*—we call him 'king'—lives in our homeland. He rules everything. Everyone works for him and he has much wealth."

Humaca nodded in understanding. He was aware

136

that, as a *cacique*, he had certain advantages over others in his *yucayeque*.

"The king," continued Antonio, "has many *nitaínos*, who in turn have *nitaínos*, who in turn have *nitaínos*. There are many layers," indicated Antonio placing his arms one on top of the other to assist his explanation. "Each layer is like *naborías* for their *nitaínos* but they also have *naborías* of their own. The difference is that the *naborías* provide work and wealth to their *nitaínos* only. Not to all the people."

Humaca's sharp mind understood the explanation and realized its implications. "How many white men are in your home land?"

"As many as the stars," said Antonio seriously. "And all the *naborí* like me, without land and without power, want to come here to get a *hacienda*."

Humaca's visage turned somber. "The Taíno stands in the way of the white men who want their ha-ci-en-da."

Antonio nodded in agreement.

"Will the white men ever stop coming to Boríken?" asked the *cacique* in a way that demanded nothing but the truth.

"I don't think so. Many white men live in misery in the homeland. They will come here to try to improve their lives."

"You have told me much that I must think about. But one thing I understand..."

"What is that?" asked Antonio.

"That you would choose to be a Taíno."

Humaca stood, wished Antonio a good night's sleep and then went to lay down on the ground on the opposite side of the fire. At once, Aimá, who had been waiting for the two men to finish their conversation, walked over and sat next to Antonio.

"It is nice to see you," he said softly. Everyone else was already asleep.

"Humaca looked sad. What did you say to him?" she asked.

"I explained about the Spanish, how they live and why they are here. It was a troubling conversation."

137

"Then listen to me. I have good news," she said with a smile that melted the Spaniard's heart. "Moné will travel with us to Ceiba after our visit. He will finally take Guaína as his wife. And it's about time!" she said in an assertive whisper. "People were beginning to say that she was getting tired of waiting. After they marry, she will move to Macao with him."

"I'm glad to hear that. It's obvious they love each other. Guaína will be very happy."

"Yes, she will," said Aimá throwing her arms around him with a coquettish smile. "Women don't like sleeping alone waiting for their men."

Antonio sensed her desire and eased Aimá to the ground next to him. In the darkness of moon shadows cast by trees, the two lovers quietly explored each other. Silently, their hands spoke and their bodies listened and responded. They clasped in the intimate embrace of lovers, their bodies screaming in pleasure that only they two could hear.

They were awakened by Moné before sunup. Reluctantly, they unsnarled their tangled bodies and loosened the stiffness that comes from sleeping on the ground. As usual, Aimá was up and about before Antonio. By the time the Spaniard got his body ready to face the day, a fire was burning and Aimá was preparing a simple tea from herbs she carried with her. Soon the group was moving, hoping to reach Macao before sundown.

The trail moved in a zigzag up the hillside. Although relatively dry, the clay mud underfoot remained slippery. Tired from the previous days' hike and his lack of sleep, Antonio lost his footing more than once. "Do all white men have problems walking on the mountains?" asked Humaca, amused, as Antonio got up from a particularly spectacular fall. "If so, this is where I'll fight them."

"Just make sure they are tired before you start the battle," responded Antonio, trying to defend himself.

"That should not be difficult. I'll have the *behique* prepare a love enchantment for the enemy the night before we meet them."

Even Moné laughed as he noticed the mud-spattered

Spaniard's embarrassment.

Antonio gained his composure. "If they do as well as I did, they will die with a smile on their faces," he said looking at Aimá as he joined the humor of the moment.

"Enough of this," said Aimá with feigned seriousness. "We have a long way to go and I don't like the tone of this conversation." She waved to Moné and the rest of the snickering men to get going.

The travelers arrived in Macao late in the afternoon to a joyous welcome. The *yucayeque*, larger than Ceiba, sat on top a long hill adjacent to a river. From the *batey* the silver thread of water could be seen winding gently to the sea. The ocean was close enough that, in the silence of night, the waves could be heard breaking on the beach. Antonio was pleasantly surprised; he didn't realize Macao would be so close to the sea.

Out of the crowd jumped a thin woman who threw herself in Aimá's arms. This must be Carima, thought Antonio. He was taken aback by her appearance. He realized that although very few Taínos were truly fat, in general they were not thin. More often they were a stocky, robust people. Carima, in contrast, was extremely thin.

"Carima," said Aimá with a forced smile that served to mask the pain she felt. "This is Antonio."

"Greetings Carima."

"Greetings Antonio. You are a brave man to be with this woman." Carima's sickly looking eyes brightened as they smiled.

"She is a challenge," responded Antonio who was getting used to this banter among Taíno friends. "But I make sure to challenge her back. We get along well," he finished looking at Aimá, gladdened to see a more honest smile on her face.

"How long will you visit?" asked Carima.

"Only a few days," said Aimá. "We will return to Ceiba with Moné. He is finally going to marry Guaína and bring her back here."

"Wonderful! I am certain he is eager to live with her. Every time he leaves for Ceiba he is full of joy and

139

anticipation at seeing her again."

Cacique Humaca approached the three friends. "Aimá and Antonio, be welcome in Macao," he said formally. "You may stay with Moné's family while you are here." He left without awaiting a response.

Aimá and Antonio looked at each other surprised at the curtness of the *cacique*. Aimá also noticed that Humaca had not greeted Carima. In fact, she thought, he had not even acknowledged her presence. "I came here to visit with you," protested Aimá. "Don't you want us to stay with you?" Aimá was sounding hurt.

Carima moved close to Aimá and took her hand. She led her and Antonio away from the other people. "You can see that I am sick," she said barely above a whisper. "The *behique* believes that at night my living spirit fights with the spirit of the dead. The battle is making me thin and weak." She looked to the floor in an effort to control her tears and then continued. "Most people won't speak to me for fear that the dead will see them and come for their spirits. Even my husband no longer sleeps in my *bohío*. Only the old woman that lives with the *behique* dares to spend any time with me. That is why Humaca expects that you will not stay with me." Carima looked up at Aimá with a mixture of hope and fear. Hope that her lifelong friend would stand by her and fear she would leave, like others had.

Aimá's movements were deliberate as she dropped Carima's hand, stepped closer to her friend and then wrapped her strong arms around the frail body of the woman who shared her childhood. Carima, so in need of compassion and acceptance, melted in the loving embrace of a true friend.

Antonio stood by, moved by the scene he was witnessing. It was easy for him to recognize in Carima the same loving, joyous spirit that made Aimá so attractive. He felt compassion for the sickly woman but also anger at the people that had abandoned her. For all his love of the Taíno, he had no empathy for the spirit talk that allowed the *yucayeque* to turn their back on one of their own. As far as he was concerned, it was all superstitions.

Carima collapsed when Aimá released her. The

emotional strain and physical effort of walking to the *batey* to meet her friends were more than her weak body could handle. Antonio put one arm around her shoulders and the other under her knees and easily lifted the woman. She weighed less than his sword, he thought. Carried by Antonio, she directed them to her *bohio* under the curious glances of those who remained in the *batey*. Antonio laid Carima in her hammock as Aimá got busy rearranging the *bohio* to make room for them. "There is no food here!" exclaimed Aimá venting her frustration. "How do you eat?"

"The *behique*'s wife brings me some food every day," responded Carima.

Just as she finished her sentence, an old woman appeared at the door. "My name is Aya, I am wife to the *behique*," she said in a voice that matched her age.

"I am Aimá and this is Antonio."

"Are you aware of the *behique*'s warning about staying with Carima. The spirit of the dead could come for any of us."

"Then tell me why you come to give her food?" Asked Aimá, checking her anger with the knowledge that Aya had been the only person assisting her friend.

"Because I am so old the dead don't want me. They know I will be leaving this world soon anyway. And, this poor girl...she needs help," Aya's voice trailed, as if she did not want them to hear the last thing she said.

"We know what the *behique* says and we are not concerned," said Aimá impatiently. "We will be staying here with Carima," she concluded, leaving no room for doubt.

"I'm glad," said Aya under her breath. She stepped carefully into the *bohio*. "This is one time when I do not agree with my husband," she whispered. A hint of fear showed in her eyes. "This girl needs care and companionship. I am glad you are here for her. I think others would come but they are afraid of challenging my husband." The frown on her face betrayed her disapproval of the situation with Carima. "Can I get you some food?"

"We would appreciate that," said Antonio. The mention of food reminded him he was quite hungry.

141

The old woman nodded and left the *bohio*. She returned shortly carrying a variety of fruits. She deposited them by the entrance to the *bohio* and left again. Next she brought two clay jars with *yuca* flour. Moving slowly, she made several trips, each time bringing a different food item. When she was finished, Carima's *bohio* was stocked with enough food for her and her guests to last several days.

"We thank you for your kindness Aya," said Aimá, somewhat taken aback by the old woman's generosity.

"The food came from many families," responded Aya from the doorway where she stood.

"Will you join us for a meal?"

"I can't. I must care for the *behique*. But I would like to see Carima."

"Please come in," said Aimá waving to Aya to enter.

The old woman walked over to the hammock where Carima lay sleeping. She gently caressed Carima's forehead, her eyes betraying her deep concern for the sick woman. Aimá and Antonio stood by, watching quietly.

"I will return tomorrow," said Aya as she turned to leave. "Sleep in peace."

Aimá stopped her. "Thank you for caring for Carima," she said.

Aya responded with a sweet toothless smile and walked out of the *bohio* into the deepening night.

Together Aimá and Antonio prepared a quick meal. After making sure Carima was comfortable they got water from the river and set themselves down to catch up on the sleep they missed the night before. No spirits came to disturb the *bohio* that night.

Carima lay awake when her two guests opened their eyes to greet the new day. "When I woke this morning, I thought that your arrival yesterday was a dream. I'm glad I was wrong."

"Be sure, we are here," said Aimá with a mockingly serious look, "and if I can get this smelly man off of me, I'll prepare you a good morning meal." She then pushed Antonio aside so he almost toppled off the hammock. He
142

reacted quickly, reaching over to regain his balance and, at the same time, pinching Aimá's buttock so she screeched in surprise.

A broad smile lit Carima's face. More than anything, she missed having people act relaxed around her. Ever since the *behique* warned people to stay away from her, Carima had not had a casual exchange with anyone except Aya. And even the old woman was nervous, afraid of her husband.

That day, Antonio and Aimá dedicated themselves to taking care of Carima. She ate better than she had in weeks and she bathed at the river. In the afternoon, Antonio offered to carry her to the beach, which she accepted joyously.

When healthy, Carima often visited the ocean spending many hours swimming, fishing or just looking out over the water to the islands that dotted the horizon. She was raised in Ceiba, snug among the inland hills. To her, even after several years of living in Macao, the vast expanse of the sea was a wondrous thing.

Antonio comfortably carried his new friend on the short hike to the beach. Aimá followed along with a woven basket full of fruits and *casabi*. She was determined to have food available for Carima. Instinctively, she associated Carima's thinness with lack of food and as long as she was there Aimá would not let her friend go hungry.

Antonio lowered Carima to a shady spot next to a cluster of mangrove trees growing to the water's edge. The ocean was calm in defiance of a steady breeze from the northeast. The beach was part of a wide bay bound to the north and south by massive promontories that dropped steeply to the sea. The river emptied into the receiving waters of the bay, south from where they stood. The onshore current carried the river sediment to the south so that the water before them was crystal clear. There were several children playing near the mouth of the river, while three men worked on a huge canoe, larger than any Antonio had seen before. Out to sea, Taíno fishermen paddled two small canoes back to shore. This, thought Antonio, was one of the most beautiful places he had ever seen.

Aimá and Antonio swam and went for a walk while

143

Carima enjoyed the day out of her *bohio* visiting her beloved beach. Off and on she fell asleep, her sick body needing rest after the slightest of exertions.

"I'm not sure what to do," said Aimá to Antonio as they walked along the beach back to their friend. "I cannot leave Carima in Macao. There is no one to take care of her."

"Why not bring her with us to Ceiba? I think Moné and I can carry her but it will take us longer to get there."

"I thought about that, but she is so weak, I don't know if she would survive the journey." Aimá looked worried. "I also need to talk to her to find out what she wants to do. We can't take her to Ceiba if she does not want to go."

They ended their conversation as they approached Carima. She slept on the sand looking sadly pathetic, her skeletal figure curled up in a fetal position. The couple turned to face the ocean. Aimá put her arms around Antonio's waist, buried her face in his chest and sobbed gently. Antonio had a terrible premonition that Carima would never leave Macao.

They returned to the *yucayeque* late in the afternoon but with plenty of daylight left to prepare a meal and make arrangements for the evening. Moné came by to visit and told Antonio that he would be ready to depart in the next two days. Antonio did not mention the idea of bringing Carima along since nothing was certain.

That evening there was a spectacular sunset. The clouds formed multiple layers, each illuminated with a different shade of gold. The meandering river reflected the light and glowed like a river of molten gold, the fantasy of Spanish conquistadors. Carima, feeling a bit stronger after eating and sleeping, sat outside her *bohio* looking at the sky and the golden hues all around her.

"I want to thank you for helping me have the best day of my life," she called out almost enthusiastically to her guests in the *bohio*.

"What do you mean?" asked Antonio, a bit confused as he stepped outside. Aimá stopped tidying the *bohio* and moved closer to hear her friend.

"I have not been treated with respect since the spirit

of the dead began to visit me," said Carima seriously. "Today you treated me like a person. That is how I grew up. That is how all people should be treated. Today I realized, more than ever, how important that is. That made this day truly memorable." With some effort Carima got on her feet and gave each of her friends a hug.

They spent the evening chatting around a small fire set in front of the *bohio*. Aya stopped by to see Carima and left without sitting down. Carima continued to drift into sleep regularly. On one of those occasions Antonio picked her up and laid her on her hammock for the night. Soon thereafter, he and Aimá joined their friend in rest.

Antonio awoke to the soft light that permeated through the reeds and poles that made up the *bohio*. He knew Aimá was up because he could not feel her warm body next to his. As he lay in the fog of near sleep he noticed the silence in the *bohio* was broken by soft gasping sounds behind him. He turned to the sound and saw Aimá kneeling over the body that once carried the spirit of Carima.

Instantly he was off the hammock and next to Aimá, too startled to speak. He knew Carima was sick, but he had hoped that their care was helping her recover. No matter how poorly she looked, Carima's death was sudden and unexpected.

After some time Aimá sat back on her feet and took a deep breath. "We must notify the *cacique* and the *behique* that one of their people has died."

"I will go," offered Antonio.

By the time he returned to Aimá the news had spread throughout the *yucayeque*. Aya was the first to arrive at the *bohio*. She stood quietly by Carima's body for a moment and then approached Aimá. "The townspeople cared for Carima," she said in a gentle voice, "but they were afraid to approach her because of the *behique*'s pronouncement. Now that Carima's spirit has gone they will honor her," the old woman paused, observing the reaction of Aimá and Antonio. She continued in response to Antonio's puzzled look. "While her spirit fought to stay with the living she never questioned the *behique*. She never put anyone at risk.

145

She was brave. The people recognize that and will honor her. Many of us also hold dear memories from the years she lived with us."

Antonio indicated his understanding with a nod.

Aimá stood facing Aya, her face stern. Her mind wrestled with her feelings with such intensity that Antonio could see her body shake. She hated the way Carima had been made to suffer, shunned from the *yucayeque*. However, she was Taíno; she knew the people were obeying the *behique* and protecting themselves. But why did Carima have to suffer so much? She thought to herself.

"You are right, Aya," said Aimá softly, but in a tone that betrayed her emotions. "Carima does deserve to be honored. I will participate in the preparations."

"That is as you want, as it should be," responded Aya. "We must begin preparations now."

Aimá nodded in acknowledgment to the old woman and turned to Antonio. "We will prepare Carima's body. You must wait outside. Please find Moné and make sure he is making arrangements for our return to Ceiba. I am anxious to return home."

Antonio caressed Aimá's cheek communicating his love for her. "I will be with Moné if you need me."

The Spaniard spent part of the morning with his quiet friend and then headed for the beach. He knew they would be leaving soon and he wanted to visit the sea once again. The beautiful panorama impressed him like the first time he saw it. If he were still looking to start a hacienda, this would be the kind of place he would want, he thought. It had the river for fresh water, high ground for protection from floods, a fertile floodplain and the ocean nearby. It would be perfect.

His mind was wandering with disparate thoughts when a boy ran up to him carrying a message from Aimá: return to the *yucayeque*. Instantly he was on his feet, walking across the sand at a quick pace. The boy kept up by trotting alongside the tall Spaniard. As they approached the *yucayeque* Antonio noticed it was empty.

"Where is everyone?" Antonio asked the boy.

"They are down by the river. I'll take you there."

Before reaching the first *bohios* the boy turned left onto a secondary trail. This trail led down from the *yucayeque* to a clearing at the edge of the river floodplain. There the population of Macao was gathered to pay tribute to Carima. Antonio felt foolish for arriving late. Aimá saw him and signaled for him to stand next to her. Quietly she touched his hand to let him know that everything was all right.

Carima's body, completely painted with different patterns and decorated with jewelry, lay on the ground next to a wide grave. At the *behique*'s order, the body was lowered to the center of the grave and laid down in a fetal position by a man who had jumped in the grave to assist. Suddenly, those gathered around the grave began handing the man a variety of items: fruits, *casabi*, several clay jars, cooking utensils, feathers and pieces of cloth. The body was then covered with palm fronds and the man climbed out of the grave.

"You leave us a warrior," said the *behique* in a stern voice. "You lived life honorably and bravely fought the spirits of the dead." The *behique* paused and a murmur of agreement was heard from the gathering. "Speak well for us in the land of the dead. We will honor your memory among the living."

With no more ceremony, the crowd began to move away, back to the *yucayeque*. Antonio, used to the lengthy prayers of the Catholic funeral ritual, was surprised at the brevity of the ceremony. He later asked Aimá about this and she explained that those who cared for her would always miss Carima, but it was more important to honor her in song than to mourn her at the grave.

XIII

THE LIVING TREES

Immediately after leaving Carima's grave the couple from Ceiba gathered their supplies for their journey home. Aimá knew that the unexpected purpose of her visit to Macao was fulfilled. She was glad to have had the opportunity to give her friend some company and comfort during her last days; nevertheless, she remained disturbed by the experience. She was anxious to leave Macao. Antonio advised Moné that he and Aimá were leaving that very afternoon and arranged a rendezvous for the next morning. They were to follow the trail west until they met the second stream from the north. There they would camp and wait for Moné to arrive the following morning.

After taking leave from *Cacique* Humaca, Aimá and Antonio quietly left the *yucayeque*. The first leg of their trek home followed the same trail they used a few days before. It was hard to believe that only a few days had passed since they arrived in Macao full of joyful anticipation. The unexpected emotional intensity of their visit made their short stay seem like it had lasted for weeks. Aimá, walking in the lead, set a vigorous pace over the flat, clear trail. She walked as if eager to put the forest between them and the memories of a dying Carima. Eventually her pace slowed as the richness of the jungle and the murmuring of the river worked to calm her troubled spirit.

They arrived at their destination as the sun began to set. Ahead of them a huge square boulder grew out of the ground on the peninsula formed by a tributary stream meeting the larger river they had been following. The couple was surprised to see a lean-to built against the boulder. Moné had been thoughtful, sending them where they would have shelter.

Hopping from rock to rock they forded the small mountain stream and approached their home for the night. A ring of stones marked the site of previous fires. Ashes and charred wood were evidence of recent use. Antonio looked inside the lean-to and found it stocked with dry wood. Palm fronds covered the ground, helping to make the shelter more comfortable. Two hammocks hung from a cleverly anchored post and a thick tree root that grew across the boulder wall of the shelter.

Before long, Aimá had a fire ready and was heating several smooth stones Antonio had picked by the river. Moving with practiced agility, she dipped the hot stones in the water held by two bowls. Thin wisps of steam told Aimá that the heat from the rocks now resided in the water. From a leather pouch Aimá produced a variety of herbs and spices which, when added to the water, resulted in a hearty-flavored warm broth to accompany the *casabi*, smoked fish and fruit which they ate that night.

They sat by the fire absorbing its warmth, comforted by its hypnotic effect. All around them the gentle song of the *coquí* filled the air. It was hard to feel alone in the forests of Borikén, thought Antonio, the tiny tree frogs were always there for company. Always singing their two-syllable *co-quí* with a multitude of voices that never allowed the song to be the same.

"When we get back to Ceiba I will need to give the news of Carima's death to her family." Aimá's voice startled Antonio, who was totally distracted by the fire and the sounds of the forest. "After that I will go to Yuquiel and tell him her story so he can make a song. Then Carima's name will be remembered in her home *yucayeque*."

"I am glad I got to meet Carima," responded Antonio. "Her life is worthy of a song."

That night they slept uncomfortably. A gentle breeze blew the cool mountain air through the lean-to. The warmth of their bodies was not enough to compensate for the inadequate protection of their shelter. Antonio was glad to see the first light of dawn. Clumsily, he climbed off the hammock and walked to the stream to relieve himself. As he looked around to re-familiarize himself with his surroundings he was startled to find Moné sitting on a rock by the river. Once his bladder was empty, he approached the quiet Taíno.

"Greetings Moné," said Antonio. "I am surprised to see you here."

"I did not mean to startle you."

"When did you arrive?"

"Not long ago. I was hoping you wouldn't sleep much longer. We have a long walk ahead of us if we mean to reach Ceiba today."

At that moment Aimá emerged from the lean-to. Paying no attention to the two men she walked to the river, removed her loin cloth and carefully stepped into a small pool of water created by a cluster of large rocks. Moments later, she emerged refreshed by the cold clean water.

Aimá nodded to Moné in greeting and walked over to the fire. After a small breakfast they restocked the lean-to with wood and began their hike to Ceiba. As usual, Moné took the lead and set a demanding pace. Aimá and Antonio followed, with the Spaniard struggling to keep within sight of his friends.

The trail followed the river upstream for a time. Where the river turned north into the mountains, the travelers continued in a westerly direction. They moved across a series of ridges repeatedly climbing and descending jungle covered hillsides. After several climbs, Antonio could feel his thigh muscles burn. He welcomed the descents, but they always seemed too short. Late in the morning they stopped to rest as they reached another of a multitude of small streams. Moné signaled that he would be right back and ran into the jungle. Instantly, he melded into the green mass of plants. Antonio moved to the stream, removed his ragged boots, and stuck his feet in the cold mountain water. His relief was instant and obvious as he let out a loud sigh.

"Are you getting old, lover?" taunted Aimá.

"I am old!" he answered laughing. "I think you need to remind Moné or you will be carrying me to Ceiba."

Moné returned with his arms full. He carried some fruits, palm nuts and carefully held three eggs in his hands.

"Where did this come from?" asked the Spaniard, impressed with the bounty of food.

"I planted some trees years ago at the top of this

hill," he said pointing at the ridge behind them. "You can travel light when you know there is food along the way."

"How about the eggs?" persisted Antonio.

"I noticed the nest the last time I walked to Ceiba," explained Moné in his calm way. "We are fortunate that the nest is being used. There were many eggs."

Aimá collected two stones from the stream, one flat, the other round and of a shape to fit comfortably in her hand. She used the flat rock as a base and with the other struck the palm nuts to crack them open. Antonio mimicked Aimá who used her fingers to collect and eat the tasty creamy pulp from inside the nut. The eggs they ate raw, sucking them out of the shell though a small hole which Moné made using the thorn from a forest palm. The sweet pulp from a fruit that Antonio did not recognize completed their midday meal.

All too soon, thought Antonio, they were on their way again. He was happy to see Moné turn to follow the trail downstream, in a southerly direction. After some time, the small stream they followed joined a larger one and the vegetation began to open up some. The air got warmer and drier as they descended from the hills. They entered a savanna environment similar to the one they had traversed on their way to Macao.

By mid-afternoon, they reached a west flowing river, which Moné informed Antonio would lead them to Ceiba. The trail moved along the edge of the dense vegetation hugging the water. At times Moné, who was intimately familiar with this route, would dart off into the forest and return with a variety of savory fruits. The warm air and easier terrain allowed Antonio to dismiss the strain of the morning hike. Even Aimá seemed more animated with every step they took closer to home, as if distance alone could assuage the pain in her heart.

The river they followed sought a way around the mountains they'd been circumventing all day. Gradually, it began to flow in a more northerly direction as the mountains opened a way for the water to reach lower ground. At times the river would meander around high ground while the trail followed a more direct route over the rise, rejoining the river

151

on the other side.

"From the top of that next ridge," said Moné pointing ahead with uncharacteristic enthusiasm, "we will be able to see the two ceibas of the *yucayeque*."

It was late in the afternoon, with the sun already low over the horizon, and Antonio was happy to hear that they were getting close to Ceiba. After the night's poor sleep and a long day of demanding travel, all he could think about was getting something to eat and climbing in his hammock.

"I think I could sleep for days," he said out loud.

"You do that old man," said Aimá looking over her shoulder with a smile. "I'll make sure no one disturbs you."

Moné started walking faster, the excitement of meeting his future bride fueling his stride. This time his companions did not try to keep up and soon he was lost from sight as he pushed up the ridge.

As they reached the base of the hill, the trailing couple was startled by Moné, running downhill towards them, an alarmed look on his face. They stepped aside as the young Taíno almost toppled trying to stop himself.

"There is a fire in Ceiba," spit out Moné so fast it was barely intelligible.

"What? What do you mean?" asked Aimá tensely.

"The *yucayeque* is burning!" responded Moné loudly, struggling to regain control. "I am running ahead. Aimá, you know the trail at this point. I will meet you again in Ceiba." Immediately he turned and ran uphill with the agility and speed of the nimblest predator.

"Let's get to the top of the ridge so we can see what is happening," said Antonio, as he encouraged Aimá to move ahead of him.

They hurried up the ridge, the pain in their muscles being displaced by dread. The panorama from the top of the hill was beautiful and terrible. Their companion river could be seen winding its way along a narrow valley. The tops of the ceibas, which tower over their namesake *yucayeque*, were clearly visible behind the masking bulge of a small hill. Meanwhile, in sharp contrast to the backdrop of another silver sunset, a large plume of black smoke filled the air around the tops of the venerable trees.

Aimá let out a shriek and started running downhill. As he started after his partner, Antonio spotted Moné about to reach the hill that blocked the view of the *yucayeque*. The next second he was in the trees, lost from view. The Spaniard ran down the steep slope of the ridge, Aimá a few steps ahead of him. All his concentration was directed to maintaining his footing in the fading light and keeping up with Aimá, who led him at a pace he knew he could not maintain much longer. In less time than he thought would be needed, they reached the hill that was their interim destination. Antonio doubled over, hands on his knees, breathing hard and dreading the climb even though it was a shallow slope. After a couple of breaths, he started moving again.

Aimá stopped halfway up the hill to wait for her friend and called him up with rushed words of encouragement. Together they crested the hill to look over a lost existence. Their worst fears were confirmed; Ceiba was burned to the ground.

But it was worse than either of them could have imagined. In the twilight, bodies could be seen lying on the ground.

"This was a battle, not an accident," Antonio murmured to himself.

The only figure seen standing was Moné, whose shock, even at a distance, was evident in the way he walked. Impelled by the need to reach the *yucayeque*, Aimá and Antonio set out at a run towards the river, which crossed their path at the base of the hill.

Aimá was in shock. The sight before her was something she could not comprehend. The events in her life offered no point of reference with which to compare this. She knew the danger of fire. Once she had witnessed a *bohío* go up in flames. The men of the *yucayeque* pushed the walls of the building towards the center and made sure no other structures were ignited. But no one was hurt, and no one expected the whole *yucayeque* to be lost. She ran as fast as she could.

This is not really happening, she thought. Irrationally,

153

she believed that once she got to the *yucayeque* and stood in the *batey* this vision would disappear, that everything would be as before. Antonio, running next to her, feared reaching the *yucayeque*. He did not want to learn the truth about what happened there. In his mind he lied to himself. This must have been a Carib raid, he thought. They were fierce enough to destroy the whole settlement. Maybe they attacked in revenge for the men we killed at the beach. His mind struggled for explanations. But he found only wishful lies to hide that which he knew was true.

They quickly forded the river and moved towards the first of the smoldering *bohios*. His feet barely out of the water, Antonio fell on his knees, his eyes focused on the ground. Aimá, not noticing, continued moving towards the *batey* to meet her own reality.

Tears came to his eyes as Antonio stretched his hand to touch the horseshoe print on the soft riverbank soil. The lies vanished. He knew the Spanish had been there. Once again, as in La Española, there would be death and destruction for the Taínos. Antonio felt foolish for daring to believe that it would be any different. He had hoped that Ponce de León would offer a new form of leadership, enlisting the Taíno as allies rather than slaves. Foolish ideas, he thought. Ponce de León was no longer an honorable soldier; he was a governor. He was embroiled in the politics of conquest. He would do whatever was politically expedient.

As his mind raced, Antonio's heart filled with bitterness and shame. He could not look up to let his eyes see what his flesh and blood had done. He did not believe he could ever forgive himself for being who he was.

Suddenly, the morbid peace was rent by a despairing scream from Aimá. Involuntarily Antonio got on his feet, his eyes still on the ground. His love for Aimá pulled him towards her. Her agonizing cry forced him to move. He had no idea how to face her but he knew he had to go to her. It would be up to Aimá to reject him for who he was.

He lifted his eyes and started walking towards the *batey* with deliberate steps. The ground where he walked was churned up, covered with hoof prints. Methodically,

154

he surveyed the scene before him. Every single structure was burned to the ground, many still smoking. Approaching the first *bohio* in his path he suddenly gagged. The revolting smell of burning flesh entered his lungs, taking away some of his own life. In the *bohio*, the carbonized remains of two adults and a child huddled together. Antonio looked away in horror moving ahead to get away from the sight and the smoke emanating from the corpses. Past the smoke, the scene that faced him in the now enveloping darkness was no less frightful. The *batey* was littered with bloodied bodies, all of them Taínos. In the moonlight he could see the clean sword cuts forced open by pressure from the innards. Other bodies were grotesquely mutilated. He stepped into the *batey* and immediately saw Aimá squatted, staring at the dead body of a man. As he moved closer he saw that it was her father. Aimá's world was destroyed. Her shocked disbelief was replaced by the despair of realization. The place where she grew up as a child, where she blossomed as a young woman, where she suffered the pain of loss and the joy of community, was lost. And the people, her people, lay dead around her, her beloved father at her feet. The terror she felt was reflected in her face.

Antonio approached quietly, stepping around the dead bodies. He stood behind Aimá, offering his support by softly putting a hand on her shoulder. Eventually, she looked up at her companion with such sadness that he could not contain himself. He bent down, lifted her slowly and led her away from the grisly *batey*. He moved towards the *conucos*, where there was less smoke. The crops the Taínos so dearly cared for were trampled and torn. The incriminating hoof prints visible everywhere in the shadows. They sat together facing the towering ceibas. Antonio was glad the trees survived the battle. More than the *bohios* and other structures, they represented the spirit of the *yucayeque*. Their silhouettes stood straight and unmovable against the backdrop of stars, a testament to permanence amid the death and chaos that surrounded them.

"What happened?" asked Aimá as she slowly recovered from the shock of what she had seen.

155

Antonio did not know how to answer. He knew the Spaniards had been there and were the cause of the destruction, but he didn't know why they had attacked. He feared she would reject him when she learned that the Spaniards had destroyed Ceiba and killed her loved ones. However, he could only tell the truth; he had no lies for this woman.

"The white men were here," he said trying to read her face for a reaction. "It was they who destroyed Ceiba."

"You warned us at Jagua," she said, struggling to regain control. "But I never imagined this savagery." The next moment her eyes filled with tears. "How can I live without my people?" she whispered in quiet despair.

Antonio sensed no accusation from her. He was torn seeing her so distraught. He could tell that she needed him. He moved closer and held her, offering what comfort he could.

They remained there for a long time, the soft trade winds providing relief from the smells of destruction. An odd silence prevailed. The frogs that lived by the river were silent; even the *coquí* were quiet. In this stillness, the scraping sound of steps brought Antonio to his feet, sword in hand. Aimá stood behind him.

"Who's there? ¿Quién va?" he said in Taíno and Spanish, not knowing what to expect.

He did not need a response. In the shadows he could see the form of two Taíno men moving slowly. He sheathed his sword. First he recognized Moné and then, beyond hope, he saw it was Taibaná, obviously injured, who leaned heavily on his friend.

"Aimá!," called out the Spaniard,."It's your brother. Moné brings him." He then rushed to help carry his friend.

"Let's move him under the trees," suggested Moné. "Their roots will provide shelter."

The two men lifted Taibaná, who went limp in their arms, exhausted from the effort of walking. They settled between two huge buttress roots just behind where Taibaná and Mayaco once had their *bohío*. As they laid him down, Aimá materialized out of the darkness. Her confused tears

156

now reflected joy in knowing she was not alone. Taibaná represented a part of her world that was not lost. Still, Aimá could not help the shock she felt at the sight of her brother. His chest and arms had numerous cuts and bruises, and most of his body was covered with blood. At times, he recovered consciousness and called out for Mayaco; or he would relive a scene from the battle, unable to contain the horror he had witnessed. Only Taibaná had survived the attack, but it was only because he was presumed dead.

With some effort, but without indecision, Aimá put her grief aside and concentrated on tending Taibaná. "Moné, you build a fire, and make it a big one. Antonio, get me water." She gave orders with newfound determination. As long as she was there, her brother would not die.

After inspecting his injuries and making sure Taibaná was comfortable, Aimá went to look for medicine. She headed for a small parcel of medicinal plants the *behique* kept near his *bohío*. There she knew she could find most commonly used remedies. If she needed other medicines, the forest held an abundance of plants that could be used for a variety of ailments. Aimá walked around the outside of the *yucayeque* staying away from the *batey*. She found Yuquiel's medicinal plants, trampled but fresh enough to be useful. She collected what she needed and quickly returned to his brother's side.

Moné had a small fire going and was feeding it wood to make it grow. Antonio was down by the river collecting water, but already two full clay jars awaited Aimá. After heating the water with hot stones from the fire, she set out to washing her brother. The blood was caked on Taibaná's skin and in some places Aimá had to use sand from the river to break it loose. As the dry blood washed into the ground the Taíno's body was exposed. The dozens of cuts and bruises told the story of his ordeal in defense of the *yucayeque*. Fortunately, none of the wounds were serious; a deep bruise on his calf was the main reason he could not walk.

Aimá was diligent in the care of her brother. Even the smallest cut was cleaned carefully and covered with the

157

medicinal paste she concocted from the *behique*'s plants. When she was finished, Taibaná was laid near the warmth of the fire to rest on a soft bed of leaves. The three traveling companions took time to rest and have some food. They sat quietly near the fire, their backs to the *batey*. None could tolerate looking into the scene of devastation.

The long day of travel was a far away memory to Antonio. Arriving at the ashes of Ceiba had changed everything. His dream of owning land and establishing a hacienda was long forgotten, replaced by the expectation of living his life with Aimá and her wondrous people. The Spanish system had made it almost impossible for him, a sailor and laborer, to achieve his first dream. Now the Spaniards had taken his new dream and burned it to the ground. Once ambivalent feelings towards the white men in Caparra gained definition in a deep-seated hatred for what they had done and for why they had done it. Antonio knew the attack on Ceiba had not been an incursion seeking to destroy a dangerous enemy, or an honorable battle in defense of land and lives. He knew the Spaniards attacked under the pretense of calming the rebellious natives in order to gather slaves for their *encomiendas*. The destroyed *yucayeque*, the torn families, the lost dreams, all this suffering in order to give some young aristocrat the opportunity to gain wealth in the new-found land.

"I need your help," said Moné suddenly. The uncharacteristic request startled Antonio, who was deep in thought. "We need to tend to the bodies in the *batey*. There are too many for burials. We will need to burn."

Antonio nodded in agreement. "How do you propose to do this?"

"As I was looking for survivors I noticed that there is much dry wood around the *yucayeque* which we can use. We will build a large fire in the middle of the *batey*."

The two men started their grisly chore, leaving Aimá behind with her thoughts and her brother. First they cleared an area and then, methodically, they moved through the *yucayeque* and collected all the wood they could find. They stripped what remained of the *bohíos*, including half burnt
158

logs. Firewood that had been intended to fuel the life-giving hearths of Taíno homes was instead used to feed the funerary pyre. Logs that served as seats at gatherings of friends and family were rolled to the center of the *batey*. Eventually, the pile of wood began to look sufficient for the task.

One by one, Antonio and Moné collected the bodies and carefully laid them on top of the pyre. When they ran out of room they stacked the remaining bodies across the legs of the first row of bodies. Antonio counted eighteen dead as they completed their morbid job.

While her companions collected wood, Aimá left her brother's side and walked into the forest behind the two giant trees. Just as the last of the bodies was laid to its final resting place, she emerged with her hands full of leaves. Solemnly, Aimá approached the cadavers and placed a leaf on their chests. Then she walked across the now empty *batey*, to the charred remains that Antonio had first seen, and placed a leaf on each of the forms as they huddled in an eternal embrace.

Antonio and Moné, the heavy work done, stood aside respectfully. They knew instinctively that Aimá meant to carry out this ritual alone. The aroma of the leaves Aimá was distributing reminded Antonio of Carima's funeral. It was there, in the midst of that burial ceremony, that he remembered having experienced the pungent aroma that emanated from the leaves.

Aimá moved as if with rehearsed steps. She walked back across the *batey* and after disbursing the remaining leaves across the pyre she stood next to her father's body. Placing a hand on his forehead and with tears in her eyes she took leave of the good man. With a determined look, she walked to the fire they had built for Taibaná and gathered a handful of lit fagots. Aimá had not been capable of handling the bodies of the people she knew and cared about. That would have been too painful. However, she knew it was her responsibility to light the fire that would fuse their bodies together and release their souls from this life. She returned to the pyre and began setting the wood afire. Once again flames licked the air and smoke rose to the skies under the

159

living trees of Ceiba. This time, however, the perfumed smoke floated straight through the massive overhanging branches, which imparted a final earthbound caress to the departing spirits of the *yucayeque*.

XIV

CAPARRA

The first dim lights of dawn appeared while the crematory fire was still raging.

"This is now a place for the dead. We cannot stay here," said Aimá to her companions.

"What do you suggest?" asked Antonio. "We can't travel very far. Taibaná needs to recuperate."

"There is the fishing camp not far downstream. We can stay there until Taibaná is well enough to walk."

No one contested the idea and they immediately set out, leaving Ceiba behind. Aimá led Moné and Antonio, who were carrying Taibaná. She walked over to the river and turned to follow a well worn path downstream. After a short time of easy downhill walking, they reached a riverside clearing containing a small *bohío*. The camp, in use until the previous day, was well-stocked with firewood and a variety of fruits and other foods which were used to snack on while working on canoes or preparing fish. The camp was situated where the river stream ceased its rough tumble from the hills and eased into a slower, more navigable disposition. There, the Taínos from Ceiba kept their few canoes, which they used for fishing and for excursions downriver. The camp was also used to clean and prepare fish, keeping the offensive smell away from the *yucayeque*.

Taibaná was laid down to rest while Aimá lit a fire. Antonio and Moné inspected the camp and found nothing out of the ordinary. Apparently everyone had run to the *yucayeque* when they heard the sounds of battle. Once Taibaná was comfortable, sleeping in the warmth of the new fire, the three travelers allowed exhaustion to overtake their bodies. They spent the next three days resting and taking care of Taibaná, who developed a fever the day after they arrived at the camp. Aimá cared diligently for her brother. Eventually his fever broke and his condition continued to improve daily.

One evening, with Taibaná almost fully recovered,

161

they sat together to share a meal. The sky was overcast, but the rain was holding off. The *coquís'* singing resonated louder than usual in the heavy air, rich with the loamy aroma from the forest. In the background, the swollen river rushed by, indifferent to any activity along its banks.

After eating, Taibaná sat up straight and faced his companions. "I am ready to tell you about the night of the attack," he said deliberately. All eyes went to the injured man. Up to that point he had been too drained by his injuries and sickness to discuss the events of the dreadful night. Aimá huddled closer to Antonio, seeking to hide from what she was about to hear. She was curious about what happened and she believed it was important that she hear the story, but she feared it because she already knew its horrible ending.

"The sun was on its way down to the horizon on a normal day in Ceiba," Taibaná began, his eyes looking through his audience to some place in his memory. "Most people were involved in chores, working in the shade of the *bohíos* or under the branches of the great trees. The hunters had returned from their morning outings. I was working with my father replacing old palm leaves on the roof of his *bohío*. From there I was one of the first to see the attackers. They had surrounded the *yucayeque* and spilled out of the forest from all directions except from right behind us, where the large trees blocked the way. I yelled but everyone was confused. They didn't know what was going on. My father and I ran for our weapons and met some other warriors at the *batey*." Taibaná paused to catch his breath.

"Some of the white men were on foot, others rode the big animals you call horses," he continued, nodding towards Antonio. "They also had dogs, very fierce, with big teeth, that helped them. They were like evil spirits." Antonio shook his head in understanding. He had seen dogs used to terrorize Taínos in the past.

"The men on horses had lit torches," Taibaná explained. "They rode around the *batey* and dropped them on the *bohíos*. Meanwhile, the men on foot reached us and we engaged them in battle. They used swords and spears. Several of their men fell. But unfortunately, more warriors

162

were dying." Once again he paused, barely breathing from the intensity of his memories. "At one point I was separated from the other warriors by two white men. I fought with them and got many of my wounds trying to evade their swords. I was able to defeat both of them. But just then I was hit from behind and lost consciousness. I woke to see the *bohios* in flames and our people being led away by the white men. They were tied together one to the other, even the children," Taibaná's pain was obvious as he recalled his first glimpse of slavery. "I then crawled away, afraid the white men would return and find me when I could not even stand up to fight. The next thing I remember is Moné shaking me awake and seeing you two," he concluded looking at Antonio and Aimá.

They sat quietly, pondering the events of the story. Antonio had many questions to ask but he knew Taibaná did not have answers. Who led the attack? Why such brutality? What is going on with the leadership in Caparra? Where were the prisoners taken? The more questions came to mind the more certain he was about his next step. The answers he needed were in Caparra and he would have to go there to get them.

After a week of rest, Taibaná felt his strength returned. He was still limping from the damage to his calf, but his many cut wounds were healing quickly, forming scars that covered his body. Aimá continued to pamper her brother, making sure his wounds were clean and feeding him well. His health regained, Taibaná became anxious to set out to find his kinfolk. That day a sun-filled downpour forced everyone into the small *bohio*. "I feel strong and able to walk," said Taibaná to his companions during the unplanned midday gathering. "I think it is time that we left in search of our people. Do you know where they were taken?" he asked Antonio.

"No," he responded quickly. "But I have been thinking about it. They were probably given away as slaves. I can go into Caparra and find where they were sent. At that time we can decide what to do next."

"That sounds very dangerous," said Aimá with

undisguised concern.

"When I first left Caparra I was supposed to return at about this time. I'll make up some stories to tell them. Then I'll talk to the men and get the information we need."

Aimá remained unconvinced.

"Don't worry, I'll be alright," said the Spaniard to his lover taking her hand in his. She nodded in acceptance, a forced smile on her lips.

"Very well then," spoke up Moné. "We leave tomorrow at dawn." His statement left no room for doubt. Moné had been anxious for Taibaná to recuperate so they could head out to find their captive friends, especially Guaína. His heart had been heavy thinking of his future wife in the hands of the white men. Now that Taibaná was better, he saw no reason to hesitate or linger. As soon as the rain let up he started collecting provisions for their journey.

The next morning Moné roused everyone in the camp before the first light of dawn. Already a fire was burning and fish stew, fruits and *casabi* were arranged for breakfast. "Eat well this morning," he told his friends. "We don't know what awaits us or when we will have another opportunity to eat a full meal."

With Moné's eagerness prodding them, the small group was on its way before the sun broke the horizon. Under the diffuse glow of the impending sunrise they followed a trail that led from their camp to the forest behind the *conucos* of Ceiba. From that vantage they could see the dead *yucayeque* beyond the trampled fields. Antonio felt a pull in his chest. It was from that location that he had first seen Ceiba, full of life and pleasing to the eye. He could still remember the joy and pride in Taibaná's voice when he announced their arrival to the *yucayeque*.

Standing close to the Spaniard, a tear streaked down Aimá's cheek. "It was a good home," said Taibaná quietly, his voice a mix of anger and sadness. Somehow they all knew they would not be returning to this place. Once again Moné, led by thoughts of Guaína, spurred them on. With the image of the majestic ceibas on their minds, they turned towards uncertainty in Caparra.

The group walked quietly through the forest, following the clearly defined path. Moné, relieved to be on the move, quickly pushed ahead to scout the trail. The other three moved together, their pace limited by Taibaná's leg injury. They walked in the shade of the dense forest, but above the canopy of leaves the sun shone brightly. The recent rains made the air heavy. Antonio sweated profusely and sought to refresh himself whenever they reached a stream. At every opportunity Aimá massaged Taibaná's calf and applied a medicinal unguent she had prepared for the hike.

In spite of Aimá's care and the slow pace, Taibaná's calf began to suffer uncontrollable spasms late in the afternoon. Taibaná could barely move his leg without provoking a painful cramp in the already delicate muscle. The group had no alternative but to make camp for the night. Once again Moné and Antonio carried their friend. At Moné's suggestion they moved to a small clearing, well hidden from the trail and next to a stream. Antonio noticed that these people, who once felt at home in every corner of their land, were now hiding from an enemy they barely knew. Their hopes and expectations had been shattered, their way of life completely disrupted. Seeing them huddled around Taibaná, Antonio thought they looked like scared children, but he knew that these children had already lost their innocence.

The next morning Antonio was the last to awake. Aimá sat by an almost smokeless fire tending the water she was heating to treat Taibaná's injury. Taibaná sat comfortably near his sister. Moné was nowhere in sight.

"You still sleep like a white man," Taibaná mocked Antonio. Aimá looked up, startled but gladdened by the humor in her brother's voice.

"It's the price you pay for getting old," responded the Spaniard. "Where is Moné?"

"He was gone this morning," said Aimá calmly. "We'll wait for him here."

Antonio walked to the river to wash the sleep off his face. He returned to the fire looking disturbed. "Did he tell you he was leaving?" he asked Aimá.

"No," she answered, unsure of why the question was asked. "I never saw him."

"I only wished he would tell us what he is doing," said Antonio to his companions. "The white men are dangerous; he could get into trouble."

Aimá started applying a warm compress to her brother's calf. "Trust him," she said, glancing at Antonio without interrupting her task. "He has never led us wrong." Taibaná nodded in support of his sister.

"I understand," said Antonio. He knew Moné was extremely capable and his loyalty was unquestionable. "It's just that I know the white people. We must be careful. If they see us they will chase us down and take us as slaves."

Taibaná and Aimá looked at their friend with sober faces. "We know how dangerous the white man is," said Taibaná gravely. Antonio felt foolish realizing he was trying to warn a man who had barely escaped Ceiba with his life. "Be sure that Moné will be back, and we," he paused, reaching a hand to Antonio's shoulder, "will be cautious."

"Here, eat something," interrupted Aimá, handing Antonio his breakfast. "We still have some walking to do."

Moné returned to camp soon after. "I went ahead to scout," he reported. "I found a place we can make camp safely while Antonio visits the white men's *yucayeque*. We should reach the place before the sun is overhead." He looked at his injured friend sitting on the ground. "How is your leg?" he asked.

"Fine," responded Taibaná. "With Aimá's good care I should have no problem getting to the shelter."

As predicted by Moné, the group reached their new camp around midday. Moné had found a shallow cave halfway up a hillside, with dense vegetation covering its entrance. Outside the cave, a rock overhang provided additional protection from the sun and inclement weather. Water from a spring above the overhang flowed in a steady trickle along a timeworn course next to the cave entrance. The location was perfect for the Taínos to await the return of Antonio.

The group spent the rest of the day setting up camp.

Moné went to collect food and returned with a bounty of fruits, nuts and two ducks, which he shot with his bow and arrow. Aimá and Antonio spent a good deal of energy convincing Taibaná to rest his leg while they went about collecting firewood and exploring the area around the cave.

Early in the evening they all sat together under the rock overhang to enjoy the exquisite meal Aimá had prepared. She had ingeniously combined different fruits and herbs to prepare an exotic tasting marinade for use with the ducks. Together with *casabi*, fruits and nuts the travelers shared what seemed like a banquet. They sat quietly, the splendor of the dying day stirring memories of less troubled times.

As they ate, Antonio looked at his companions. They represented what he loved best about the Taíno: their openness and honesty. These gentle people had accepted him without prejudgment or prejudice. In a matter of weeks he was working and living in Ceiba like any other member of the community. Now, he felt great apprehension returning to Caparra to face the arrogance of the Spanish, who considered themselves a superior civilization even though most of them lived in squalor.

"I will leave in the morning," said Antonio breaking the silence. Aimá stopped eating and looked at him. Even though this had been the plan all along, she seemed to be taken aback by Antonio's announcement. At the lack of response Antonio continued. "As soon as I find out where the people from Ceiba were taken I will return here. It will probably take me several days. Make sure you are not found by the white men. We've seen signs of them, so we know they visit this area."

"You don't have to worry about us," said Moné. "This is our home, we know how to keep hidden. It is you who walks into danger. It is you who must take care."

Antonio was surprised by the concern in Moné's face. He rather expected this kind of reaction from Aimá, or maybe Taibaná. "Remember," said Antonio with all the confidence he could muster, "the white men were also my people. I'll know how to live with them and get the information I need without much problem."

"We will wait for you and then we will find our people," interrupted Taibaná bluntly, betraying his dislike of any negative talk about Antonio's mission and expressing full confidence about the order of events to come.

The last hints of a silver sunset eventually gave way to a remarkably clear night sky. In the absence of the moon, stars engulfed the world with their ethereal light. Aimá moved close to Antonio and leaned against his chest. From their vantage, under the rock overhang, they could sees the top of the trees all around the cave. They sat against a rock absorbing the night in a peaceful, intimate embrace. Later, after their companions had retired to sleep, they made love under the stars, like their first time. But this time they moved slowly, deliberately. Not knowing what the future held for them, they immersed themselves in the present and in each other.

The night passed too quickly for Aimá, who lay quietly next to Antonio listening to the morning sounds. She found it difficult to associate Antonio with the Spaniards, even knowing he was one of them. Every other story she heard or news she received about the Spaniards was corrupt in some way. This contrasted strongly with the character of the quiet, honest man who received her love. Aimá wanted Antonio to stay with her, but knew that she could not be selfish. She feared for Antonio, though he reassured her that he would be all right. Antonio held the key to finding the people of Ceiba and that was as important as having water to drink. What use is life, thought Aimá, if you could not share it with your people? How could anyone envision a life without their community?

Aimá shook these disturbing thoughts from her mind and set out to prepare a morning meal. She was surprised to find that a fire was already burning and went on to prepare a broth to have with *casabi* and fruit. Taibaná and Moné had risen early and stood outside the cave looking out over the forest. Eventually, Antonio woke up, and after greeting Aimá, walked outside to join the other men.

The group exchanged pleasantries over breakfast, none of them wanting to face Antonio's departure directly.

Moné shared his thoughts about the weather for the day and Aimá distracted herself by preparing some food items for Antonio to take along. Taibaná sat quietly, focusing on the future, visualizing the return of his friend.

Soon after breakfast it was time for the Spaniard to leave. Antonio hid his anxiousness about returning to Caparra behind a nervous smile. He quickly said good bye to Taibaná and Moné. Then he embraced Aimá and held her for a long moment. Tears streaked down her face as he released her.

"We will see you again soon," said Taibaná, fully assured. "Don't delay your return."

With a wave of his hand, Antonio turned and headed down the hillside to join the trail leading back to his past, back to Caparra. As he walked, his mind moved from one scenario of his return to another. Young settlements like Caparra changed quickly. Sometimes they grew, other times they suffered when faced with disease or war. What would he find there? Beneath his anxiety there was nervous energy and the deep desire to succeed in his mission.

After walking for an hour, the path he followed became wider, allowing Antonio to maintain a quick pace. He knew he was getting closer to his destination when he began to recognize tracks left by Spanish men and animals. In the solitary monotony of the hike his imagination wandered. It was curious, he thought, how the Taíno could walk through the jungle without so much as leaving a footprint while the white men left an imprint everywhere they went. This thought transported him to the disaster he had witnessed in Ceiba. What did the people of the *yucayeque* think when they saw the huge horses charging towards them, nostrils flared and their riders belting battle cries? What terror must have gripped the women and children when they saw their husbands, fathers and brothers cut open by swords and mowed down by the huge beasts? The anger in Antonio grew more intense as his thoughts lingered on the ruin of Ceiba. His pace accelerated. "Bastards!" he cried out loud, disgusted at the images in his mind. He pounded the trail, head down, the desire for vengeance filling his heart.

Lost in his thoughts he walked through the forest, oblivious to his surroundings. Suddenly, he was wrenched to reality by the brilliant steel of a Spanish sword pushing against his gut. He looked up to find himself surrounded by eight soldiers with weapons drawn. For an instant, the images of battle in Ceiba became tangled with his present reality and he felt a sense of panic.

"Identify yourself," commanded the officer who held Antonio's life in his hands.

"I am Antonio Dos Santos," he said, recovering quickly from the surprise encounter. "I return to Caparra after a mission for the governor, Don Juan Ponce de León." He figured that mentioning the governor would give him some leverage with the officer. "Who are you?"

"I am Lieutenant Villa and I will ask the questions," he responded sternly. "How long have you been away?" asked the young officer as he slowly lowered his sword signaling his companions to do the same.

Antonio was not sure what to respond. He had not been keeping track of time other than by noticing changes in weather patterns. "What month is it?" he asked.

"July."

"Is the year 1511?"

"Of course!" responded Villa, his patience running short after realizing he was answering questions again. "How long have you been gone that you are not even sure what year it is?"

"Close to eleven months."

"We will escort you back to Caparra and verify your story," said the Lieutenant with a knowing smile. "A lot has changed while you've been away. You may be interested to learn that the status of Ponce de León as governor is not certain. Rumor has it that Juan Cerón and Miguel Díaz will be returning to take command." Swiftly the officer turned away from Antonio and started barking orders. In seconds, the column of men began moving single file along the trail.

Antonio didn't know what to think about the news that Ponce de León might lose his position as governor. The return of Cerón and Díaz, allies of Don Diego Colón an avowed enemy of de León, meant nothing but trouble for the governor. It was unlikely that the two men would be incarcerated and sent back to Spain for a second time. Surely they would have a plan to prevent that from happening again. Not that it mattered much, thought Antonio. His fate was no longer connected to that of the governor. He only had to play along in order to get into Caparra without suspicion and obtain the information he sought.

Antonio and his escort reached the Spanish village shortly after midday. Caparra had not changed much since Antonio saw it last. There were several additional barracks and two new wooden homes, undoubtedly for use by well-positioned officials. The group marched across the settlement, attracting the attention of people they passed. Antonio recognized several men he used to work with but received no acknowledgment from them. He knew the military escort kept the curious at a distance.

The soldiers led Antonio to Ponce de León's house, which continued to be the only stone house in the village. The company stopped outside the gate of the perimeter wall surrounding the house. Lieutenant Villa gave orders to wait for him and walked through the gates and into the house. A moment later he showed up at the door. "Dos Santos," he called. "The governor will see you now."

Antonio gladly moved away from his escort. He did not enjoy feeling like a prisoner. Lieutenant Villa, moving inside the house, led him to the governor's office.

"You may leave Lieutenant," said Ponce de León from his desk chair. "And thank you for bringing Dos Santos back safely." The lieutenant bowed and exited the small room.

"Please come in and sit down," said Ponce de León to Antonio with an amused smile. "I was wondering if I would ever see you again. With all the Indian unrest, I feared for your life."

"The Taínos are good people," said Antonio. "Once you make contact and they know you are not a threat, there is really nothing to fear."

"Tell that to Cristobal de Sotomayor," shot back

the governor, suddenly angry. "He died at the hands of the Indians."

Antonio tensed at the governor's reaction. He took a moment to respond reminding himself that all he needed from the governor was his blessing to return to Caparra as a regular citizen. Obviously, the governor was tense. Probably, thought Antonio, because of the tenuous political situation surrounding the governorship of the island. "My apologies sir," said Antonio. "I did not mean to insult the memory of Don Cristobal."

Ponce de León gestured the apology away and leaned back on his chair with a scowl on his face. "Tell me what you found."

Antonio did not have a clear idea about what to tell Ponce de León. Until that morning he had no idea he would find himself seated in front of the governor immediately upon his arrival. After a couple of breaths, Antonio stilled himself and began to describe some of the lands he had seen. He took care not to mention the location of any *yucayeques*. Using his travels over the last several months as a template, he invented tales of traveling to the south side of the island and seeing lush mountains and valleys. Ponce de León expressed his desire to find pasture for cattle and asked about the lay of the land, whether it was lowland, forested or grassland. Also, like many of the settlers, he was concerned about gold and asked questions about rivers where the precious metal could be found. Antonio, somewhat nervous at first, eventually got more comfortable responding to the governor's inquiries with fabrications.

The interview did not last long. During a pause, when Ponce de León was considering what to do with the information he just acquired, it occurred to Antonio that the governor may be able to provide information concerning the events in Ceiba. The thought of questioning the governor sent a warning tingle traveling down his back. It didn't take long for Antonio to feel the apprehension and fear elicited by the strong hierarchical structure kept by the Spaniards. In Caparra, Antonio knew his place, and that was very close to the bottom. His personal audience with the governor was an

172

intimidating and rare occurrence. The idea of questioning Ponce de León could backfire if not done with extreme tact, especially since the governor had shown he was in an irritable mood.

"With your permission sir," said Antonio. "As I traveled back to Caparra I came across a destroyed *yucayeque* about a days' walk from here," Antonio stopped to gather his thoughts. "What is our present situation with the Taínos?"

Ponce de León looked at Antonio for a moment before responding. As much as he liked his men and felt a kinship with the foot soldiers, he did not care to discuss political matters with them. These issues were too complicated, he thought, for the uneducated to understand. However, he realized that Antonio had been out of touch for an extended period time and decided to answer his question.

"All *caciques* must agree to cooperate with, and follow, the dictates of the crown," responded the governor in a serious tone. "Those who do not are considered our enemies. We cannot afford to have renegade Indians disrupting our peaceful settlement of this island."

Antonio nodded his head as if in agreement. "I suppose the people of the *caciques* that don't comply will go to work in the *encomiendas*."

"That's right," said Ponce de León casually. "No different than we did in Española. Now," said the governor loudly to change topic. "I want you to report to your old barracks. Tell the foreman to assign you to a work party."

Antonio became tense; he feared that he would lose the opportunity to learn the whereabouts of the people of Ceiba. "Don't worry, I remember my part of the bargain," said the governor incorrectly interpreting the nervousness of his guest. "I will send you with a surveying expedition to the region you explored and you can pick land for yourself. You've earned it."

"Thank you," said Antonio hesitantly. Then, out of nowhere, Antonio got an idea to get the information he needed. "If I may sir, the people from the *yucayeque* I saw destroyed, to what *encomienda* were they sent?" Antonio waited for Ponce de León's reaction. As expected, he saw

173

the suspicion in the face of the governor. "You see sir," he continued meekly. "I met this woman and..." he let the sentence linger in the air, assuming no need for further explanation.

Ponce de León's face lit up and he laughed out loud. "I tell you, if I could offer a woman as a bribe to every one of my men I could have Caparra looking like Seville in less than a year. What was the name of the *cacique*?"

"That was *Cacique* Gurao of Ceiba, sir."

"Those Indians were sold to the Ramirez and Ochoa *encomiendas* west of here. You must understand however," the governor continued with a smile still on his lips. "The Indians belong to the *encomienda* owners and you will have to buy your woman back once you find her."

"I understand that sir. Thank you for your help," said Antonio continuing his deliberate deference to the governor.

"You may leave now," said the governor, his attention returning to the paperwork on his desk. "I will call you if I need you."

Antonio stepped out of Ponce de León's office feeling euphoric. He had obtained the information he wanted in less time than he anticipated. Now all he needed was the location of the two *encomiendas*. The bright mid-afternoon sun led him to seek shelter under a tree near the barracks. A thick, curved root made a comfortable seat while he determined what to do next. Before meeting with Ponce de León, he planned to use his hidden money to get some of the men drunk and talking. Caparra was a small settlement and it was hard to keep a secret. There's nothing better than liquor to loosen the tongue, he thought. He decided this was still a good approach to find out where the people of Ceiba where being held. In addition, he thought, who knows what else he could learn from a group of drunken men.

Making sure he remained unseen, he quietly walked beyond the barracks to the spot where he buried his money months before. The area remained undisturbed and he had no difficulty finding the coins. He returned to the village and headed for the small commissary across from the barracks.

"Dos Santos!" came the call from behind. Antonio turned to see several men from his old work crew. The men approached, curious about the return of their work mate. "We thought you had been captured and made into stew by the Caribs," said a short, heavy man called Gaspar who Antonio remembered as the clown of the group. The men chuckled.

"They didn't like the way I tasted and sent me away," said Antonio returning the jest. "Now you owe me because the Caribs think we all taste terrible and they won't bother us again." The men laughed enjoying the exchange of taunts.

"Tell me," said Antonio changing his tone. "Is Silvio still the foreman?"

"He sure is and ugly as ever," answered Gaspar.

"I must report to him later. I'll be joining your work gang again."

"Poor bastard," whispered Gaspar sounding almost serious. "I'll be happy to have you back. These other guys," he said pointing behind him, "are driving me nuts. Maybe you can help me with them." The men jeered and one of them slapped Gaspar's head from behind.

"You better go before they hurt you," said Antonio. "I'll see you later at the barracks." He waved at the group and continued on his way to the commissary.

The supply store occupied a small, nondescript wooden building with a thatch roof. Inside, a thin old man wearing a worn-out military uniform sat behind a makeshift counter.

"I need a shirt and a pair of pants," said Antonio to the attendant.

The old man leaned over the counter to gauge the size of his customer and then moved to the back of the store. He returned carrying a yellowing white shirt and brown pants. Antonio didn't waste time haggling and paid the asking price for the clothes. "Where can I buy some rum?" he asked.

"I happen to have some from La Española which I can sell at a fair price," responded the old man.

This time Antonio played along and got the rum for a third the asking price. He bought two large jugs that

175

he wrapped in his old shirt before stepping outside the commissary. After casually walking past the barracks, he hid the rum under some bushes where he could easily find it that night. Anticipating a long night, Antonio bribed the camp cook for an early meal of stew and bread and then found a shady spot away from the town where he could rest through the afternoon.

That evening Antonio presented himself at his old barracks, well groomed and rested. About a dozen men were gathered outside the building, sitting around a sparse campfire under the branches of a mahogany tree, socializing after a day of work. Antonio greeted them and then walked into the barracks and over to the corner of the building where the foreman lived. Silvio was a tall, heavy, unkempt man well known for his sour disposition and short temper.

"I was ordered by the governor to return here and work with you," announced Antonio. Silvio grunted in acknowledgment. "However, I don't expect to be here long. I may be called again at any time, like the last time." He knew this last comment would upset Silvio, who was resigned to being a foreman for the rest of his life and hated when his men talked of their plans and ambitions. But it also served to set up a screen for the next morning, when they would wake to find him gone.

"Sure, sure," said Silvio condescendingly. "If you are so important why do they keep sending you back to do more labor? Bah!," he exclaimed. "Just grab a bunk and don't bother me. And, Antonio," he paused, flashing a sarcastic smile of rotten teeth, "welcome back."

Antonio turned away from Silvio feeling amused. There was something comfortingly familiar and predictable, he thought, about the foreman's gruff, insulting manners. Carefully, he stepped to the back of the dark building to claim a bed. He placed his travel bag on a bunk but did not empty it. He had forgotten how dreary these buildings were. The stuffy smell of sweat hung heavy in the poorly ventilated air. The lack of interior walls and the overcrowded conditions gave residents little private space and made the barracks feel cramped. Compared to the ample *bohios,* these

176

barracks resembled torture chambers. Antonio hurried out of the building, taking a deep breath as he stepped out to the fresh open air.

Seeing no reason to delay his plan, he walked over to where he hid the rum and pulled out the jugs. As he approached with a smile on his face, the men under the mahogany went quiet. "Gentlemen," he said with mock seriousness as he presented the jugs of rum. "I'm back. I think we should celebrate."

Gaspar jumped to the front of the group and grabbed one of the jugs. "To you sir," he said lifting the jug in a toast. "Our best wish for you is that you get a chance to leave again soon." He then took a long drink while the others laughed and cheered. Several cups materialized in front of Antonio who wasted no time at filling them. Soon everyone had some rum and the men where ready to speak their truths. After some gentle prompting, they were telling Antonio all that had occurred in Caparra since he left.

He was told of the ships that had made port in San Juan. He learned that his old friend Rodrigo had visited Caparra the previous Christmas day under orders from his captain, who forced all his men to attend church that day. Rodrigo had inquired about Antonio to some of the men but learning of his absence had returned to the *Santa María* in all haste. "He called Caparra a 'village for dogs'," said Gaspar. "That man is only happy when in his ship's kitchen surrounded by food." Antonio smiled, knowing that Gaspar's statement was quite accurate.

Antonio steered the conversation to obtain details about the threats to the governor's rule, and the battles led by Ponce de León against the rebellious *caciques*. It all started, according to the men, with what happened to Cristobal de Sotomayor. The young nobleman had strived to make his *enconmienda* a success. He faced many challenges, including lack of manpower and a poor choice of location for Távara. The village was located near a great harbor on the southwest of the island; the same that was so admired by Captain Gil during the original trip to San Juan. But mosquitoes were not concerned with that, only with the newcomers. Before

177

long, Sotomayor was forced to seek a new location for his settlement closer to the west coast of the island. All these delays frustrated the young captain and led him to push hard on the few Indians he managed to get from the local *cacique,* who was no other than Agüeybaná the Brave. Sotomayor thought the Indians were lazy, weak and disobedient. What he didn't know was that the Indians thought no better of him – arrogant, disrespectful, ungrateful and cruel. Eventually they tired of the white man and planned an attack. Juan González, who accompanied Sotomayor as an interpreter, tried to warn his young leader. However, the Taínos were right about the Spaniard's arrogance. Instead of escaping the war-minded Indians, Sotomayor decided to face his enemies in broad daylight—there would be no question of his bravery. He died proudly and gallantly along with all his companions except Juan González, whose lack of pride was balanced by an abundance of common sense. The not so gallant translator managed to survive the attack and eventually reached Caparra with news of Sotomayor's fate.

"The governor avenged Sotomayor in battles against Agüeybaná the Brave," explained Gaspar. "That seems to have quieted the Indians, but there continue to be minor encounters with them."

Antonio discovered that his drinking companions, all of whom sought wealth through land or gold, also had strong opinions about the different *encomiendas* that had been granted by the governor. The Ramirez and Ochoa *encomiendas,* they informed Antonio, had been granted recently.

"Those two stand to become rich now," said one of the men.

"They got some of the best available land. I hope they know how to use it," said another.

"Captain Ochoa went out and got himself some slaves," burst in an overanxious young voice, talking fast as if wanting to have his say before being told to shut up. "I was a page for his lieutenant when he attacked *Cacique* Gurao."

Antonio's head turned sharply to look at the bearer of this news and saw a brown haired boy, not yet seventeen but trying hard to look older. He had crept up on the group of older men, too curious to stay away. He stood tall, looking proud, as he told the group he had been present at the battle.

"This is Sebastián," said Gaspar introducing the boy. "He's a little like a fly, always around, never wanted." The men laughed making Sebastián's wide-eyed face turn angry and red.

"Don't be so harsh, Gaspar," said Antonio. "We've all acted like flies at one time or another.

"Tell me more about your big adventure," he continued, changing his attention to the boy.

"I helped to carry weapons and equipment," said Sebastián, somewhat nervous. He was excited that someone wanted to hear his story. "The Indian village was at the far side of a clearing. The pages, we hid in the forest when Captain Ochoa gave the order to charge. The soldiers were almost to the first houses before the Indians saw them. There was a great battle and then they brought everyone to work at Ochoa's *encomienda*."

"Ochoa? I was told those Indians were to be shared by Ochoa and Ramirez," interjected Gaspar.

"On the way back to Caparra I heard Ochoa bragging that he won the Indians from Ramirez in a game of cards. He said that he felt so bad for Ramirez that he gave him two cows to cover for the loss of the slaves."

"That sounds like Ochoa," said Gaspar. "He's an arrogant bully. Ever since the Indians killed Sotomayor he's been out to kill as many of them as he can."

"Why is that?" asked Antonio.

"As I understand, he used to be one of Sotomayor's favorite officers. Whatever riches Don Cristobal was to make, Ochoa was sure to share. He was off getting supplies near Aguada when Sotomayor was killed. It is said that he found the body of Don Cristobal. His head was bashed....,"

"Hush!" one of the men sharply interrupted Gaspar in mid-sentence. "We have guests."

They all looked up in unison. Three soldiers approached and joined them around the small fire. One of the soldiers stood half a head taller than everyone else.

179

"That's Ochoa," whispered Gaspar to Antonio as he signaled to the tall man.

Antonio could not help but be impressed by the man. Dressed in full uniform, including a polished breastplate and a curving helmet, he cut an imposing figure. His broad shoulders and square jaw radiated physical strength and confidence. Everything about him seemed to be made of bone and muscle, nothing soft, nothing weak.

"Who is Antonio?" asked Ochoa in a booming voice that startled Antonio.

"I am," came the response, sounding weaker than he wanted.

"I understand that you are to thank for the rum."

"Only a small gift to celebrate my return to Caparra," said Antonio with greater confidence.

"To your health," said Ochoa raising a metal cup to the air and then drinking from it.

"How about a story, Captain," requested Gaspar. "Tell us what you've been up to."

"Unfortunately, I don't have much to tell," said Ochoa, obviously enjoying being the center of attention. "These last few weeks I've been trying to break those Indians I got from *Cacique* Gurao. I tell you, I'd do more work with a couple of Christians with horses than with an army of those Indians. And they are so stupid that teaching a turtle to jump would be easier that teaching them to drink water."

The men laughed at the remarks of the soldier, but Antonio became stone faced and quiet. His mind, however, was a maelstrom of memories and thoughts, evoking feelings of disbelief, rage and undeniable hatred. A hatred that until now had remained diffused, targeted to a whole people and to no one in particular. That hatred had found a concrete beginning and end. It could now be focused in one place, on one person, in one name – Ochoa!

"....but I tire of that life." Antonio's attention returned to the present and to Ochoa who continued with his monologue. "I am a man of action as you all know. I'm hoping that the governor will have orders for me to go to battle again. The sooner we conquer the savages and put them under our rule, the sooner we'll be able to transform this land for the glory of the King and the Church....and the sooner we'll be able to go out and make our fortunes!" his closing statement, after a well calculated pause, drew a cheer from his listeners.

Having conquered the crowd, Ochoa signaled to his men and walked away with an arrogant smile on his face and a swagger to his step.

Antonio could feel his heart burning with hatred. The images of dead bodies, sliced and burned, filled his mind. Ceiba, the once idyllic *yucayeque*, lay in ruins. Its people, uprooted, slaves to a man who thought of them as no more than animals. These were the same people with whom he ate, sang and danced. These were the family and friends of the woman he loved. These were a people with dignity who deserved to be treated with respect and compassion. Instead they were slaves to a bigot who would think nothing of killing them. A man who was now looking for other *yucayeques* to rape, other lives to ruin.

Antonio's thoughts and feelings converged in one desire, singular and final—the death of Ochoa. Whether he sought revenge for Ceiba and its people, or to stop Ochoa from achieving his murderous goals did not matter. Both reasons seemed good enough to him. One thing was certain, clear in his mind as the images of death in Ceiba: Ochoa would not leave Caparra alive.

Before going in the barracks to get some sleep, Antonio found out Ochoa was staying with a friend, a government-appointed lawyer, who lived in a small wooden house near the governor's home. He also found out that Ochoa's *encomienda* was located a half-day's walk west of Caparra, near the coast, along the same Toa River he had visited when he first arrived in Borikén. Ochoa's *encomienda* was considered a rich reward for the soldier since the Toa River was believed to be rich in gold and its valley was flat and fertile.

Antonio was alone in the barracks when he lay down to sleep. Outside he could hear the boisterous, rum-induced chatter. The noxious air in the barracks and his troubled thoughts kept him awake. After tossing for a while he grabbed a blanket and his bag and stepped outside. Unnoticed by the drunken men, he walked to the wooded area behind the building, cleared a small patch of ground and once again lay down to sleep. He focused his thoughts on Aimá, finding peace in the memory of her expansive, loving spirit. Before long he was sleeping, if ever so lightly.

From the campfire outside the doorway Antonio looked at Aimá sitting inside her *bohío* in Ceiba. The *yucayeque* was eerily quiet, as if abandoned. He looked up and saw the huge branches of the twin ceiba trees moving, extending down, reaching to the ground and taking up all of the *yucayeque* in an embrace. The scene changed abruptly and he found himself standing in the forest looking at Aimá who sat at the mouth of the cave where he left her only yesterday. She was looking towards Caparra longing for his return. Her face looked pained—the same look she carried while they were cremating the bodies in Ceiba. Antonio waved to Aimá but she could not, or would not, see him. Then, out of the cave came Taibaná with Mayaco and they stood next to Aimá. Moné, hand in hand with Guaína, also came out and stood by his friend. One by one all the people he knew from Ceiba came out of the cave and crowded together under the entrance. They all looked in the same direction, bonded in the pain of what they were seeing. Antonio was confused. What where they looking at? Why didn't they see him?

"Aimá!," he called out. Aimá did not respond. He started walking towards the cave but every time he looked up, he saw that he was getting no closer. He began to panic and started running. He could feel the earth under his feet, he knew he was running, but he was not moving any closer. He called to Aimá repeatedly with no success. His panic had grown to despair. He gathered his breath and shouted to Aimá with a force that made his chest ache. He willed his voice across to his lover who heard the call and turned towards him.

"I hear you calling my love," said Aimá in a whisper Antonio could hear clearly. With tears in his eyes, he waited
182

for her to say more. "We met and shared a short, but joyful, time together. Now the end is approaching, we can see it coming. We will go and you will remain and neither of us will be better for it." Aimá looked melancholy as she spoke. "I love you. Please don't try to come to us. You will live only if you stay there. It's where you where born, it's where you will survive." As she finished, she looked longingly at Antonio, gestured farewell and turned to gaze in the distance as before.

Antonio stood still, mesmerized by the voice of Aimá. When she stopped looking at him he began to cry in deep painful sobs. Tears gushed from his eyes. His feet gave way under him. As he fell to the ground he woke up with a start. He had been crying in his sleep grieving as if he had just witnessed the death of Aimá and all her people.

He wondered about the dream as he looked around to gather his bearings. All was still. Trees rustled gently in the soft wind while the song of the *coquí* permeated the humid air emanating from the jungle. The drunken men were unconscious; the rest of the town slept. Only the guards along the town's defenses were awake.

She warned me not to go back, he thought. But I'll be damned if I stay here. My life is now with Aimá and the Taínos. Whatever 'the end' is, he reasoned, I would rather face it with them than stay here with the likes of Ochoa.

At the thought of that name a rage built inside of him. He could feel his gut tighten as the adrenaline flowed through his body. Suddenly, it was very clear what he had to do.

He pulled out his knife and tucked it in his belt. He wrapped all his other possessions in the blanket he used to sleep. Walking barefoot he silently moved in the direction of the governor's house, careful to stay in the shadows cast by a half- moon. "The house right behind the flowering tree," the drunken man had been happy to share directions to Ochoa's quarters and Antonio had been thankful for the rum. Walking with great care to be silent, Antonio approached the back of the small house. The windows, with open shutters but no glass, were low to the ground and Antonio had no problem
183

spying the inside. A man and a woman occupied the first room he came to.

Probably the owners of the house, he thought.

Further along, he came to a window that opened to a hallway. Antonio could see across the house to a large room in the front. Moving to his right he looked through the next window into a second bedroom. There he found what he sought. Resting against a chair was an armor breastplate. It looked bigger than he remembered without the massive shoulders of Ochoa diminishing it. There was a single bed placed against the corner of the outside walls of the room. Ochoa lay there, his feet dangling over the end of the wood frame.

Antonio was suddenly overcome with nervousness and doubt. He took a step back to compose himself. His thoughts went to the night before, he could see Ochoa bragging and vowing to kill more Indians. Suddenly he understood what Aimá meant in the dream when she talked about 'the end'. She was referring to the Spanish killing the Taínos. She and her people were staring at the death of their culture, their end as a people. The image of the funeral pyre in Ceiba appeared in his mind. The grief. The tears. Aimá's pain.

Ochoa was only one man, but he was driven to kill and had already shown how ruthless he could be. Deep within, Antonio knew he needed to be stopped. With new resolve Antonio set out to complete his objective. Nimbly, he climbed through the window, careful not to make any noise. He pulled out his knife and looked down on Ochoa, who lay on his back. Without hesitation he held the giant's head down as he ran the knife across his neck in one swift motion. "Like butchering a pig," he murmured.

Unexpectedly, Ochoa jerked violently. With the instincts of a soldier, he grabbed Antonio's shirt in a powerful fist and pulled the intruder close. For an instant Antonio could see the despair in the dying man's eyes. "You will kill no more Taínos," whispered Antonio. He was not sure if Ochoa heard. The deep cut had already served its purpose.

184

Antonio released his shirt from Ochoa's death grip and, as quietly as before, crawled out the window with not even a glance at the dead man. Once outside he took a deep breath, shaken by what he had just done. Sweat accumulated on his brow. His gut was in a nervous knot and a wave of nausea shook him. He knew he should not linger. A voice in his mind kept insisting to move, to get out of there. He retraced his steps to where he slept earlier. Silently he put on his boots, strapped on his sword, stuffed the frayed blanket in his travel bag and strapped the bag on his back. As he looked around to make sure he left no traces of having been there, he realized that once and for all he had shut the door to his Spanish heritage. The decision he had made in his heart and his mind now had been irreversibly confirmed in action. From this moment on, his fate lay with the Taínos; the white man would always consider him an enemy.

XV

BREAKING THE CHAINS

Moving through the trees and using the shadows to keep hidden, Antonio had little trouble slipping past the guards at the edge of town. Well beyond sight of the village he reached the trail that would take him back to the company of his friends. His mind quickly flashed to the same trail months before; leaving Caparra with Taibaná and Moné, dreaming of becoming a landowner. How things had changed, he thought. This time I leave Caparra running away from my old life and with no possibility of returning, he told himself.

On the trail he pushed himself to walk fast. By daybreak he wanted as much distance as possible between himself and Caparra. The death of Captain Ochoa would not be taken lightly and Antonio knew that, because of his absence, he would immediately be considered a suspect. If nothing else, the Spaniards were perseverant; they would do all they could to find him. Remembering his previous experience on this trail, Antonio kept alert. Unconsciously his ears searched behind him for sounds of pursuers. Meanwhile, his eyes, long adjusted to the diminished light within the forest, scanned the path ahead. He moved at a slow rhythmic trot he found easy to maintain. The cool morning air was revitalizing as it brushed past his body, helping him sustain his pace. As he ran, he focused on his breathing and the cadence of his feet hitting the ground. He noticed the first rays of sunlight as they filtered gradually through the foliage to reach the forest floor. He could see farther ahead with every passing moment and felt more secure as he moved along the trail.

He could imagine what was going on in Caparra. The government lawyer, or his wife, would find Ochoa, his neck slit open and blood running to the floor. In minutes the whole town would know what happened. Someone, probably Silvio the foreman, would notice Antonio was missing. After searching the town they would send a detachment of soldiers with dogs to hunt him down.

The thought of dogs chasing spurred him to run faster. He stopped at streams to get a drink and catch his breath. Cursing the climbs and blessing every downhill stretch, Antonio ran, not daring to slow down. Every sound reminded him of the hunt and made him forget the shortness of breath that was slowly catching up with him.

In less time than he had dared hope, Antonio began to recognize the landscape around him. Away from the lowlands the soil was less fertile and the vegetation adapted to the harsher environment. He knew he was close to the point where he needed to leave the main trail to reach the cave. He strengthened his pace encouraged by his progress. The rhythm of his breathing adjusted to the new tempo as he moved under the thinner canopy. For a moment his thoughts drifted. He was still troubled by the previous night's dream and was eager to reach Aimá and hold her in his arms. In his mind his hands could feel her skin; his back tingled just at the thought of her touch. An anticipatory smile crossed his lips when a sound just behind him instantly returned his mind to the present. Footsteps, he thought, and from the sound they were close behind and moving fast. Swiftly Antonio planted one foot and, without breaking step, spun around while unsheathing his sword. There, an arms length from the ready tip of his blade, stood Moné.

"Mierda!" Antonio cursed out loud in his native tongue as he lowered his sword. "Why did you run up to me like that?" He yelled. "I almost killed you!" .

"I did not expect you would be looking to kill anyone," responded the impassive Taíno in a calm voice. "It's good to see you again."

"I don't understand you," said Antonio shaking his head, as he regained his composure. "But, never mind that," he continued, leaving behind the recent incident. "How far are we from the cave? I'm sure I'm being followed. We must leave right away."

"Did you find where they took our people?" asked Moné, disregarding Antonio's concerns.

"Yes. They are west of here, working the *conucos* of a white man." Antonio was impatient to get going but

187

he understood the need for Moné to find out if he had succeeded in his mission.

Moné nodded. "The cave is just ahead," he said as he turned to lead the way.

When they reached the side trail Antonio stopped. "Give me some time," he called to Moné. "I need to do something to distract the dogs and keep them from following us." Antonio pulled the old blanket out of his bag and threw it on the ground. Then lowered his pants and urinated on it. Moné stood by with a puzzled look. He had heard of dogs and had seen them in Caparra. However, he did not know that they could be used to track a scent.

Antonio smiled when he saw Moné's expression. "Dogs can smell where people have been," he explained to Moné as he gestured to his nose. "I will take this smelly blanket further down the trail and hide it. That way they will follow its scent and hopefully miss us."

Moné understood right away. He knew about using his sense of smell while hunting and moving through the forests. "I will take it," he said reaching down for the blanket. "You go to the others." Instantly he took off, running at a pace that Antonio never could have matched.

Antonio started off for the cave, with a strange feeling that he had been away for a long time. As he approached, he looked up and recognized the same scene he had seen in his dream. There, above him, was the cave with Aimá sitting outside its entrance. This time however, unlike in the dream, she did not ignore him. He called out and instantly she was on her feet running down to meet him. His heart was full as he buried himself in her embrace.

After what seemed like a very short time he released her and tried to step back. Aimá fought him as he pulled away from her. She had settled into his arms and was letting the joy of his return wash away the tension that she accumulated since he left for Caparra. Now she felt such relief that she did not want to move, not for a long while. But he insisted.

"Aimá, listen to me," he said gently. "We must leave this place now. I believe I'm being followed."

"What do you mean? What happened?"

"I'll tell you everything later, with the others," he responded trying to convey his urgency. "Right now we must prepare to leave. Where is Taibaná?"

"He's in the cave."

"Good. Let's get him and get going," he said turning towards the cave. "I already met Moné on the trail, he will be along shortly."

In a matter of minutes they were ready to leave. Aimá prepared a travel pack that included food and the few utensils they carried along. Taibaná, having greeted Antonio, collected his weapons and erased any traces of their stay in the cave.

"Before we go you must tell us what you found out," said Taibaná to Antonio as soon as Moné arrived.

"Later, I will tell you everything that happened," responded Antonio. "For now you must know that all the people from Ceiba were taken to work in the *conucos* of the man who led the attack on Ceiba." Antonio noticed the two Taíno men tense at the news. "His land is on the Toa River along the main trail leading west from Caparra."

"Why are you being followed?" asked Aimá, impatient to find out more.

"I killed the man who led the attack," answered Antonio directly, knowing his companions needed to know why they were running. "His name was Ochoa. He was a fierce and respected warrior for the white men. Now they look for me to claim their vengeance."

Antonio's revelation was initially met with silence. Then, Taibaná, followed by Moné, approached Antonio and grabbed his forearms firmly in a quiet gesture of support and gratitude mixed with admiration.

"Let's go find our people," said Moné. "I know the area called Toa. We can get there tonight if we don't waste time." He then turned and entered the forest followed by his three companions; Aimá first, Antonio, and Taibaná at the rear.

Antonio was again impressed at the way his friends knew their way walking through a forest that presented few

189

landmarks or other points of reference. Moné led confidently, pausing at streams to drink and periodically presenting his companions with fruits he collected along the way. They walked through mid-afternoon without stopping until they reached a wide trail marked with hoof prints and cart tracks, clear evidence of frequent use by Spaniards.

"In that direction is the white man's *yucayeque*," said Moné pointing east, referring to Caparra. "We will move faster if we follow this trail towards the sunset."

"That's fine," said Antonio who recognized the trail as the principal westward route from Caparra. "But remain vigilant; any meeting with white men will surely mean trouble."

The vegetation was dense on both sides of the trail so that only those approaching from ahead or behind would be able to spot them. Moné ran well ahead of the group to scout in advance. The others followed together, walking quietly and listening for sounds of anyone approaching from behind. The trail followed a line of hills that marked the southern edge of a broad plain extending north to the ocean. At times the trail would climb across the hills, giving the travelers a view over the vegetation at the lowlands and the clearly delineated coastline in the distance.

Moné startled his companions when he appeared from around a bend running full speed. "There are men approaching our way." he said catching his breath. "They ride horses and have dogs."

"Quick, into the forest," ordered Antonio.

They ran uphill into the woods and stopped to hide behind a cluster of boulders overgrown with vegetation. The men pulled out their weapons and held them close. Laying flat on the ground they kept perfectly quiet. Antonio peeked from between two boulders, waiting for the riders to come within his line of sight. It did not take long for the characteristic sound of horses walking and the men's muffled voices to reach their hiding place. Antonio could see four riders. They wore the distinctive uniforms of the military and were armed with swords and long spears. Two large bloodhounds walked alongside the lead horses, their
190

noses close to the ground.

As the band approached the area in front of the boulders the dogs became excited. Antonio cursed under his breath. The dogs had found their scent, he thought. The leader of the soldiers ordered the men to halt. Antonio noticed how the same man gave a hand signal that sent one of the riders galloping ahead with one of the dogs trailing. Those that remained behind scrutinized their surroundings looking for whatever it was that agitated the dogs.

Waiting in the heat and humidity of the jungle Antonio struggled to keep thick drops of sweat from entering his eyes. Next to him the Taínos lay on the ground quiet and perfectly still; their bronze skin a perfect camouflage against the foliage around them. Below, the remaining dog continued to sniff at the edge of the trail, moving back and forth nervously. Antonio's only thought was for the animal to stay on the trail. If it decided to track the scent into the woods the soldiers would follow. Just as the dog started to venture off the trail a call came from the rider that had been ordered ahead. The three soldiers regrouped and advanced to meet their comrade, the suspicious dog following eagerly. Antonio, afraid the soldiers might return, signaled for everyone to remain in hiding. After all sounds of the riders were lost and they were convinced that the threat was passed, they stepped out from behind the boulders.

"The small animals are dogs," explained Antonio to his Taíno friends who were looking at him questioningly. "They have keen noses and are used by the white men to track animals when hunting. They can also be used to track people."

"And what are the big animals?" interrupted Aimá, who had never seen any of the animals brought by the Spaniards to the island.

"Those are horses. They are used to carry people and to help move heavy objects," he said in response.

"I've heard about horses but didn't realize they were so big."

Leaving Aimá to her thoughts Antonio continued. "I think that the dog that went ahead picked up our scent

191

further along the trail and they decided to follow it that way. Hopefully they will be moving away from us." He could see his companions nodding in understanding. "I suggest we walk in the forest for a while to confuse them in case they decide to return to track us in this direction."

Moné grunted in agreement and went off to be the lead man once again. Antonio walked over to Aimá. "Are you all right?"

"Yes. Why do you ask?"

"I thought you might be afraid from seeing those animals."

"I was surprised to see them, but I was not afraid," she explained simply. "We better go. Taibaná is calling."

They walked through the woods and rejoined the trail at a point where it crossed a river. The water was waist deep on Antonio and with a strong current, which challenged everyone to keep their balance while crossing. Once across, they stopped to rest and eat before nightfall. Antonio, who had been up since before dawn, welcomed the opportunity to rest. He laid down on a smooth, sun-warmed rock and could not keep himself from falling asleep. Meanwhile, his companions busied themselves preparing a meal. Moné set off to scout the trail ahead and to search for some additional fruits or nuts to supplement the food they carried with them.

The soothing touch of a hand caressing his forehead brought Antonio back from the world of sleep. Upon opening his eyes he was startled at the sight of a starry sky above him. He felt like he had slept for only a few minutes. "How long have I slept?" asked Antonio.

"Long enough for the sun to hide," said Aimá with a smile. "Come eat something," she invited in a soft voice.

Antonio sat up and was greeted by many long forgotten muscles. Sleeping on the hard rock after a full day of exertion made his whole body feel stiff. He stretched and moaned to the amusement of his friends who found his rough awakening rather humorous.

A silent riverside fire provided warmth for the two

Taíno men who sat around it. Lying on a palm frond on the ground next to the fire was an improbable feast. Antonio was surprised to see fruit, *casabi*, nuts, fish and shrimp. "Where did this all come from?" he asked.

The men looked at each other wondering if they heard correctly. "The forest and the river," responded Taibaná. "Where else?"

"Of course," said the Spaniard, feeling a bit foolish. Even after all these months, Antonio continued to marvel at the Taíno's limitless adaptability. Their knowledge and ability to extract sustenance from their natural surroundings seemed endless. Expressing his gratitude for the food, he sat to eat.

"We must decide what to do tonight," said Taibaná to his companions. "Moné climbed a hill and said he could see light of fires in the distance. He believes that is the place we seek."

"How far is it?" asked Antonio, who continued to enjoy his meal.

"We could reach there while the moon is still overhead," said Moné. "I say we go tonight. Any delay prolongs the time our people are slaves."

It was obvious to Antonio that if Moné were alone he would have reached the *encomienda* by now. His concern for his people, and especially for Guaína, showed in his every move.

"I agree," said Taibaná. "I fear for my wife. I feel I have gone too long without her at my side."

Aimá nodded in agreement, sufficient response for her brother.

"I feel rested and strong, thanks to this food," said Antonio. "We go tonight."

In a matter of minutes Antonio finished eating and the group headed out again. The trees along the trail shaded any available night light. They walked in total darkness, surrounded by the silhouettes of the dizzying variety of plants found in this tropical garden. After a while when their eyes grew accustomed to the darkness and, as Antonio's stiff body loosened up, they began to make good progress. In the privacy provided by the darkness, the Spaniard focused on the night song of Borikén. He was mesmerized by the complex sounds of *coquí* singing, insects chirping and birds calling. It was as if the island awoke at night to speak to the stars in a voice of incomprehensible beauty. From time to time the babble of a mountain stream joined in the night chorus, providing evenness to the intricate music.

At one point the trail began to climb steeply, crossing a ridge that ran in a north-south direction. At the top of the ridge they could hear the sound of rushing water far below. Downhill the trail followed a gentler grade along the side of the ridge. At the bottom they came upon a fast flowing river. To their left, upriver, a tumbling waterfall was made clearly evident by the roar of its waters as they splashed down from the mountains. Where they stood they could feel the cool spray from the falling waters. Moné waited a few steps ahead.

"This is the Toa River," he announced shouting over the background noise. "The trail splits here. The main trail continues to the west. Another follows downriver. I believe the place we seek is downriver."

"Let's go that way then," said Taibaná.

"Go with care," said Antonio. "After the death of their master the white men are probably going to be alert. Chances are they have posted sentries."

Moné nodded in understanding and moved once again to take the lead. He disappeared in the darkness as the others followed. The side trail was narrower than their previous route but nevertheless it was well used and easy to track. Aimá, Antonio and Taibaná walked close together. Trees continued to hug the trail, keeping it in darkness; off to the left flowed the river. The narrow valley, which held the Toa River, opened up onto a wide plain. As the ground leveled the river became wider and its waters slowed. It was near that point that Moné met his companions.

"We've arrived," he announced. "Further ahead, the trees end and the white men have four buildings."

"Did you see anyone?" asked Antonio.

"Two white men sitting by a fire in front of one of

the buildings."

"Did you see any of our people," asked Aimá.

"No."

"Let's go closer, I want to see this place," said Taibaná.

They remained on the trail until they got to the edge of the clearing. Then they moved into the woods and crouched behind trees to survey the homestead before them. Antonio recognized the layout of the buildings from other farms he had visited. From his vantage he could see four main buildings, two side by side on the left and two on the right, all facing an open yard in the center. Beyond the buildings the clear night sky allowed enough light to see that there were cultivated fields. The buildings on the right side were single level houses. The far one was an unadorned small house probably used by the Spanish laborers, the other, closer to Antonio and his companions, was twice as large, with a raised porch overlooking the compound. The buildings on the left side of the compound sat overlooking the river. They were rectangular in shape, with shuttered small windows. Antonio guessed that these were used as barns. They were also the only place where slaves could be housed.

As Moné said, there were two men sitting by an open fire across from the smaller of the two houses. They were talking and taking turns at teasing a large mongrel dog with a piece of rope. Antonio noticed another dog sleeping on the porch of the large house. Pulling back from the trees the four companions gathered around close, squatting low to the ground where they could whisper to each other. Antonio explained the function of the buildings and where he thought the people from Ceiba were being kept.

"I say we kill the two men and get everyone out," said Taibaná in an excited whisper. He was impatient to take action.

"We don't know how many white men there are," said Antonio. "There could be many more than us. And with their weapons," he paused to think. "We don't want to get into a battle. We don't even know if our people are actually here," he said putting a hand on the young warriors arm.

"What do you suggest then?" asked Taibaná.

"Let's wait until the men go to sleep. Then we can look for our people. I think they are in one of those buildings," he said pointing at the barns. "Then," he continued quietly, "we can let the people out and quietly move into the forest and away from here."

"What if the white men awaken?"

"Then we must be ready to fight," responded Antonio soberly. "But we risk everything if we go in there and confront them directly."

It did not take long before the two men by the fire went inside the small house. Patiently Antonio and his Taíno friends waited until all lights were out and everything was quiet. Antonio noticed that the dogs slept outside and worried about them sounding the alarm. Fortunately the animals were upwind from them; still, he knew that the slightest sound could alert the dogs of their presence.

"Prepare your arrows," he warned Moné and Taibaná. "If the dogs see us you must kill them before they can wake their masters."

Together they walked in the direction of the barn buildings, making sure to remain within the shadows of the forest. Aimá remained at the forests' edge where she could help direct the people about to be released. The three men crept close to the river's edge and, keeping low to the ground, used the river bank as cover until they reached a point behind the first building. Approaching the building, Antonio looked in one of the windows and was startled when he came face to face with a horse that poked its nose at him. The barn had a second horse and some equipment but no prisoners. With his heart racing, he returned to his friends and signaled to continue to the next building. Once again they retreated to the river and approached the second building from the back. Quietly they crawled up to the wooden structure. Antonio reached for a window hardly wider than his hand and, after removing a stout crossbar, opened it. Inside the building it was completely dark, so his eyes could tell him nothing, but the smell of human sweat and waste was inescapable.

"They are in here," whispered Antonio.

They quickly stepped around the side of the building facing the horse barn. Under Antonio's guidance they removed the crossbar keeping the double doors locked and the slaves in captivity. As the doors opened a sickly stench emanated from the interior. The three liberators gasped as they tried to step in the building.

"Taibaná?" said a voice out of the darkness in total disbelief.

"Be quiet," he whispered over the growing commotion. "Walk out quietly towards the forest."

Already Moné and Antonio were busy helping people up and offering quiet words of encouragement. They were beginning to realize the poor condition of the prisoners. Many were coughing, others had injuries and all were terrorized. The children cried, not knowing what else to do, their shattered lives too confusing for them to understand. Antonio was completely occupied with helping people up when he felt a presence behind him. He turned his head to see the two dogs standing by the doorway, teeth barred and growling menacingly. He could feel the people cowering behind him. Obviously they had learned to fear these animals. His mind was rushing through a maze of ideas on what to do when the sound of two bows releasing almost simultaneously broke the air. In an instant the arrows found their marks and with a sharp squeal the dogs were down. Before Antonio could exhale, a second set of arrows finished what the others had started. Antonio stepped outside and after a moment of listening and looking towards the houses determined that all was clear.

The death of the dogs seemed to free the prisoners from the grip of terror. For the first time they had seen their oppressors put down and proven vulnerable. The death of the animals was a victory for them, a symbol of hope. They began to walk out of their prison like they were being reborn. Their bodies were broken and sick but for the first time since their capture they felt that not all was lost.

Aimá, standing by the forest, was beginning to fear the worst after she saw the dogs cross the grounds in the direction of her companions. She had started to leave her place and approach the horse barn when she saw a woman holding a child appear out of the darkness. Her heart raced as she recognized an old neighbor just from the silhouette of her body. Energetically, she waved at her to approach. She hugged the woman when they met and helped her to the edge of the woods.

"Go through the woods to the trail and head inland," she instructed. "We'll meet at the waterfall." The woman nodded in understanding and went off. Aimá repeated her instructions and gave encouragement to the others as they approached her. Tears streaked down her face when she saw her mother walking towards her leaning on a teenage girl, but she could not tell if it was happiness she felt or sadness because of her mother's terrible condition. As with the others, she helped them to the woods and sent them off.

It did not take long for Taibaná and Moné to realize that their mates were missing from the prisoners. "Jima," Taibaná called out to a cousin. "Where are Mayaco and Guaína?" he asked, afraid to hear the answer.

"I thought someone had told you," she responded shyly. "They were taken to the main house, along with two other women. We've only seen them in passing since we got here."

"Thank you Jima," said Taibaná. "Go on with the others." Moné, Antonio and Taibaná exchanged looks, each thinking of what to do next. The two Taínos wrestled with anger and anxiety.

The three men pulled the dog carcasses inside and closed the doors of the empty slave barracks. They then gathered behind the building, where they would be out of sight, to decide what to do next. Deliberation was short.

"Everyone has reached the forest by now," said Moné. "I'm going for Guaína and the others." He felt he had waited long enough. Always he placed the needs of others ahead of his own. No longer would he be denied. Guaína was in the big house and that is where he was headed.

Taibaná was not going to stop his friend, but the question of whether he should go with Moné or help his
198

freed family and friends reach safety did cross his mind. However, he knew Mayaco needed him and that this would be his only opportunity to help her. If Moné failed, he had to be there.

"Go with Aimá," Taibaná told Antonio. "We'll get the women and meet you with the others."

Antonio wanted to somehow discourage them, or come up with a different plan. But he had none. He knew there was nothing he could say that would dissuade them from looking for their mates. "I need to go with you," he said, knowing that something as simple as a door latch would be new to his friends. They also had no idea who they would find in the house. "We don't know how many people are there and you may need my sword."

With a nod of agreement, Taibaná led them to the far end of the barn. They then ran across the compound and, with great care to be silent, gathered behind the small house. Fortunately the same night song that distracted Antonio while they hiked helped to mask any noise they made. A glance through the open windows showed that four men slept in the small house and no Taínos were being held there.

They proceeded to the next house and approached the first window they saw open. Like in Caparra the windows had shutters but no glass. Inside there was a lone, older man sleeping. Past that room, in the middle of the rear wall of the house there was a door with a small square window with thick tinted glass. Antonio climbed the steps leading to the door to get a look through the window, but the tinted glass erased much detail. The layout of the house seemed similar to the lawyer's house in Caparra, except in this house, the center hallway served four bedrooms, not two. Gently Antonio tried to open the door, but it was latched from the inside.

Taibaná, already looking in the next window signaled for Moné. Antonio hurried over. Inside the room there was a naked man sleeping on a bed. On the floor, at the foot of the bed, slept Guaína. Moné did not hesitate. Using Taibaná for support he nimbly climbed to the windowsill, stone club in his right hand. He dropped to the floor of the house and in the same motion smashed the club on the sleeping man's head. Guaína had barely opened her eyes when Moné covered her mouth and whispered for her to be quiet. She wrapped her arms around him with such force that he fell backwards against the bed. They held each other for a moment before getting up to leave the room.

Taibaná and Antonio moved on around the corner of the house to the next room and found another white man with a Taíno woman. Taibaná climbed inside the room and, as swiftly as Moné, disposed of the white man, who died in his sleep ignorant of his fate. Antonio entered the room after his friend and found Taibaná comforting a scared young girl who was crying in his arms. Holding his sword ready, Antonio walked past them and carefully opened the door to the hallway. He stepped out of the room at the same time as Moné at the other end of the hallway. They looked to both sides and were startled to see the old man they had seen sleeping, lacing his pants after having urinated out the back door.

The old man's legs almost buckled under him when he saw Moné approaching with his club raised. He took a step back and fell out of the house through the back door. Energized by fear he quickly got to his feet and ran to the laborers house calling out for help.

Antonio saw what happened and knew there was no time to waste. He burst into the remaining bedroom not knowing what to expect. Mayaco was crouching, terrified, on the opposite corner of the room. A tall man with a long nightshirt stood on the far side of a bed, struggling to pull his sword out of its scabbard. He was fast enough to parry Antonio's first stab even though the sword was still sheathed. However, Antonio was faster on the second blow, sweeping his sword on a wide arch to the right and slicing across his opponent's ribs and into his lungs. In a single motion he pulled out the sword and sank it into the man's heart. Taibaná had the girl by one hand as he reached to help his wife to her feet. She cried as she hugged him, even as he carried her out of the room.

200

"Where's the other woman?" asked Antonio.

"She is dead," answered Guaína. "She resisted the white men, so they beat her until she died." Moné instinctively pulled Guaína closer to him.

"We must leave, the other men are coming," he reminded his companions. Even now his cool mind was always aware of the next step.

Antonio rushed ahead of the others, pushing chairs and a table out of the way. He opened the front door of the house and stepped out. Seeing that all was clear, he jumped off the porch and signaled for the others to follow.

In the next house the men were slow to get up. The old man was so excited he could hardly talk. By the time they got out of bed and collected their weapons the raiders next door were leaving the house.

Aimá waited nervously leaning against the animal barn. She had seen the shadows of the men as they headed away from her and crossed the compound to the houses. She knew what the men were doing since she too had asked Jima about Mayaco and Guaína. Now she saw them coming out of the big house and she could not contain herself. Aimá waved her arms as she ran towards the houses joyful at seeing her good friends safe. It was then that the first shot rang out and a malformed iron ball hit her on the chest. Her Taíno heart burst open and she collapsed instantly.

"No!" Antonio cried out, rushing to her side.

As he reached her he heard the sound of a second shot and he felt a bullet tear though his tattered shirt and bite into his left side. He came down on his knees within reach of his lover's body. Crawling, he managed to reach her side. He pulled her head close to him and kissed her cheek.

"How much I loved you, woman." An intense sadness overcame him as his mind raced, thinking of his time with Aimá and their lost future.

Taibaná ran over, shocked with disbelief, and knelt over the two bodies lying on the ground. "You are alive," he exclaimed in surprise when he saw Antonio looking up at him. "Come with me," he said reaching down to take his friend's arm.

In a desperate effort Antonio reached up with his right arm and grabbed Taibaná by the chest squeezing his skin in a painful grip. "You will leave here now!" spat out Antonio. "Aimá is dead. I'm dying. Go to your people. Now!"

The suddenness of Antonio's move and the intensity of his plea shook Taibaná, who knelt motionless trying to make sense of what was happening. It was Moné leading the three women who brought Taibaná back to the present by placing a hand on his shoulder. Moné did not stop as he walked by, seeing Aimá dead on the ground and looking Antonio directly in the eyes, the pain he felt clearly etched in his face. Guaína and Mayaco cried out when they saw Aimá's body, and in the background Antonio could hear Spanish voices. He knew they were all in mortal danger. "Leave brother," he pleaded softly to Taibaná. "Leave!"

Taibaná stood up, his eyes going back and forth from Antonio to his sister. Another shot was fired and a bullet hit at his feet. As if heeding a last warning, the Taíno warrior turned gracefully and ran off, daring any bullet to catch him.

XVI

THE CELL

"Here," said Antonio, reaching up with his right hand. "Help me lay down. This injury is very painful."

"Of course," said Rodolfo, grabbing Antonio's hand and supporting his back. "I have some questions about your Indian friends."

"They'll have to wait," said Antonio in a low voice. "I am very tired."

"Of course, you go ahead and sleep. We'll talk later." Rodolfo then took off his vest, rolled it and put it under Antonio's head to use as a pillow.

Antonio was thankful for the steady stream of fresh air that was blowing from outside under the cell door. He pushed his face closer to the gap under the door, imagining himself outside. He looked around at the dense jungle and took a deep breath. He was surprised that his wound did not hurt. Ahead of him ran a trail not unlike the ones he had walked over the last year. Sensing a need, he started walking. It felt good to be outside and smell the perfumed air of the jungle. He found walking to be an effortless and joyful experience. He was enjoying himself thoroughly, his senses fully awake when, unexpectedly, the forest ahead of him vanished. He was standing at the edge of the *conucos* overlooking the two huge trees that covered the *yucayeque* of Ceiba. Close to the trees there was one *bohio*. All signs of destruction were gone. An iridescent green grass covered the area where the rest of the *yucayeque* used to sit. Antonio's heart was gladdened by the sight.

A woman stepped out of the *bohio* and began searching the edge of the forest with her eyes. When she spotted Antonio, she waved. It was Aimá! He started running to her and in an improbable two steps was holding her in his arms.

"I'm glad you didn't take long to find me," she said.

"However long I've been away from you, it has been too long."

203

They embraced filling each other's souls with love.

"Where is everyone?" asked Antonio, looking around at the empty site.

"They will come," she answered simply. And he understood.

That evening Rodolfo called out for the guards. "I'm afraid there won't be an execution tomorrow," he said.

"What the hell are you talking about?" responded the guard, angry that the prisoner had interrupted his card game.

"Dos Santos is dead."

"Oh, shit."

The guard left, grumbling, and returned with another man and a priest. He unlocked the cell and opened the door, hinges squeaking from the rust. The other man grabbed the body by the arms and dragged it out. The guard slammed the door shut and went to help carry the dead man away.

"Hey, father," called out Rodolfo. "Make sure you say a good prayer for him. Dos Santos was not as bad a character as people are saying."

"But he was a killer," said the priest, taken aback.

"I tell you in confidence that I talked to him," explained Rodolfo. "He had reasons for doing what he did."

"If you are correct, then he has nothing to worry about. Final justice is not of this world, but it will know to account for everything we did while we were here."

Hija de las Antillas... ¡Borikén!
Su corazón late sin disimulo.
Su sangre surge desde lo más profundo.
El amor que trae en su alma
Fue creado por toda su gente...
Las de antes, las de ahora, y las del futuro.

Francisco Xavier de Aragón
From his poem '*Hija de las Antillas*'

AFTERWORD

I am no different than the authors of most books in that I received inspiration and support from many sources. For taking the time to read earlier drafts of this book I would like to thank Julie Simmons-Lynch, Dwight Mengel, Leslie Schill, Gino Locardi and my dear cousin Marta Larrieu. Robin Cisne and my talented friends, Norma Helsper and Mihal Ronen, generously offered detailed editing suggestions for which I am very grateful. I am also thankful for the enthusiastic support of my brothers Eduardo de Aragón, Francisco de Aragón, and my parents Orlando and Lillian de Aragón, who read draft manuscripts and encouraged me to continue with the project. Two students of early Puerto Rican history, Drs. Elsa Gelpí Baíz and José R. Oliver were generous with their time and provided valuable advice and information during my research. Finally, I wish to acknowledge the support of my wife Jacki Thompson who put up with me talking about this book for many years before it became a reality. Without her support this work would not have been completed.

This book is a work of fiction based on historical events leading to the initial settlement of the island known as Borikén by the indigenous Taínos, San Juan Bautista by the early Spanish settlers and currently known as Puerto Rico. *Dos Santos* aims to offer a glimpse of Juan Ponce de León's expedition and of the Taínos who inhabited the island through the eyes of a fictional character, Antonio Dos Santos.

In general, Part I of the book follows historical events as reported in a variety of historical records. The visits to Yuma, Mona Island and Cacique Agüeybaná, as well as the two hurricanes encountered during the voyage are recorded history. The difficulties in finding a final settlement location are also based on recorded events.

The main plot of Part II of the book, including Ceiba and its inhabitants, are entirely fictional. However, many of the background events that propel the plot line are historical.

These include the story of Anacaona and the events leading to her death; the story of Cristobal de Sotomayor, his death and retaliation by Spanish forces; the attack by Caribs in Santa Cruz; and the challenges faced by Ponce de León for the governorship of San Juan. I also borrowed the names of several historical figures and placed them in a completely fictional context in order to enhance the historical ambiance of the story. These include *Caciques* Mabodamaca, Guaraca, and Humaca, Spanish translator Juan Gonzalez, Capt. Juan Gil Calderón and Governor Ponce de León.

In order to simplify the storytelling, I use the name Carib throughout the book to identify the native peoples that inhabited the Lesser Antilles. These people are also known as the *Kalinago*, for the men, and *Callipuna*, for the women; or Island Caribs, to distinguish them from Caribs in the South American mainland. My research shows that many questions remain as to the origin and lifestyle of the Caribs in the early 16th century and their relationship with the Taínos. There is evidence of trade between Taínos in Puerto Rico and Caribs. But there is also evidence of Caribs raiding Taíno settlements, kidnapping residents and inspiring fear in Taíno chiefdoms. The Kalinago/Caribs can claim to be the only native Caribbean island population to survive the European conquest with some measure of cultural continuity. This is an extraordinary accomplishment that commands my respect, especially when considering the fate of neighboring pre-Columbian island and mainland cultures.

I write these words exactly 500 years after the main events in this book were considered to have taken place. Much has happened in that time that has transformed the American hemisphere from an 'unknown' land, and so much of it has been incomprehensively tragic.

One of the most tragic consequences of the European conquest of the lands they called the Americas has been the loss of native knowledge accumulated by the First Peoples of the hemisphere over millennia. We live in an era when we seem to adversely impact nature with every breath we take and we know enough to realize we are causing damage. I can't help but compare our explosive modern lifestyles with the way Taíno life was so beautifully in tune with their environment.

It is important to continue to study, write about and imagine the Taínos and other lost indigenous cultures. They had much to teach us and it is a worthwhile effort to seek to recover that knowledge, incomplete as it may be. I believe there are lessons from the Taínos that could help a modern Puerto Rico redefine its relationship to the world around it. The Island was once home to a perfectly sustainable culture; why shouldn't it strive to reach that lofty goal once again?

Fernando de Aragón
Ithaca, NY
September 2010

SOURCES USED BY THE AUTHOR

Although no pretense is made that this novel is an academic work, every effort was made to present events and places as accurately as possible. To that end I used a variety of sources to help educate and inspire myself. The principal of these are presented below:

Fuson, Robert H. *Juan Ponce de León and the Spanish Discovery of Puerto Rico and Florida.* The McDonald and Woodward Publishing Company, Blacksburg, VA, 2000.

Gelpí Baíz, Elsa. *Siglo En Blanco, Estudio de la Economía Azucarera en el Puerto Rico del Siglo XVI (1540-1612).* Editorial de la Universidad de Puerto Rico, 2000.

Emmer Pieter C. and Carrera Damas, German. *General History of the Caribbean*, Volume II. New Societies: The Caribbean in the long sixteenth century. UNESCO Publishing, Paris and Macmillan Education, LTD, London, 1999.

Hernández Diaz, Fernando. *Anacaona.* Editora Corripio, C.por A., Santo Domingo, Dominican Republic, 2003.

Jiménez de Wagenheim, Olga. *Puerto Rico: An Interpretive History from Pre-Columbian Times to 1900.* Markus Weiner Plublishers, Princeton, 1998.

Murga Sanz, Vicente. *Juan Ponce de León.* Editorial Universitaria, University of Puerto Rico, 1971.

Oliver, José R. *Caciques and Cemí Idols.* University of Alabama Press, Tuscaloosa, 2009.

Siegel, Peter E., editor. *Ancient Borinquen: Archaeology and Ethnohistory of Native Puerto Rico.* The University of Alabama Press, Tuscaloosa, 2005.

Sued Badillo, Jalil. *General History of the Caribbean, Volume I Autochthonous Societies.* UNESCO Publishing, Paris and Macmillan Publishers, Inc., London, 2003.

Sued Badillo, Jalil. *Agüeybaná el Bravo, La Recuperación de un Símbolo.* Ediciones Puerto, San Juan, 2008.

Tió, Aurelio. *Dr. Diego Alvarez Chanca (Estudio Biográfico).* Institute of Puerto Rican Culture. Interamerican University of Puerto Rico, 1966.

Wilson, Samuel M. editor. *The Indigenous People of the Caribbean.* University of Florida Press, 1999.

Zayas y Alfonso, Alfredo. *Lexicografía Antillana, Volume I & II.* Molina y Cia. Havana, Cuba. 2nd Edition, 1931.

GLOSSARY OF TAÍNO WORDS USED IN THE BOOK

The Taíno were the first indigenous group with whom Europeans coexisted in the 'New World'. Their rich language provided names for plants, animals, objects and locations that were all new to the Europeans. Not surprisingly, many words were adopted by the new settlers and remain in common use to this day.

Ano River   currently Cibuco River in northern Puerto Rico.

Areito   celebration with dance, music and storytelling.

Aytí   Taíno name for Hispaniola, the island that currently includes the countries of Haiti and the Dominican Republic.

Barbacoa   a structure used to to cook meat over open fire. It was also used to store fish to be dried.

Batey   ceremonial square or plaza used for areitos and ball games.

Bato   ball game played in the *batey*. Some references indicate that *bato* was the name given to the ball and the game was called *batey*, as in the place where the game was held.

Bohio   usually round dwellings built of small tree trunks, with a conical thatch roof.

Behique   shaman or holy man.

Borikén   Taíno name of current day Puerto Rico.

Cacique   chief.

Caney   a *cacique's* dwelling made of wood with thatch roof; often more elaborate than *bohios* and varying in shape.

Canoa   Canoe. Taíno canoes varied in size. The are

reports of canoes that held 150 men. Canoes were used by Taínos and other peoples of the Caribbean to travel between islands.

Carey — Hawksbill turtle (*Eretmochelys imbricata*).

Cayabo — area of south central Borikén ruled consecutively by two brothers who shared the same name, Agüeybaná, in the time period covered in this book, from 1508-1511.

Casabi — unleavened bread made with *yuca*.

Cohoba — ceremonial snuff made from seeds of the Cojobana tree and other ingredients, including tobacco.

Conucos — mounds of soil used for planting vegetables and other plants. Large land areas were covered with *conucos*.

Cemí — idol figure made of stone or wood; often taking a human shape, but also animal or plant shapes.

Chicha — fermented corn drink.

Dujo — ceremonial chair used by the *cacique*.

Guanín — mixed metal composed of mostly copper, gold and silver. Also, the name given to jewelry made of *guanín*, particularly a pendant used by *caciques* or others of high rank.

Hamaca — Hammock.

Huracán — Hurricane.

Naboría — the common or working class among the Taínos.

Nitaínos — higher ranking class, sub-chiefs, among the Taínos.

Toa River — currently Rio de la Plata in northern Puerto Rico, east of the Cibuco River.

Yuca a root vegetable (*manihot esculenta*), also known as cassava, that served as a staple food for Caribbean, Central and South American indigenous populations. It continues to be a vitally important crop around the world.

Yucayeque Taíno village.

Made in the USA
Columbia, SC
22 July 2017